The Human Element Trilogy
The Clade

Van Camp, Kevin

The Human Element Trilogy/ by Kevin Van Camp – 1st ed.

p. cm.

Summary: Zeke Laufor discovers he has an incredible ability. After realizing what he can do, he is kidnapped by a man wearing a black cloak by the name of Marcus. He is taken to the Clade, an underground society filled with other individuals with abilities.

ISBN-13: 978-0-615-47779-4

ISBN-10: 0-615-47779-4

Printed in U.S.A.

First edition, April 2011

The text was set in Garamond font

Book Cover design by Eddie Conlon and Phillip Sanks

"In a war, I learned that true power comes from what you are fighting for. Not how big your muscles are."-Zeke Laufor

Special Thanks to,
Holly Heacock, Eddie Conlon,
Phil Sanks, Wade Osterberg,
Jake Van Hecke,
And everyone else who enjoys this

Please keep in mind that I had to use non-book writing software. Some pages may contain extra space at the bottom due to this. Thank You.

Chapter 1

Hi, to everyone who is interested in my story. I will have to admit that it is far stranger than anyone else's, so heed this warning. My story is filled with suspense, danger, and secrets. Enclosed are big secrets; secrets that if anyone would take advantage of, it would put you and everyone else like me in danger. These secrets destroyed my home, family, and my friends. So, if you are still interested, let's begin.

My name is Zeke Laufor. I am currently enrolled as a sophomore at Middleton High School in Connecticut. My mother and I live in an apartment on the 7th floor in the city of New Haven. It is about 3 blocks north of the peninsula that leads into the Atlantic Ocean. My father was a Lieutenant in the marines and was killed in a helicopter crash when I was 2, so I really have no memory of him. My mom told me that he did amazing things while he was away. She told me about his rescue missions and about his other noble acts to the soldiers. Even though I have never really met him, I am still proud of him.

So now that you are familiar with who I am and where I come from, you can begin my story. Just remember my warning; however, if at anytime you feel this is too deep, and you feel that your existence may hang in the balance, stop reading immediately.

The day it all began was March 30th 2010, just one day away from my 16th birthday. I woke up to my alarm clock blaring its second ring and rolled over to look at the time on my nightstand and realized that I had only 10 minutes to get to school.

"Oh crap!" I yelled out loud to no one.

I jumped out of bed and hurried to my closet. I figured I could bear without a shower that morning. I really didn't care if people thought I smelled rank or not. There was no way I was going to miss this day.

This was the day that I was going to ask Trish Dawson to the spring dance. I know what you're thinking. The Spring Dance? Don't tell me this is another boring, old, love story where in the end the couple gets torn apart, but finally get together at the end. It's alright, that is not what this story is about. Well, this dance was important because the couples at the end of that dance would spend most of the summer talking, and I have wanted to be with Trish Dawson since before I can remember. Believe me, I would not have skipped a shower and tried to get to school on time if I knew that that day wasn't my best chance to finally get her.

I threw on some jeans, a t-shirt, and a sweatshirt and ran down to the hall connected to the kitchen. I threw my sleeping t-shirt and shorts on the floor next to the heaping pile of clothes in the far corner that already needed to be washed, and I ran out the door into the kitchen.

My mom was getting ready to go to work herself when I got downstairs. She works at Memorial Remembrance Hospital about 5 blocks east of my house. She watched as I ran into the cupboard next to the refrigerator and grabbed a Poptart and my coat and headed for the door.

My mom is absolutely amazing. She does everything for me or tries to at least. That's what counts, though, right? Just trying to give you what you want? Like one time I asked for a puppy for my seventh birthday, but we are not allowed to have pets in our apartment besides fish. I already had a little goldfish named Shwimmy. His name is Shwimmy because I couldn't pronounce my words very well when I was five. Anyways, my mom ended up taking me to a zoo and bought me the right to name any animal I wanted to. I was pumped at the time, but now my giraffe Geronimo just walks around. I haven't been there in a long time. The main point is my mom is pretty sweet. She caught me on my way out.

"About time you got up. I thought you were going to sleep the day away." My mom said.

"Well," I replied, "You could have woken me up a half an hour ago."

"And do what? Miss my chance to watch this exciting morning show? I think next time you should pay more attention to the clock Zeke."

"Yeah Yeah, I have to go. I'll see you tonight for dinner."

"Okay honey. Good luck with Trish."

Oh my goodness, did everyone know about her? Okay, I did tell my best friend, Thomas, but really, he isn't that big of a blabber mouth? Oh well, I didn't have time to think about whoever is stalking me out there, I had to get to school. So I sprinted out the door and down the flights of stairs before anyone could question me about her again.

After reaching the ground level and heading out of the building, I turned left on my street, Wilcox. It is always filled with the sounds of people complaining, engines running, and horns honking. I guess that is what I get for living in a city, huh?

I sprinted down the street not caring about what anyone thought of me at the time. I took the next left three blocks down on Carrigan and stopped at the school three more blocks away. I was out of breath, and my watch read that it was 8:10.

"Okay," I told myself, "Not the worst on timing, I will just be a little late for history."

I walked up the short row of stairs and entered school slowly not caring how long it took anymore.

But, Ms. Johnson, on the other hand, did care.

She is one of our secretaries in the main office of the lobby. Pretty much all of the kids in the school dislike her, but I feel like she is out to get me more than anyone else. The other secretary is Mrs. Johanson (a big difference one "a" can make when it comes to kindness). She is the one we hope will be working on days that aren't going our way. She will write us a pass to go to our class and excuse us. Mrs. Johnson, on the other hand, will make you stay after school and watch documentaries on the fifties. Not exactly the greatest thing to do after school.

Mrs. Johnson saw me come in and walked over to me from behind her desk. Standing only five-foot-four, she isn't exactly intimidating…that is until you meet her.

"And what, may I ask, which I will, is your reason for being late?" She asked not really looking for an excuse.

Alright, so I couldn't tell her the truth about how my clock wouldn't ring, she would tear my head off. Instead I thought quickly and said something she HAD to believe.

"My bird pooped on my homework last night, and I needed to finish it because school is very important to me." She had to believe that. I mean, come on, who wouldn't?

"Are you trying to be funny with me, Mr. Laufor?"

Crap.

"No ma'am. I am telling you the truth. My bird flew out of its cage and pooped on my homework."

"Mr. Laufor, do you take me for a fool? I happen to know that you are not allowed, by your landlord, to own any pets besides small aquatic animals in your home."

Does she study my file? How did she know that?

"I expect you to know that I will tell the principal exactly what happened here today. Now, GET TO CLASS!"

She didn't have to tell me twice. Anywhere was better than with her. I didn't look back as I quickly walked to history.

I stopped at my locker on the way to class to drop off my backpack and grab my history notebook. My locker was the eighth from the end in the hallway straight back after you enter. New Haven High School is a perfect square with the freshman lockers by the lobby, the sophomores at the end of the straight hallway, the juniors are in the right hallway, and the seniors are in the left. The left and right halls are the best mainly because there are staircases at the end of them. All of the classes are upstairs so that means you can talk to your friends longer and get to class on time. I was just happy I only had to finish that year, and then I could get out of the desolate area.

I grabbed my things and ran up the junior hallway staircase. History was the second door on the right. At the end of the hall was the balcony where students could walk all around the upper floor and look down on the lobby. I walked in to class to find Mr. Turtish at his podium giving a lecture.

Mr. Turtish is an awesome teacher. He is fairly skinny standing at approximately six-foot-one. He always says cool stuff and gives you advances on your homework if you need it. He also doesn't care if you are late to his class because he feels that that is your responsibility.

I quietly sat down in my desk in the third row fourth desk back behind my best friend Thomas. He is short, at least shorter than me by a few inches, and I am five-foot-ten. He always wears his glasses instead of contacts. He is a dweeb but my dweeb, and I would always stand up for him if he needed it. He turned around and whispered to me quietly.

"Nice timing dude, I was starting to think you bailed on the big day."

"No way Thomas, I am asking her today after fourth period when I pass her in the sophomore hall. Then, she will finally accept the fact that we are made for each other and that we are going to go to the Spring Dance together."

"Sounds a little far-fetched to me, but I have complete faith in you. Good luck later." Tommy said a little louder than a whisper. This caught Mr. Turtish's attention, and he looked up at us.

"A little loud aren't we boys?" He asked in a very sweet and polite tone.

Thomas answered, "Yeah, sorry about that Mr. Turtish. It was my bad, and it won't happen again. I promise." He then held up the Vulcan Salute to him, and everyone snickered a little. Thomas didn't care. He likes who he is, and I respect that about him.

Mr. Turtish just looked a bit longer at the two of us and then turned his attention back on teaching the class about the Cuban Missile Crisis or something along those lines. I really wasn't paying attention because I was too psyched about after fourth hour.

History ended, and as bored out of my skull as I was, I was excited because that meant that I was one hour closer to asking out Trish.

The next few hours flew by. English was as exciting as it is everyday, not very. Geometry also was not very fun. Something about polygons I never really cared for. Maybe I had the thought in my head that I will never use them. Hopefully, I am right.

Then, finally, it was fourth hour, Phy. Ed., and like anything you want in life, the hour right before seems to take a lifetime. It ended eventually, and I changed my clothes without taking a shower (which I should have because I hadn't taken one that morning) and walked down the sophomore hallway to lunch.

I was too excited to think at the moment. What would I say when I see her? "Hi how are you? I am a nervous wreck?" No, No, that wouldn't do. I had to be smooth and on top of my game. I can't have her take me by surprise, and I need to respond right after she asks me a question or expects me to talk because, oh man, there she was, right on cue.

Trish is, how would you say, a catch. She has everything going for her. First, she is beautiful. Not like "oh cute" beautiful but exquisitely beautiful. Her brown hair flows to just below her shoulder blades, her deep gray eyes sparkle in the light, and the way she walks catches my every time. She is also great at sports, hilarious, and super smart, like 4.0 smart. Straight A's. Me, I am just above a "B" average and not exactly getting any college letters any time soon.

I watched as she went to go to her locker and put away her class materials. I waited for the most opportune moment for me to go up to her. She had just put her last folder in her locker when I decided it would be now or never. I walked up to her cautiously yet remained determined. I couldn't be intimidated. She was my height, so eye contact wouldn't be a problem. I stopped just short of her and began speaking.

"Whaz Up?" Whaz Up? Oh God I'm done before I even beginn.

"Hey Zeke, how are you?" She replied not skipping a beat. Good thing too, I had just dodged a bullet.

"I'm just wondering how your day has been?" I replied. It was a nice save, and now I would just have to speak off of what she said.

"My day has been… productive. I finished my project in Advanced History, and I started my essay for Writing and Composition.

"That's exciting." I spoke back.

"So," she responded looking a little uneasy, "Why are you talking to me? I mean, not in a bad way, it's just that you haven't really spoken to me since Christmas."

Okay, she had caught me. I was nervous. I began to sweat, and my knees began to shake under me. I hoped she wouldn't notice because I had only one shot at this and I just couldn't fail after all my mental preparation.

"I was wondering, actually, if you were interested in going with me to the Spring Dance on the 3rd?" I spoke, dangling the question out there for her to decide. Yes or No. Oh please, be the first one.

"Actually," She said, "I was already asked by Matt, you know the captain of the football team?"

Houston, we have a problem. All of my hope of ever being with her just vanished from right in front of me. I knew I didn't deserve a girl like her, but really, I had lost her to the captain of the football team? How cliché. Also, Matt is dumber than a pile of dumb rocks, and rocks were already dumb to start with! I decided to just respond as if it didn't matter.

"Oh, that is okay. I was just wondering if you were interested." I lied.

"Well, I'm sorry. Don't feel too bad. You are a nice guy. I'm sure you'll find someone else to go to the dance with, but I am going with Matt to this one. In the future though, maybe we can go to one?"

What was that? A little hope? That was better than expected, honestly. I knew I had no chance with her, but as parents always say, "Just think positive, and it will happen." Yeah right, that's a big load.

"Okay, I will talk to you later then." I added with nothing left of me.

"Okay, see ya later Zeke."

And with that, she left with nothing more to say or to give me hope for. It didn't take a rocket scientist to figure out that I was a mess. She had to see it even though I didn't say it. Yeah, she had to. God, I'm a loser.

And with that last thought, I headed for lunch.

Chapter 2

Our high school lunch room, like any other high school lunch room, has a caste system. Over to the far left are the jocks, then the preppy kids, followed by nerds and geeks, and finally my table, consisting of a whole Thomas, Brandon, the kid who can't live without an inhaler, and me. As you can guess, my table isn't exactly the coolest in the lunch room.

I sat down at the table after what seemed like a lifetime in the pizza line and found Thomas giving me 'the sign.' Basically, 'the sign,' which was developed in third grade when we wanted to speak to each other privately, was putting your two thumbs together and flapping your hands like a bird.

"Yeah? What's up?" I asked.

Thomas replied, "How did the big proposal go for you? Brandon and I were talking about the possible outcomes. We decided that she would just laugh then make some rude remark about your looks and walk away."

"Well, thank you for all of your support guys. Actually, It wasn't like that, but it still wasn't what I wanted to hear," I said.

"Hey, man I'm sorry to hear that. Want some of my pizza to cheer you up? It's pepperoni... I think?" Thomas said with a small laugh.

'No thank you, I'm fine," I replied also with a small laugh.

That Thomas, always trying to cheer me up even though he knew there would be no chance for me to be with a girl like Trish. Maybe that's why we decided to become best friends all that while ago.

"You know," I said," Maybe this is for the best. I mean in like what? Two years, I'm leaving anyway."

"That is true," he replied.

"But still, it makes me angry thinking that she could go for someone like Matt."

As I thought about the possible ways I could torture Matt, something very odd happened. The lights in the school began to flicker on and off, and the microwaves began heating and cooling. Pretty much anything electronic was malfunctioning in some way, and no one knew why. Everyone in the lunch room was watching what was happening to the lights, phones, and the other gadgets. Someone's electric pen even shocked him in his pants.

Even stranger still, there was this man. Well, I didn't know who he was, or what he was or, even if the thing was a he, but I thought I saw a person wearing a jet black cloak, like a cult member, standing in the middle of the lunchroom. I didn't see him again after that because the next time the lights turned on he was gone.

The lights began to steady themselves and stay on. I turned to face Thomas and gave him 'the sign.'

"Did you see that man, the man in the black?" I asked Thomas.

"Umm... are you feeling okay? There was no man in black down here. The lights turning on and off was probably just someone playing a practical joke or maybe even a short in the wires." Thomas said.

"A short that just so happened to possibly put the whole school on the fritz?"

"Who knows? Maybe?"

We didn't get much time to think it through because the bell rang, and I was off to fifth hour chemistry.

The rest of the day went by smoothly. Chemistry was boring and physics was basically like watching grass grow, but biology was actually quite interesting. Thomas and I were partners, and we were working on heart dissections which were the coolest things in the world. Trish was in that class too, so that always made class a little better.

People were still talking about the lights freaking out at lunch. It was the topic of the day, and everywhere I turned I heard someone telling their theory of what had happened. I kept thinking of that man in the black cloak. Nobody else has said anything about him, but I was sure I had seen him. In fact, it had looked as if he had been staring right at me. Then again, how come I was the only one who actually saw him? I kept thinking of the possibilities and decided to just drop it and that it was all just in my imagination.

It was a long walk home, mainly because traffic was backed up, so I had to stop and wait for a multitude of cars to drive through an intersection before I could cross. Stop and wait, stop and wait. They should make dodging traffic a sport because I would be an Olympic athlete in it. When I finally got home, I found a note from my mother waiting for me on the kitchen table.

Hi hunni,

I will be home late tonight. I left you some leftovers in the refrigerator, so you can help yourself tonight. Happy Early Birthday

P.S. I love you no matter what happens

"'I love you no matter what happens?'" That was kind of ominous and strange at the same time. Mom was probably just worried that she wouldn't be able to make it home tomorrow morning for my driver's test.

The next day would be my 16th birthday, and I would finally get to take my driver's test. I was starting to get super nervous. It's the same for everyone though. You over check the mirrors, go way too slow, etc. I had been planning on taking Trish to the dance in my mom's station wagon, but I guess that is out of the picture.

I took my mom's advice and put some leftover spaghetti in the microwave and watched some T.V. We didn't have cable, so the only show we really got was the news. I was drifting between my meal and the news broadcast trying not to focus too much on the news, but I caught a few snippets about an accident that had happened the week before. "Last week, an apartment building on Sycamore Street burned down, killing Jake Van Hecke and Wade Osterberg. They died, however, to save the life of three children on the fifth floor. There will be a memorial to them on Tuesday at-." I clicked off the T.V. and finished my meal. Too many bad things happen to good people.

When my spaghetti was gone, I put the dishes in the sink and began washing them. Once I finished with that, I started on my homework that was due the next day. When I had gotten about halfway through, I heard a thumping sound coming from my bedroom followed by a crash.

I jolted up and looked down the hall into my room. I noticed that the door was slightly ajar. I got up from my homework and walked down to the door to take a peek inside. What I saw was almost horrifying.

My bed wasn't made from that morning, and my mom was going to kill me.

I opened the door and walked inside to make my bed. I noticed that my window was open, and realized that it had blown off my lamp creating the crashing sound. I walked up to the window and looked outside. I looked out at the dark sky and the traffic below me and shivered a little. I shut the window, and then looked back at the lamp broken on the floor.

"How could the wind have blown a lamp off my end table? The wind wasn't that strong." I said out loud to no one.

And, of course, I had to open my big mouth. When I looked across the room again, I saw the man in the black cloak standing there staring at me.

I froze in my shoes. I was afraid to do anything believing that this guy probably wanted to kill me and I was done for. I quickly got a hold of myself and bent down to pick up a shard of the broken lamp to hold it out in front of me as a weapon. The man just stood there looking at me from under his black hood.

I didn't know what to do. I could jump out of the window and make it easier for this guy in black to kill me, or I could try attacking him with the shard. He probably was prepared for something like that though. What was I supposed to do? "Who the hell are you!?" I finally screamed.

He just stood there with his arms folded in the doorway to my room. What was he thinking? I'm sure he wasn't there just to check out my bedroom. It had to do something with me because I had seen him at school that day. Hey, maybe I wasn't just seeing things.

"Who are you and what are you doing here?" I asked in a more controlled tone.

He still stared at me for about a minute longer. Finally, he spoke to me through his hood. "Please put the shard down before I put it down for you."

Yikes that didn't sound pleasant. I slowly put it down on my bed in between us. I then looked up at him and asked, "Who are you?"

"Do not be worried about your safety. I will not cause you any harm."

"And why should I believe that?" I asked.

He took his hands and put them on his hood and began to pull it off. He was pale (well hiding under that hood will do that to you) with short, blond, spiky hair. He had a skinny face and blue eyes like ice. I was still afraid of this guy because he looked somewhat like a killer. If looks could kill that is.

"My name is Marcus, and the reason I came here is to recruit you," He said.

I was concerned. Usually a robber would take something and just run, or a kidnapper would take someone without telling them first. Who is this guy?

"Recruit me? Recruit me for what?" I asked.

"There really is no time to explain. I have already taken too long and my leader will surely punish me for this but now we have to hurry. Please just come now."

This guy, Marcus, was working for what seemed like a business. Not any normal business though. I'm pretty sure normal companies don't just break into people's houses and tell them that they want to hire them. "Why, what is the rush. Wanting to go before my mom gets home, huh?" I spoke with a slight sneer.

"Oh, I am not worried about her. After all, we did ask her to raise you," he said.

"What do you mean "raise me"? She is my mom. She is supposed to," I said.

"Listen I don't have time to explain. If we don't leave now, you are going to have visitors that won't be as kind to you as I am being right now." He said

"Why? What do you need me for?" I asked him.

He stood for a few seconds as if he was thinking about answering or not. I decided to speak first. "Was it you today who caused the lights to go psycho at school?"

"No, that was not me. It was you Zeke. Now please come with me before I make you," he said getting irritated.

"That couldn't have been me. I'm just a teenager and that kind of stuff isn't possible." I said

Before he could respond, there was a knock on my apartment door. Marcus turned his head around towards the door.

And that was when I ran.

I jumped across the bed and shoved him into my mom's room across the hall and shut the door.

"Wait," he yelled, "Don't answer th...," and I shut the door on him.

I ran to the door and opened it. At first I thought it would be my mom, but I was wrong. It was a man wearing a business suit, and he was big, like 6 foot 5 big. He was muscular too. He looked down at me and asked, "Excuse me boy, is you mother home?"

I looked up to him and lied, "Yeah, she is in her room right now though."

He gave a small laugh and a wide smile. "C'mon now Zeke. Didn't your mother ever tell you not to lie?"

He knew my mom wasn't home, and he knew my name. What is going on here? I was going to make a snappy come back when I thought about Marcus still in my mom's room. I only pushed him in there. He should've charged out ready to kill me by now. Well, if he didn't do it, I was sure this guy would.

"Zeke Laufor," the man said.

"How do you know me?" I said

"Zeke we have been watching you for some time now, and I have to say we are impressed. Who knew that the second generation would become so powerful," He said.

"What are you talking about?" I said, starting to cower and back away from the door.

The man took a step in towards me. "Zeke Laufor," he said definitively, "you are under arrest for tampering with the city's electricity for possible terrorist reasons."

I was about to run when he pulled out a taser. Right before he was about to fire, however, a rush of air went over me, and the man stumbled a bit.

You had to be there to believe this, but I swear that the wind began to morph and take shape. He twisted and turned until the air was visible, and then, out of that air, a man was formed. It was Marcus.

"Go, run for it, now!" he yelled to me.

I took his advice and scrambled out the door and down the stairs. I could hear Marcus and the other man in my apartment. I could hear the man in the suit say, "Well, well, I wouldn't say that this it is a surprise to see you, Marcus, having found the boy before us."

Marcus told him, "Yeah, well, it really isn't my pleasure to be seeing you again. It's a good thing that you're going to-"

And that was all I heard. I ran out onto the street and saw the man in the suit's black Mercedes sitting on the curb. I ran over to it and looked inside and saw that the keys were in the ignition.

"Yes!" I thought. Something good was finally happening. I ran over to the driver's side when I heard a loud, electric-like, sound from my building. I looked at my window and saw blue flashes of electricity going through the room. I thought about the man shocking Marcus with the taser, but I was wrong. The next thing I knew, the man in the suit was being flown from my apartment and out the window. He screamed as he fell to the ground. His arms flailing and legs kicking, but that all ended when he landed on top of his car. It made a sickening thud against the car. The car's roof buckled and collapsed under his weight.

I guessed that I wouldn't be driving that anytime soon.

Frightened, I looked back up into my apartment window, and I could see Marcus peering down at me. I ran as fast as I could. I didn't know where to go, but I knew that I had to run and fast.

I sprinted hastily away from my attacker and into the night.

Chapter 3

"I'm coming!"

I knocked on Thomas' door rapidly just hoping he would be awake and would answer. It was about 11 o'clock at night, and I had been running from Marcus, or whoever he was, for an hour. I didn't know where to run to, so I decided to run to Thomas'. He lived in view of the school in an apartment just a bit bigger than mine which makes sense since it is just my mom and me in my apartment.

I wished for my dad at that point. He would've known what to do.

Thomas answered the door. "Zeke? What are you doing here this late at night? Don't you know we have school in, oh, nine hours?" he asked me standing in his Captain America pajamas.

I walked in and spoke hastily, "Look, I don't know what is going on, but there are people chasing me. A man was murdered at my apartment, Thomas, he was thrown out of my window by the man in the black cloak who-," he cut me off.

"Zeke, do you know how bizarre this sounds. Are you sure it wasn't just a bad dream over what happened with Trish today?"

Actually I had totally forgotten about her and about what had happened today. It seemed like so long before.

"Listen, would it be possible for me to stay overnight just for tonight? I'm kind of freaking out here" I said.

"Sure," he said, "Just let me put out a sleeping bag for you. Does your mom know you are here?"

Mom. What had happened to her? Where was she? The note she left had said that she was at work, but Marcus had said something about 'asking her to raise me.' I knew that something weird was definitely going on, and it had something to do with my mom and me.

"Yeah, she knows." I lied.

"Okay, let's just get to bed. I'm tired, and it is your birthday tomorrow. You should at least be sane enough to enjoy it," he snickered a little.

I didn't want to argue with him. I was just thankful I could get a good nights rest without being worried about someone breaking in to kidnap me or something.

I walked with him down his hall and into his room. I crawled under the thick, blue, sleeping bag and thought about how the next morning I would be sixteen. The only problem was that I wasn't sure my life would be the same once I woke up.

I woke up to Thomas' alarm. He lived closer to school, so I didn't have to wake up as early as I usually did. I got up and walked around the room. I noticed that Thomas was already in the shower and that I was alone in his room. I sat on his bed and thought about the night before. Maybe it was all just some weird dream. I was sure my mom would be home after school, and I could just talk to her then. Actually, she was probably having a heart attack after noticing I wasn't in bed last night. I decided to call her. The phone rang, and rang, and rang, and then got to the answering machine. Now I was starting to become nervous.

Thomas' mom walked in, "Happy Birthday Zeke," she said cheerfully, "I didn't know you stayed overnight."

I replied, "Yeah, it was a heat of the moment thing. Sorry that I did."

"It's okay. I'm surprised your mom let you come stay over since it's your birthday today. Shouldn't you be going to get your license at some point?"

I realized that I was supposed to be going for my license in an hour. This was a perfect excuse to run home before school to see if it had all been a dream or not. "Yeah," I said, "she told me to come home before school so that she could drive me to my driver's test."

"Okay, good luck. I'm sure you will pass."

With those last few encouraging words, she left. I watched Scott and Ben, Thomas' younger brothers, run down the hall into the kitchen for breakfast. Thomas walked in behind them and said, "Happy Birthday! Do you feel like yourself again or do I have to knock some sense into ya?" He laughed.

"Thanks man. No I think I'm okay. I am heading out soon to go take my drivers test. I'll let you know how it goes," I said.

"All right, do you need to take a shower first? You have plenty of time before Scott tries to jump in," Tommy said.

I decided to take him up on his offer for a shower. I smelled pretty rancid after not taking a shower since two days before, and the shower was right there where no possible harm could come to me. After the shower, I grabbed some toast from Thomas' mother and began my walk home.

The morning was bitter since it was March and since we lived on the Northeast coast. When I walked on the sidewalk with everyone else, it looked like a mass of tiny breath fogs blinding my way. Sadly, I was only wearing my Middleton High long sleeve shirt and some jeans, and I was a little chilly.

The long walk home got me thinking about what had happened the night before. I couldn't help but think about it even though what happened usually classifies as "not normal." A MAN had appeared out of thin air. Or at least, so I thought. That kind of stuff is impossible. Maybe that guy in the suit had tasered me and he had never flown out of my window. Perhaps, I was lying on a cold, steel, table in a dark, FBI, room with electrodes and other gizmos implanted into my head. "I hope I'll wake up soon then," I said to myself.

I was a block away from my building when I noticed that the black car that was crushed by the man in the suit had disappeared. "No way," I thought. I ran over to the spot where the car was, carefully avoiding other civilians, and noticed that there was nothing. Nothing at all remained from that car. There was no framing or glass, not even a broken antenna. Nothing. How had everything been moved and cleaned up after that guy had fallen from my window? Then I decided to look up.

It was fixed. The window in the sliding door on the balcony was fixed. The night before, a man had flown threw that window, and now there were no remains anywhere that showed that any of it had even happened. I rushed into the building and up the stairs to the 7th floor. I stopped in front of my apartment and prepared myself for whatever was waiting inside. After a few deep breaths, I turned the key and went in.

It was breathtaking. My apartment was perfect. I quickly checked my room and found that my lamp had been fixed too. Everything was as it was the night before, before the craziness had begun. "It must have been a horrible dream," I thought to myself.

I walked back into the living room and looked at Shwimmy swimming around his bowl on the table. He looked okay. Maybe everything had been in my head. I went behind the counter in my kitchen, grabbed some fish food, and opened the top to feed him; however, one more thought came to mind. "What about the note," I thought to myself. I went over to the kitchen table and looked down at the note.

Hi hunni,

I will be home late tonight. I left you some leftovers in the refrigerator, so you can help yourself tonight. Happy Early Birthday

P.S. I love you no matter what happens

Wow, mom was right about the last part. "Where was she," I said aloud to myself.

"I told you last night, she was just here to raise you," said a voice from the hallway.

I quickly turned around and saw Marcus standing there with the same black cloak on as he had worn the night before in my dream. His hood was off again, so I could see his face in the sunlight. He looked as intimidating as I had thought he was in my dream.

"You are probably thinking that last night was a dream," he said to me, "but I assure you, it was all real."

I just stood there with my mouth open. How was he still there? And yes, I had thought it was all a dream, but now...

"How did this all get cleaned up?" I asked first.

"My friends came and cleaned this all up before any cops decided to show up. We have to remain low-profile for what we do," he said.

"Your friends?" I asked, "I don't care who you are, just get out. Now!"

That's when it started again. The lights began to flash, and the bulbs began to shatter. This was much stronger than before. Why does this keep happening? Am I really the cause? The microwave was starting and stopping. The T.V. was changing channels so fast that it short circuited. Everything was going hay-wire and all I knew was that someone a short distance away might want to kill me.

"Hey!" Marcus yelled. "Stop it or you are going to attract them back here."

But I couldn't stop. I was afraid and angry for this guy messing up my life. I was now 16, and all I know is that I can possible create some sort of electric field. I wasn't going to stop. I was intent on trying to scare him away with my amazing on-and-off powers.

However, I didn't scare him away. Instead lightning began to emit from my fingertips. I yelled and fell over backwards waiting for the pain to begin, but I felt absolutely nothing. It was amazing. This kind of power and no recoil.

That's when I noticed Marcus was running at me from down the hall. I pointed my fingers at him to keep him away, and he vanished into the air again like he did last night. "Where did he go?" I thought.

I stood up and the electric storm began to subside to nothingness again. I spun 360 degrees and saw no one. I ran towards the door, but when I opened it, there he was just grinning.

"Sorry I have to do this," he said, "but you really need to come with us. Our lives may depend on it."

I looked down and saw a taser coming for my chest. I couldn't react fast enough and was hit with enough volts of electricity to keep a man down for a week. I felt the volts surge through my body and its appendages providing a tingling sensation to my limbs. I thought I was going to fall down and black out, but that didn't happen.

I held my chest and looked around and then back up to Marcus who seemed as surprised as I was. "That was weird," I said shocked. "How did I withstand that?"

Marcus replied, "I guess your body can withstand high voltage of electricity for tasers." He looked down at the floor and around the living room.

I almost forgot that this man was still in my home. He wanted to kidnap me, so I began to sprint around him and out the door.

"Hold on!" He yelled as I began to descend the flights of stairs.

I wasn't going to let this guy get me. I took the steps two at a time until I reached the next floor, and then continue my run all over again. The floor numbers flashed in front of me as I ran down the steps. 6...5...4...

When I reached the 3rd floor, I heard Marcus yell down, "Heads up!"

I foolishly looked up to see the cover of a toilet seat coming down and whacking me in the head. The knock hit me so hard I tipped off my feet and blacked out. This guy had me.

Chapter 4

Being bonked on the head isn't fun; it feels like you're passing out. You feel like you're falling away into nothingness, and then you realize that you have no idea where you will be when you wake up. However, unlike passing out, when somebody purposefully knocks you out, it's more likely that you will end up in a scary place. And trust me; it isn't what you want to be doing on your birthday.

When I woke up, I didn't know how much time had passed since I had last been in my apartment on my birthday. It had been maybe a few hours, days, weeks, maybe. I thought that I might've been given some sort of sedative to keep me knocked out while the people in the cloaks "experimented" on me. Either way, I wasn't home anymore.

I woke up looking at a bright light hanging from the ceiling. I squinted a bit until my eyes were fully adjusted, and then I looked around. The room was made out of concrete, and the ceiling was black. The room had an eerie feeling almost like it was where a mad scientist kept his "subjects." I was lying on a steel table, and I noticed that there were many other steel tables lying next to mine in a row and then in another row across a little aisle. I turned my head to the left and noticed another boy was there with me. He looked about fourteen and had short, blond hair and a rounder face. It looked like I was a bit taller than him, but he looked a little bit thicker than me.

I decided that I should get out of there before the people came back and found me awake. I tried to get up, but my wrists and ankles were locked onto the table by padded cuffs. "What are they doing to us," I asked myself, frightened.

I turned my head over to the other boy and asked him, "Are you okay? Are you awake? We need to do something to get out of here."

He let out a small grunt and forced his eyes open to look at me. "Where are we?" he asked painfully. "I was at home with my dog when a woman in a cloak came and told me to come with her."

His story was starting to sound a lot like mine. "What happened?" I asked him.

He took a few deep breaths and blinked a lot, then said, "I decided to run. I ran out the door and across the field behind my house. She was fast though. It was as if she was floating on air."

His story was so far exactly like mine. I only needed to know one other thing to make sure. "What did she say about your parents?"

A tear began to form in his eye. "She said that they were only there to raise me, to make sure I matured correctly in the direction *they* wanted. Eventually, she got me with a taser. How did you get here?" he asked.

I told him what happened to me: the power surge, the man in the suit, and the man in the cloak who could vanish into the air. He nodded as I went on with my story. I finished, and he said, "Wow, sounds like you were having troubles too with things out of your control."

"What do you mean?" I asked him

"Well, I was recently on the run from cops for burning down my day-care. It was a terrible place, and the caretakers had us on a tight leash. We couldn't even play football in the back," he said. "Then, one day, I just got so angry, and I wished the place would just burn down, and… it did."

He began to cry softly. He was having the same problems as me but, apparently, with fire. I guess he had it worse than I did. At least I didn't fry the school and all the students. I felt really sorry for him, and realized I didn't really even know who he was. "What's your name?" I asked him.

"My name is Gabriel, Gabriel Mason, but my friends call me Gabe," He said softening up a little.

"My name's Zeke," I replied back to him.

"So," he said quietly. "How do you suppose we go abou-",

He was cut off by a man and a woman walking into the room wearing black cloaks. Whatever was about to happen to us, we were about to find out.

I looked closer at the man that had walked in, and, of course, it was Marcus. The woman, however, I have never met before. She had black hair that fell just below her ears and had a small face. Her eyes were gray, and if you looked into them for too long, it seemed as if she was peering into your soul.

Marcus walked over to me, and the unknown woman walked over to Gabe a few tables down. I lied on my back looking up at him waiting for whatever they were going to do to us. Marcus just looked down at me and then over to the woman. It appeared as if they were waiting for something, like one of us to speak first. So, I decided I shouldn't let them wait any longer.

"Hey Marcus, long time no shocking me," I said to him rudely.

He just looked at me then smiled and chuckled a little bit. The girl next to him also gave a little laugh, but it was much more reserved than Marcus'. Marcus kept his eyes on me and dug into his pocket on the side of his cloak. I thought it was going to be the taser, and I got myself ready for the pain to start again, but instead it was a golden key. "I am going to release you," he said to me, "but do not try to run. We are your friends whether either of you believe me or not. Agreed?"

We both shook our heads and said, "Yes."

He reached down and unlocked my ankles first and then the left wrist. "I could grab him," I thought, "then again, he could just vanish again and tase me. I better just follow along." I looked over to Gabe and mouthed to follow them at least for a while. Gabe nodded, and we were both free.

"Now," the woman spoke for the first time, "get up and follow us. We have a lot to tell you before you begin training."

"Training?" I thought. What do we have to train for? We are not soldiers; we are kids who were captured by random hoodlums in cloaks. "What do we need to be training for? We are not soldiers, and we can not use any weapons."

The girl spoke before Marcus. She seemed very intimidating, even towards Marcus. "You are both very strong. You, both of you, are like us. Well," she said turning to me, "maybe not like us at all."

I didn't know what she was talking about, but I was worried. Being stared down by a woman who looks like she would beat the crap out of you is not the greatest feeling in the world. In fact, a little gulp escaped from me.

We both stood up and stretched a little bit. Then, Marcus and the other girl led the way out for us into… somewhere. I looked over to Gabe walking next to me and asked, "What's her name? She's kind of scary."

Gabe replied, "She told me her name was Juliette, but I really wasn't worrying about her name before. Why?"

"I was just wondering," I said, "but I think Marcus seems trustworthy enough, at least for now. I say we follow them around and amuse them until we figure out how to get out of here. These people are dangerous.

We followed Marcus and Juliette out of the room and into a well lit hallway. The hallway seemed to stretch out for quite a while and had many rooms to the left and right. The walls itself weren't like the walls in the room we were just in. They looked like the ones in actual homes with drywall and stuff like that. I forgot about this and continued following.

As we kept moving, I noticed that many of the rooms had hardly anything in them. Every once in a while, we would come across a room with a table or a box in it marked *fragile* or *do not open*. We followed the hallway to the end and made a left turn. We continued to the elevator at the end of the hall. As we waited for the elevator, I asked, "So, Marcus, what's going on?"

He looked to the floor and said, "I wish I knew for sure, but I can tell you that we are like mutants. We have powers that are out of our control until we reach our teen years, and, even then, they are unstable."

He appeared to be just as lost as I was, but I think he knew more than he was letting on. The elevator arrived, and we stepped in. The monitor showed that we were on the basement floor.

Juliette said, "We are in an abandoned hospital on the very northern tip of New York. So, if you were planning on escaping, which is impossible anyways, where will you go? Besides, the FBI will probably get you anyways."

"Juliette," Marcus said quickly, "Don't scare these kids. They are very important to us." Marcus started to fade after that, but I could still barely hear, "Zeke is supposed to free us. Remember? That's the plan. The President won't be happy if you scare him away."

Whoa, save them? What was going on here, and why did they need me? Also, who was this president they spoke of? Was he running this whole super powered cult? I was beginning to become nauseous when we reached the third floor. The doors opened, and we stepped into a hallway filled with other people in black cloaks.

The people seemed to be all, at the very least, in their teens or above. There were a few teenage boys a little older than me, and a few teenage girls a few years older than me. There were also many older individuals. Some even looked like they could be sixty. Either way, these individuals were all like us.

They had powers too.

We walked past about thirty of them down the hall when we stepped into an exercise room. The room was filled with medicine balls, weights, bicycles, and other fitness equipment. We walked to the back and opened the door to a little larger room with padding all around the walls, including the floor. As we stepped in, Juliette closed and locked the door behind us. Marcus walked us to the center and said, "You boys are special, like everyone else here."

"So," Gabe said, "you can all... you know," he began to whisper, "throw fire?"

Marcus replied, "No, some of us, yes. We all have special abilities that have to do with the elements. Some have power over water; some over fire. Some can control the earth, and some can move through the air, like me. Juliette has the ability to push air and cause it to penetrate into people. It is very powerful considering it is almost invisible, and it can piece through a living person."

Marcus walked into a closet in the back of the room and pulled out a wrestling dummy. "Juliette, why don't you provide these young learners with an example?"

Juliette obliged and walked into the center of the room. She stared down the dummy and breathed in deeply. As she did this, she pulled her hands to the center of her chest. At first, I saw nothing but then I saw a small quiver or a shake in the air in front of her. It almost looked like a spear. Then, she quickly pushed her hands towards the dummy, and its chest EXPLODED. I couldn't believe my eyes. The dummy was nothing more than legs after she just pushed air at it.

Marcus stepped back into the center of the room and said, "Pretty powerful, right?" with a slight smile.

Chapter 5

"So," Gabe said, "we all have a power that has to do with the elements? You know, fire, water, air, and earth?"

"Yes, Gabe, that is exactly correct. You can throw flames just by thinking it." Marcus took a slight pause, "I'm sorry about the day-care, but if we hadn't shown up then the other men in the suits would have gotten you."

I thought this over for a little bit. "Wait, what about me then? You never said anything about lightning and electricity." I asked him.

Marcus looked over to Juliette, and she replied, "Yes, you are… different… even more than us." She said with a small chuckle.

"What Juliette is *trying* to say is that we don't know exactly how you came to be." Marcus said.

"What do you mean 'how I came to be?'" I wondered.

"I will talk to you about it later, but, for now, just listen to what we say. First, I want to see what you two can both do," he walked to the back and pulled out another dummy, "Alright, Gabe, let's see what you can do. Just aim at the dummy, and think of him on fire. Really want him to be on fire, Gabe."

Gabe walked in front of the dummy, turned to the two in the cloaks, and said, "I don't know. I'm kind of afraid." So far, Gabe reminded me of Thomas back home. I hoped that Thomas knew I was okay. He was probably really worried and same with my mom. What had happened to her? I couldn't believe that I hadn't thought of them before then.

"Its okay, Gabe," Juliette said encouragingly, "If you misfire, then we will all burn," Juliette said with a big smile.

Gabe was beginning not to look too well. He turned and faced the dummy; however, and he focused. He stared at the dummy for about ten minutes when, *WHOOOSH!* A large fireball erupted where the dummy was standing.

Gabe walked away from the dummy slowly. He was as stunned as I was that he could do that. We were in the same boat there.

"Very good," said Marcus, "Now, all we need to work on is being able to do it faster," Marcus turned to me and said, "Alright, Zeke, you're up. Now, try to keep it under control. I don't want to have to tase you again," He said with a laugh.

I walked in front of the newly placed dummy and stared at it. Five minutes and nothing had happened. Ten minutes, nothing happened. Time seemed to take forever. After about twenty minutes, Juliette said, "Okay, Marcus did you recruit the wrong kid?"

Marcus turned to her and said, "No, maybe it only works out of anger." He turned to me and asked, "You were always angry, were you not, when you had electrical storms?"

He was right. "Yeah, actually, I think so. The first time I was jealous, and the second time, well, I thought you wanted to kill me."

Marcus just laughed and said, "Don't worry, I get that a lot. We will just have to wait until another time when you are angry."

And with that, we left and went back into the hall filled with the other people like us.

We went back into the elevator and rose to the 3rd floor of the hospital. Marcus took me and Gabe to a room straight down the hall from the elevator. Juliette left us and went back to the basement floor.

The room we walked into had two bunk beds. One on each side of the door. There was a window in between the beds on the furthest wall that was boarded up. I guess when they choose an abandoned place; they choose a place where they can't be found even from close up.

Marcus walked a short distance to the left side and pointed out two duffle bags. "These are your clothes from home. We don't bring you here with absolutely nothing, believe it or not."

We strode over to the bed and opened the bag. I found my pajama pants and a few t-shirts on one side and jeans and sweatpants on the other. All of my hygienic stuff was there too. These people really did think of everything. Marcus went over to the small closet in the tiny space between our bunk beds and the far wall. He opened it and pulled out two dark cloaks. He handed them to us and said, "You will receive more information tomorrow, but for now, you should rest. It is getting to be 10 p.m. and tomorrow we will run through more tests."

We listened to him and crawled into bed. I let Gabe get the top bunk, and I took the bottom. As we relaxed in bed, Marcus turned off the lights and said, "Good night gentlemen, and, also, Happy Birthday Zeke. Welcome to the Clade."

And with that, the lights were out, and I was asleep before I knew it just waiting to see what tomorrow would bring. Also, it was still my birthday.

We woke up to the sound of an alarm going over the loudspeaker. "Good morning," said the voice smoothly, "it is April 1st and the Agents are coming to get us right now... April Fools! Have a wonderful day."

I woke up slowly. I was hoping that I would wake up and find myself laying in my own bed in my apartment back in New Haven, but I didn't think that was going to happen ever again. A boy could dream though, can't he?

Gabe got up first, and then I did. We put on some new clothes and looked at the cloaks that were hanging in the closet. We decided that since we were members of "The Clade," we should put them on. They were actually very comfortable. The material was light and pliable. It was also very free feeling, as in, it felt like it wasn't even there at all.

We stepped out into the hallway hoping to find somebody to tell us what to do, but it seemed like everyone had already started their day. We walked down the other halls looking into open rooms and noticed that the majority of people, mainly teens, slept on the 3rd floor. Each room contained two bunk beds and two closets. I could tell they were mainly teens because the rooms were pretty messy. As we walked down another hall looking through rooms, a voice shouted behind us, "Are you boys lost or something?"

The voice was feminine, and we turned around to see that I was correct on the assumption that the voice belonged to a girl. She was a tiny little girl. She was skinny and only about 5-foot-3. The cooler thing still was that she had purple highlights in her black hair. The girl reminded me of some rebels back at Middleton High. I thought that she might be the same thing here.

Gabe and I walked over to her, and I said, "Hi, I'm Zeke, and this is Gabe. We are new to the Clade… or whatever this place is called."

"Aaahh," she replied, "so what got you here? Did you almost drown a school just using water from a water fountain? I hope not. That is what I did. On accident of course. I can move water. I'm like a telekinetic only with water. So would that be a *hydrokinetic*?" She seemed very energetic and uppity. She acted like she was about to start a mile race any second. She was very nice though, and Gabe and I decided to tag along with her.

The girl spoke first. "So what're your abilities? You, the one on the left, go first." She pointed to Gabe.

"My name is Gabe, and my ability lets me create fireballs just by thinking it," said Gabe.

"Okay," replied the girl, "that sounds very exciting," although she didn't look very interested. "How about you?"

She pointed to me, and I told her, "I'm Zeke, and I'm from Connecticut-"

"Only Connecticut," she broke me off, "You didn't have to come far at all. I'm from Colorado."

"Anyway," I continued, "I can cause electrical storms."

The girl's jaw dropped and turned to me. "What?" I thought. I knew it was different, but I didn't think I was that different.

The girl began to walk away with her jaw still partially hanging. I quickly asked her, "Hey, what's your name?"

She turned around slowly and looked at me with serious eyes. "Sarah, my name is Sarah Ubancs. Well, maybe we'll get to work together sometime in the future, but right now I have to go eat and train. That's all we ever do around here. If you are going to fit in around here, Zeke, I would recommend you get that power of yours working. You don't want to see what they do to the ones that aren't like us." She turned away and said, "See you later!" in her energetic tone again.

The ominous feeling that my power only works when I feel in danger wouldn't go away for the rest of the morning. Gabe and I went downstairs for lunch in the cafeteria, and then went to go train with Marcus and Juliette. Once again, my power decided that it didn't want to show up again today. Gabe, on the other hand, shaved a solid five seconds off of his time. I didn't want to show that I was scared about my power not emerging. Fear is a sign of weakness, and I am definitely not weak. These people would crush fear anyway.

After lunch, we went back down to the training area. We sat and waited on the cushion floor for Marcus and Juliette to show up, so we could train. "So, what are we going to do about the whole escaping idea?" Gabe began suddenly. "We have to get out of here. These people will kill us if we don't."

I thought it over. Escaping would be great, but I felt like I was finally somewhere that I belonged. Gabe was from the Midwest anyway. If he tried to run, it wasn't as if he could run all the way back home, and these people would still find us once we got there. The whole idea of leaving seemed idiotic to me. "I don't know if we should. Where would we go to? These people would just catch us again, or those other guys," I replied.

"So, are we just going to sit here and take whatever they give us? I don't know if I could do this all day. It's just constant training," Gabe said.

"Yeah," I replied, "We will just have to tough it out. It will only get easier."

"But, what if your power doesn't show up? What are we supposed to do? I can't stop them from taking you away. They seem really interested in yours," Gabe said.

"It will. I know it will." I decided to change the subject and get off of the depressing one, "So, where are Marcus and Juliette? They should have shown up by-" I was cut off. A man came into the room, but it wasn't Marcus or Juliette. It was a man in one of those government suits.

Like the one back at my apartment.

"Hello Gentlemen. Listen, would you two like to come with me?" he said.

I knew their game. He immediately pulled out a taser right after I thought that. I panicked and pushed Gabe out of the way. The man in the suit pulled the trigger, and the darts flew across the open space and hit me in the neck. The pain began immediately. I yelled and screamed. "Wait?" I thought, "I can scream." I noticed that the darts only gave a small pinch of electricity. The taser wasn't powerful enough to tase us.

I got up, and the man was stunned. "How did you do that?" he said, "I have enough volts in you right now to stop your heart."

I stood fully up and then I noticed little sparks emanating from my body. Yes, my power had finally arrived. I charged up and got angry. Lightning shot across every part of the room. I just hoped I didn't hit Gabe by accident. The lights shattered overhead, and the taser overloaded in his hand. I felt like the electricity was part of me and pushed it into my hand. My hand emanated with light blue electricity. I looked up to the man still stunned standing there, and I pulled back and sprinted at him. He didn't move. There was no point. He wasn't getting away from me. I pushed my hand towards his chest, and it was grabbed by someone standing behind the door.

It was Marcus.

"Thank you Ezekiel," he said, "That will be all."

"Oh thank God. I thought I was dead," and Ezekiel left.

Just then, Juliette came out from behind Marcus and said, "Well, you got me Marcus. I guess you did find *him.*"

"Wait, what just happened?" I said.

"Well," Marcus started, "I knew fear would bring out your power. So, Ezekiel volunteered to be an agent and scare you. In fact, I think you scared him," He laughed to himself.

"So, this whole thing was a set-up? All of it. Did you get what you want? That was absolutely TERRIBLE. I thought we were dead," I said angrily at him.

"Yes," Juliette said, "In fact, we got more than we bargained for. That taser really was set to kill you. So, congratulations, you survived your first near death experience."

I walked out of the room and up to my bedroom. I laid in bed for what seemed like forever, but the clock said thirty minutes. I had dealt with enough death in my time: My father, who I was still thinking of even here, my grandparents, who died in a car accident and were old anyway, and my mom, if she was dead, for all I knew. Those were the only people in my family. No cousins, no girlfriends, not anyone. That's maybe the reason I only had one real friend, and now Gabe.

I hoped Thomas was okay.

The dinner bell rang, but I wasn't hungry. I just laid in bed for another hour, and then Gabe came in. "Hey, you missed dinner like an hour ago. Are you okay?" he said.

I sat up on my bed and said, "Yeah, I'm just upset about their whole set-up for me at training today. I really thought we were in trouble."

"Hey," he replied, "look on the bright side; at least you're not getting kicked out, or worse."

I couldn't argue with him about that. I flopped back onto the bed without saying another word. I could tell Gabe was feeling sorry for me. He was a good guy. In fact, one of the better persons I had ever met. He was just like me: his parents disappeared, he was kidnapped, and, even worse, he burned down a day-care center. I thought that I should begin to toughen up a little. Things would only get worse if I didn't.

I fell asleep right away exhausted from the day. I was hoping to be able to sleep in for about an extra three hours, but that didn't happen. The people there ran on a tight schedule, and if any freshmen dared to try to overturn it, they would be toast.

Chapter 6

The next week went by pretty much the same way as the first. I stopped getting tricked into using my electric storm of death, which was a bonus. It started to function properly on its own without the help of adrenaline and the fear of dying. Gabe and I were destroying dummies left and right. Granted, we weren't really all that strong yet. It still took Gabe a good eight minutes before his fire would kick in, and I still had to at least fake being afraid. Marcus and Juliet watched us everyday and gave us pointers on how to use our supposed "gifts" more quickly and accurately. Actually, none of their pointers had really been working to that point, but don't tell them that.

The one nice thing about living in a hospital with a group of people just like you and not with your parents is that I don't have to make my bed. My room was starting to have the feeling of a teenager. It was the good kind of filth for a boy my age though. My clothes lay in a pile next to my closet, and I could throw my boxers wherever I wanted and not worry about getting in trouble.

One of the bad things about living in a hospital with a large number of individuals is that the bathroom space is limited. After the wake-up alarm, everyone races to the bathrooms on the 3rd floor to get a spot in the shower. Gabe and I just waited a little bit longer in bed because we would get pushed to the back anyways because we were new.   Man, this newbie thing is no good.

I had been thinking a lot about how Thomas and how my mom were. I hoped they knew I was okay. Did they have any idea about my powers or about who I was? Marcus wanted me to believe that my mom did, but, at the time, I didn't believe him. I still thought of her as my mom, but really who was she? Thomas, I was pretty sure had no idea. He was just with the wrong friend at the wrong time. Actually, Thomas didn't have many friends besides me; unless you count Brandon, but he really didn't like to do anything fun with us outside of school. He liked to keep to his Star Trek and video games.

Training ended, and Gabe and I headed to the cafeteria for lunch. We were escorted by Marcus and Juliette to the elevator. In fact, they escorted us pretty much everywhere. I didn't see any of the other kids with their instructors ever. Something had to be going down. But what could it be? I decided that it was probably just an orientation thing and began to think nothing of it.

We had just gotten to the elevator when Sarah and her instructor intercepted us. They came from a side hallway off of the main one we walked down to our training room everyday. Sarah's instructor looked as strict as all the other instructors here. He was about 6-foot-3 with a short white beard and a broad forehead. He was probably around fifty. He gave Marcus and Juliette a look and gave them both a little wave with his head that meant "we should talk in private away from these kids." I don't think I was supposed to see that, but he made it look pretty obvious.

Juliette looked at us when we got to the elevator and said, "You three go on up to lunch without us. We need to discuss some issues. We will be right behind you."

She pushed the level three button for us. The doors shut, and we began our ride up. Sarah looked at us both and asked, "So, how have you boys been?"

That seemed like an easy enough question, so I answered, "Pretty good. Although, I have only been here for a week. No offense to anyone here, but I really do miss my family," Gabe agreed with me.

"Well, that feeling will fade soon. These people are like family, so everyone feels warm and welcome," Sarah said.

We were silent the rest of the way up to the third floor. The elevator dinged and the doors opened. For an abandoned hospital, the place sure did run well. Gabe headed off to the cafeteria doors at the end of the hall, but I turned to Sarah before she left, and I asked, "How long have you been here, Sarah? It must have been pretty hard to forget your parents, huh?"

She looked at me long and hard. I felt as if I hit a nerve with her that I shouldn't have hit. After a long time, she answered, "They haven't told you yet, have they, Marcus and Juliette?"

"What," I asked, "What didn't they tell me?"

"They weren't our real parents. They were just hired to protect us."

I told Gabe in the lunch cafeteria about what Sarah told me. He couldn't believe it either. How could someone fake that they loved you since the day you were born? They must have hearts of stone, or else the Clade gave them something in return for all of their hugs and kisses. I waited for Marcus and Juliette to walk through the cafeteria doors before I jumped them about it. I waited and waited and waited. After about twenty minutes, they finally walked in.

I ran up to them in front of everyone eating, which was pretty much the entire Clade, and shouted, "Where are my PARENTS!"

At that point, it sounded like everyone's silverware dropped all at the same time. Marcus glared at me for a second, but I just kept staring him down. I was mad. I followed all of their rules, and I didn't even try to run. I could. What was preventing me? Nothing. Nothing was preventing me from leaving the place and telling everyone about them.

Marcus still didn't answer so I asked again, "*Where* are my parents!" This time not as loud.

Finally he answered, "Meet me in the training room after lunch, and I will tell you," and then he walked away to get in line for food.

Gabe and I entered the training room after lunch and found a table set up with four chairs placed around it. It looked like the kind of meeting your parents would call if you got in trouble at school or had a really large cell phone bill. Apparently, I didn't have parents though, so the thought just made me saltier.

We waited the usual two hours until Marcus and Juliette finally came in and sat down across from us. Juliette kept her arms folded on the table looking as if she meant business; although, if anyone was to mean business, it should be Gabe and me. Marcus kept his arms under the table and began to look at both of us.

Finally, after about five minutes, I spoke, "So, who do you people think you are?" I asked in an angry tone.

Juliette was about to yell at me for speaking to them like that, but Marcus stopped her. Juliette began to fume at us from behind her closed mouth. Marcus just looked back at us and said, "What do you mean Zeke? We have done nothing wrong."

Like I would believe something like that. However, before I could speak, Gabe did, "Just tell us. No more lies or "you'll find out later" stuff. Where are our parents?" I could tell Gabe was upset. He loved his parents. I loved my mom too, but I only had her. My father died when I was young, but Gabe would talk about what his parents would do with him almost every night before bed. He talked about how he and his dad fished down in the creek behind their house; although they never caught anything, he still enjoyed the time with his dad. I never had had those memories.

Marcus took a big breath and then said, "Your mother and father, Gabe, same with your mother, Zeke," he turned to me and then back, "were hired when you were both born to make sure that you were kept safe until your powers emerged. If you are asking whether or not the people that raised you were your real parents, then no, they were not your real parents, but they acted like they were."

I heard Gabe give a little whimper then quiet down. I am assuming it's hard on a child when his or her parents get a divorce, but finding out that they were never your real parents to begin with and then gave you up, is even harder. In a divorce, at least you still get to see both of them. Gabe and I would probably never see the people who raised us again. A thought emerged in my head, and I asked Marcus, "Wait, how did you know that we would have powers?" It didn't make sense. They knew before we were born. I think I knew what he was going to say, but I still wondered.

Marcus said, "We knew that you two would be special, just like all the rest of the teenagers here, because your biological parents were. At least one was; it seems to be a dominant trait."

"Why couldn't they just raise us then?" Gabe asked.

"They couldn't let you know about the Clade, their powers, or your powers. It would have only put you into even more danger with the Agents, and if you would've fallen into their hands, you would've prayed for death," Marcus said slowly.

I found it hard to believe that we would've prayed for death if those guys in the suits captured us, but if the

Clade took the precaution of being stationed at an abandoned hospital out in the suburbs of New York, then I guessed they weren't kidding. Plus I had seen what one of them had wanted to do when he found out that I could produce an electrical storm.

I looked over to Gabe, and I think we both had the same question, "What happened to our parents? Also, how did this even start to become so... so... strange?" I asked.

Marcus paused for a few seconds as if he didn't know how to respond to the question. He eventually said in a low voice, "Gabe, your parents were killed when you were about three. They were on a mission to gather intel on where the Agents were located outside. We have been here for twenty years, and the Agents have never found us, but they are getting close. We have a Wall of Honor for those who were lost in the fight between the Agents and us. I'm sorry Gabe. They loved you very much." Marcus seemed very sincere when he said this. Gabe looked depressed, as if someone had just taken away his chance at being with his "real" parents again. I soon thought that my dad may not have died in a war.

"What about me?" I asked.

"You, Zeke," he paused, "your parents' story is tough to explain. First, they were both terrific people with amazing abilities. Second, what your "mom" in Connecticut said was true. Your father was killed in war, but not the war regular individuals would think of. He was killed when a bomb blew up one of our transport trucks. He was the only one in the truck at the time, so the overall loss was small, but we lost a good man." He paused. I guess he was letting me take it all in. He began again, "your mother was an average individual with no powers. She was attending UCONN at the time. As members of the Clade, we highly disapproved of this, but your father was relentless. He loved her too much. Three years later, you were born. Your mom was caught by the Agents, and we never heard from her again." He paused again.

I started to think about my parents. My dad must really have loved my mom to have gone against all of these scary individuals. "Wait." I started. "Does that mean my mom could be alive?" I didn't actually want to know the answer. I just needed a little hope that my biological mom could maybe be alive.

Marcus looked over to Juliette. Juliette then said, "It is possible, but the odds are low. The Agents would do anything to get to us." I was hurt. I still believed that she could be alive, but with all of that against me, it was hard to believe. I still loved my mom who had raised me, but it's hard to turn away from the mom that had actually given life to you.

Marcus continued, "Zeke, I am sure you have thought about your gift. We all have control over the elements: fire, water, earth, and air. I am sure people have given you funny looks when you told them you can control electricity in the air and in your body. That's because… you are different. We have never seen another individual like you. Lightning was never an idea by the people who created us, and they probably couldn't have predicted it; however, they should have."

I was starting to get confused. I have an ability that no one else has. Also, what does he mean by 'the people who created us'? I was ending up with more questions than answers, but I took whatever I could get. "What do you mean by 'the people who created us?'" I asked.

"Nothing," Marcus said, "that is for another day, but understand Zeke that you are extremely important to us and to our hopes to be free. You are something that the Agents, until your little outburst at school, have not seen coming. We think it is a mutated version of what we all have; however instead of controlling just one element, you control something all the elements have, some sort of atomic structure. You can control the electrons in the air and your body, and you can use them as a weapon. It is incredibly powerful. A taser set to kill only stung you a little. Everything that we hope to achieve: freedom, rights, anything, comes down to your incredible gift.

After a pause he added.

"You, Zeke, will be the one who frees us."

Chapter 7

Gabe and I sat on our beds after the meeting with Marcus and Juliette. Neither of us spoke a word. There was a dead silence in the room until the loudspeaker lady told us it was time for bed. It wasn't very hard to go from sitting on our beds to laying on them. Gabe jumped down from the top, turned off the light, and crawled back up.

As I sat in darkness, I thought about my parents and imagined what they were like. I bet my mom was smart, being that she was in college, and my dad muscular and intimidating because that's what these people breed here: scary individuals with unique abilities. And now they want me to be one. They want me to be their leader and to save them. I'm too scared to even save myself from one man in a suit. They must have the wrong person. I'm not special, at least on these people's standards. I'm a sixteen year old boy who can't even drive a car. All I want to do right now is be home with my mom; the mom I had growing up, the mom who had all those birthday parties for me, and the mom who would tuck me into bed at night. That's where I want to be. Not here in this mess where people talk about death and despair and training for war. I'm definitely not built for that.

Surprisingly, I found sleep quickly, or it found me. Either way, I was out like a rock. I had a dream about my real parents, and how they met for the first time. My mom looked beautiful, and my dad, dare I say, looked ripped just like I had imagined. They looked so happy together. It was like looking at a black-and-white movie playing out in front of you. It seemed so surreal that my biological parents were dead.

It was surreal that the person I thought was my mom wasn't at all.

Why did they have to do that? I love my "mom" and all, but I think my real parents could've raised me just fine. When they had to go out to do a "mission" or whatever Marcus calls them, I could have been watched over by others in the Clade, kind of like babysitting. Of course, there's nothing I can do about it now; my father is dead, and my mom is probably dead too. I can't believe that though. I don't want to. I think she is alive and just waiting for me to find her.

Another thought burrowed deep into my mind. Who were these Agents that everyone kepts talking about? Marcus and Juliette weren't the only ones who talked about them. I overheard conversations in the cafeteria about Agents being posted near our position looking for suspicious activity. To be honest, I'm surprised they haven't found us yet. They had found me pretty easily. I'm sure they had some way to track us down, like if someone used their power on accident in the open, I'm sure then they would swarm this place.

Before I realized I was even asleep, I woke to Sarah staring at me from the edge of my bed. "Ah!" I yelled causing me to jump up and hit my head on the bottom of Gabe's bed, waking him up too. "Sarah," I continued, "what are you doing in here? It's... four o' clock. Shouldn't you be in bed?"

"No," she retorted, "I like to wander around at night exploring the hospital."

Now that Gabe was up, he looked down at Sarah and responded, "You walk around at night? Isn't that against the "Rule Book of the Clade" or something?"

Sarah just made a face at him and said, "Nah, I do this almost every night. It's hard to sleep with my roommate, Betsy. She creates mini earthquakes where she walks, so if she rolls in her bed, the rumble wakes me up." She kept staring at us as if she was possessed. "So," she added, "would you like to come with me? I can show you some cool stuff that the heads of the Clade are only allowed to see."

I was intrigued by what she said. I was sure there were a lot of things that we weren't supposed to know about around here. After a few minutes of thinking, I decided to go for it. "Sure, let's do it. Gabe, how about you?"

Gabe sat up and replied, "I don't know. We have only been here for a few days, Zeke. We don't want to get in trouble already and be on Marcus' bad side. I know I don't want to do anything to piss off Juliette. She will annihilate me."

I said, "Oh c'mon, Gabe. Don't you want to check out this place? Maybe they are some cool things hiding around here. Perhaps, even a way out so we can get back home.

Gabe let this sink in. He wasn't too happy with the idea, but any way to get back home no matter how dangerous was a good idea to Gabe. "Yeah, I guess I'm right behind you," he answered.

As Gabe and I got dressed quickly, Sarah sat on the bunk across from ours looking at the room. There really wasn't much to look at other than the gray walls and the steel bunk beds. I asked her as I was putting on my cloak, "Um, what are you looking at?"

She looked over to me and said, "Nothing. To be honest, my friends, back home, thought I was some kind of a weirdo." She flipped one of her descending bangs out of her face revealing a few purple dyed strands of hair. I finished putting on my clothes and thought, wow, hit the nail on the head there.

"We're ready," Gabe said.

"Okay, let's go," replied Sarah.

We opened the door and stepped out into the halls of the Clade after hours.

The only thing different between the hospital during the day compared to at night is that, well, it was dark. Other than that, not much was different. We walked around the 3rd floor on our tip toes to make sure no one heard us. It was dead silence, the kind of silence where if a pin dropped a hundred feet down the hall, it could be heard from the other end. Gabe and I followed Sarah as she headed towards a thick wooden door with a small window along the edge in the corner of the hall. She slowly pushed it open hoping no one would hear it and then told us to come. We followed behind Sarah as she moved down a staircase.

"Where are we going," I whispered to Sarah.

"I saw something," she replied, "Something that I think both of you need to see."

Gabe looked to me and then asked, "Why do *we* have to see it?" He seemed a bit anxious. I guess he never snuck out that much back home. But then again, I had only snuck out once back home to go see a rated "R" film with Thomas. It was called "Blood Lust," and it wasn't even very good. The only thing that made it "R" was nudity, and any movie can have that in it and make it "R."

Sarah stopped at the next door. The sign in front of it read "Level 2." We were on the second floor. So far, since arriving here, I had only been on the 3rd floor and in the basement. I wondered why, or who, was on the other floors. I didn't even know how big the hospital was.

Sarah said, "Okay, no one is allowed to be on the 1st or 2nd floors. The only ones who ever do are the instructors; for everyone else, it is forbidden to use the staircase which is the only way to get to these floors anyways. The elevator won't open up on them."

"Wait, so we are severely breaking the rules being up this late, not to mention wandering in forbidden territory. If we get caught, they're going to execute us," I said sounding a bit nervous.

Gabe was slowly starting to back away from the door, but Sarah grabbed him and said, "Don't worry. I was down here last night. I saw... something. I don't know what it is, and you guys are like my best friends. Also, I think it has to do with you, Zeke."

I was flattered to hear that we were her best friends. At least, now, it wouldn't be me and Gabe alone the whole time not knowing what was happening. Plus, she had been here the longest out of all of us. I was surprised she hadn't gone crazy yet with no one else to talk to, well, besides Betsy.

We agreed and followed her. The halls were even darker than the ones on the 3rd floor, mainly because the lights in the corners of the hallways were broken. It was almost pitch black.

I asked, "Sarah, do you have a light to see where we are going?"

"Yeah," she replied, "I took one off of the check in counter on the 3rd floor."

She pulled out a flashlight and clicked it on. The beam was extremely luminescent. If someone were to look at the light, they would be blinded for at least a minute or so.

We followed behind her down a long hallway with no turns at all. It gave me a creepy feeling that she was leading me to a gruesome death like in some horror film. I turned to Gabe to see that he was just as afraid as I was about this floor.

We finally reached a point where the hall went in three different directions with a reception desk in the center. She pointed the light up to the directory on the ceiling. The sign read: *Laboratory-Left, Pediatrics-Right,* and

Podiatry-Forward. We walked to the left and down another long, dark hallway.

As we walked, I looked to Sarah and asked, "Sarah, you never told us how long you have been here?"

Sarah kept walking as if she hadn't heard me. I was about to ask again when she said, "I came here three years ago when I was thirteen. Girls mature faster than boys, so I got my powers when I was much younger than you."

I nodded my head up and down listening to her tell her story. "Can you continue, please? I'm curious," I told her.

"When I first arrived here, Nathaniel began to instruct me on how to use my ability of moving water with my mind. I think you've seen him. He's the tall man with white hair. Anyway, I found out the same thing about my parents as you did; the only difference was that they're still alive. Nathaniel told me they are stationed at their main base of operations which is classified to those who are not instructors or leaders. I asked him how people can become instructors or leaders, and he told me, 'In order to become a leader, you must be elected by everyone in the Clade, and to become an instructor, you must survive many battles against the Agents and be voted in.' After that, the only thing I can focus on is training and mastering my ability to the point where I can become an instructor, and then I will be able to find out everything about this place, especially how we got our powers."

I liked Sarah. Even though she was thrown into this, alone even, she was still good at things like finding out who we all are. She's a big dreamer, and I could only break a smile at her.

We walked a little bit more in silence. We eventually stopped at room 241F. The door was shut, and I was anxious to find out what was inside that Sarah was so keen on telling us about. Gabe spoke first, "Sarah, what exactly is in here."

"I told you," Sarah said impatiently, "it is important to you both but especially you, Zeke. I think you will be shocked when you look inside."

I walked over to the door and turned the medal handle. It was as cold as ice on my skin. I slowly pushed down on the lever until I heard a click.

I began to slowly open the door.

The only thing that stopped me were the hallway lights turning on.

Chapter 8

I quickly shut the door, and we all ran inside an open laboratory door across the hall. We sat in silence and waited for whoever would show. Lights don't just randomly turn on, unless you're me, I guess, but that was besides the point. Someone was coming to check up on *something* but what?

We waited for about ten minutes, and we were about to walk out and slowly make our way for an exit when we heard footsteps. No, it was a pair of footsteps, two people were coming. We crouched even lower behind the door. I could feel Gabe breathing heavily on my back. Then I saw the feet come into view.

It was Marcus and Nathaniel. Surely, they couldn't have known we were down here unless they checked up on us and found out that we were not in our beds, but they had never checked in on us yet in the week we had been there, so why start now? All three of us watched as they stopped in front of room 241F. They waited, looking around to see if anyone was watching. We sat quietly in the darkness behind the door, waiting. Finally, they began to talk.

"How has the boy been doing so far?" asked Nathaniel.

"He is coming along faster than expected," Marcus replied, "we just had to find what brings out his power."

"Amazing," Nathaniel said. "That one of us would mutate into something even more powerful, it's hard to believe considering we are all mutated."

"I agree, it's a good thing the Agents didn't get a hand on him. That would be disastrous for the Clade."

They walked into the room and shut the door behind them. I slowly stepped out from behind the door and tip-toed behind the door they had just entered: room 241F. Gabe grabbed the back of my shirt and asked, "Are you sure we should be doing this? We should get back to bed before they find out we're not there."

I replied, "I have to. I'm sure they were talking about me back there, and if it is about me, I have a right to know."

"Zeke," Gabe said, "maybe it's not about you. It could be about... I don't know.... Lewis?"

Lewis was a fifteen year old boy who had the ability to have water drip from his fingers. It wasn't exactly the most powerful ability, but he had still gotten sent here for it. I felt bad for him. It would be hard for him to even fight in a war if something ever came to that. Oh goodness, listen to me, I've only been here a week and I'm already talking about an imminent war.

"Who else could they be talking about in there?" I replied a little irritated, "I am the only one who could do something different than everyone else. Believe me, Gabe, I didn't ask for this. I wish I was home right now playing X-Box with my friends, but that's not how it is, so I have to find out what is happening in there."

Sarah stood behind us just listening to us bicker. Gabe got fed up and said, "Fine, I'm going to bed. There is no way I am getting caught down here after hours, especially if it is off limits." Gabe looked over to Sarah, "How about you?"

Sarah replied with a slight nod of the head. She and Gabe left and left me alone to listen.

I was still crouching by the door, but thanks to Gabe, I had missed most of the conversation. I reentered the conversation when Nathaniel said, "The Agents are closing in. We can't stay here forever. 40 years has been a good run but enough is enough, Marcus. We can regroup at the headquarters and find a new place to base our operations there."

"No," replied Marcus, "I think we can take them if they choose to make an assault. I will make sure Zeke is ready to fight by then. I am going to send him out on a mission soon to gather another gifted child. The experience will be beneficial towards his skills in the field. He will soon become a great leader in the war against the Agents."

"Hear reason, Marcus. If the Agents do choose to make an assault we will be overrun. Many lives will be lost. Valuable lives. Think of the children who are finally getting used to the Clade, to find out that their leader is a war hungry monster. What if Zeke were to find out what was in here? What would become of him? He will no doubt try to run away or turn over to the Agents," Nathaniel said pleadingly.

"I have made up my mind," replied Marcus, "If they attack, we will fight. But I do agree that Zeke can never know what we are planning for him. He is a valuable asset that the Agents don't see coming."

There was a pause, and then Nathaniel finished, "If Zeke's father finds out about what you are going to do to his son, you will be no more."

Marcus replied after a short pause, "Zeke's father? I do not fear him and his ability, and, for Zeke, I am sure he would appreciate the opportunity I am giving him once he becomes loyal to the Clade. Zeke Laufor is our key to freedom."

I heard them start walking towards the door, so I went and hid behind the door across the hall again. They stepped out and locked the door behind them. I slowly creeped out until they were out of sight and then ran over to the door. I tried turning the knob but it was indeed locked.

I wasn't worried about that at the moment. I could only think about what they had just said, especially the part about my father. He *was* alive. These people had been lying to me since the moment I had arrived. All they wanted me for was to fight in their army. I wasn't going to be a part of any army any time soon. Nathaniel was right, I'd run away if I had to.

My new job was to find out what was behind that door that they didn't want me to see. I was sure Gabe would forgive me with the information I was about to give him. I started to walk down the hall towards the main hall and then to the exit, when I was hit with a terrible thought.

They had turned on the lights.

That meant they could also turn them off.

I began to walk faster but no sooner did I think about it, the lights went off.

I was stranded in the dark.

I was left lost in the 2nd floor all night until someone came and caught me trying to find my way out. She said her name was Maya, and she could melt into water. Not a bad gift for sneaking under doorways. At that point all I could think about was finding out what was in that room. Well, that and sleep.

That was until Maya led me right to Marcus' office.

Being a leader of this portion of the Clade, Marcus had an office on the far end of the 3rd floor. I think it used to be a surgeon's office until whatever made them close down.

"You have violated one of the strictest rules of the Clade. Do you understand what I am saying, Zeke?"

"Yes, sir"

"Good," Marcus said, "I was going to let you go out on a mission to retrieve a girl your age with an ability. The exact ability is still unknown, but we know it deals with fire, but now, I don't think you deserve to prove you are worth your weight around here, pulling stunts like this. Most members would be killed or worse…turned over to the Agents."

"Marcus, to be honest with you, you never said anything about going onto level 1 or 2," I said.

He thought this over for a few moments. He never had. I would've remembered if he had said that I couldn't go onto the 2nd floor. I probably would've snuck down there quickly until he said it was punishable by death. That would have been the dumbest move I would have ever made. But what was he hiding down there that no one could know anything about?

Marcus finally replied, "That may be true, but you would not have known about the 2nd floor unless someone told you. Who is it?"

Crap. I couldn't rat out Sarah. She was a good person, and I felt sorry for her. She had been here before everyone else. What else could she do besides roam around the hospital. Sarah had no one her age to be with, and, of course, my curiosity got the better of me.

I made up an excuse, "I had to find the bathroom, and it was dark." It was a lame excuse, I hoped that he would fall for it.

"Really? The bathroom? Zeke, tell me the truth. Who wanted you to go down to the 2nd level?" Marcus asked with a slight sneer. He thought he had caught me, so I decided to just play dumb and hope for the best.

"No, I really did have to pee. Too much caffeine in one day will do that to you. You should moderate the soda machine near the registration desk," I said. My plan was to keep playing dumb and hopefully he would just drop it.

Marcus stood up and slammed his fists down onto his desk. His face turned red with anger. He reminded me of a pot boiling over the top. Marcus exhaled slowly and closed his eyes trying to calm himself down. "Okay," he said, "it doesn't matter anymore. No one got hurt. I will still send you on your mission to gather a freshy."

"A freshy?" I asked.

"Yeah, that's what we call all new members until they prove their worth. The girl lives, surprisingly, in your home town. Tomorrow, Nathaniel will go with you to New Haven, and you will convince this girl to come with you."

"Okay," I replied, "And what if she doesn't want to come, like I didn't?"

He smiled and said, "Then do what I did to get you here. If she does try to run, a taser would not hurt her, but it would knock her out for a good time. Although, now that your power is starting to mature, you could be your own taser."

I was worried. I really didn't think I was strong enough to actually shoot someone with my electricity. I knew Marcus was using me to defeat the Agents and lead the Clade to some sort of "Promised Land," but I wasn't going to tell him that I had overheard Nathanial and him talking about me last night.

I thought it over for a few minutes and then he asked, "So, what is your decision. Are you ready to start showing the Clade what you are made of?"

I answered with a surprising, "Yes."

"Good," Marcus said with a smile, "Here is her file and you will leave tomorrow at first light. Good luck soldier."

I opened the door and left his office. I had survived Marcus' wrath, and now I was going to have to apologize to Gabe before I left. I didn't want to be rude to him, but I had had to stay and listen. I'm sure he would've seen my point of view if they were talking about him through the door to room 241F.

I walked into my room and lied down on my bottom bunk. I rolled over and picked up the file lying on the floor. "Another one of us," I said aloud. I already felt sorry for her and for what she had to be thrown into.

I opened the file a crack when the door opened and Gabe walked in. I sat up and looked at him. He stared back at me as if he was waiting for an apology.

Maybe he could also read minds.

"Hey Gabe," I said, "How have you been?"

Gabe rolled his eyes and said, "Just dandy, how about you?"

"Okay," I paused, "Gabe, I'm sorry for what I said last night. I didn't mean to hurt you, but I was just too curious at the time to care. Please forgive me. You are my only real friend in this place."

I waited for him to respond. He put his hand out in front of me and said, "I forgive you, don't worry. I just wanted an apology. I would've been freaking out too if I had found out that I was being used."

I grabbed his hand, and he pulled me off the bed. I had to give it to this guy. We had only known each other a little longer than a week, and he had already forgiven me for my mistake. He's a good guy.

"Hey," he said, "How about we find Sarah and grab some lunch, and maybe then you can give us an update on what happened last night?"

"Sounds like a plan!" I said excited.

"Finally," I thought, "Things were making sense and I was starting to feel like a regular boy again; well, a regular boy with lightning at his fingertips."

We were about to leave when I saw the file lying on my bed. "Hey Gabe, before we go can I look at the freshy I have to get tomorrow?" I asked.

"Freshy?" he asked back.

"Yeah, that means a newbie until you prove your worth."

"Ah, I really don't care," he replied, "I'll see you in the cafeteria."

Gabe left and shut the door behind him. I sat back down on my bed and picked up the file. I opened it up and immediately dropped the file.

I was stunned. Too stunned to even move or close my hanging jaw.

Because I knew the person in the file.

It was Trish. Trish Dawson.

Chapter 9

I sat down at the lunch table with Sarah and Gabe and threw down the file. They looked back up at me kind of hesitantly. I could tell that they somehow knew that I had a connection with this. They were right.

Trish was the girl that I was going to ask to the spring dance. Unfortunately, I was shot down, and she went with Mike, the quarterback, instead. It had happened at lunch that day that my powers had manifested and I had began the crazy adventure I'm on now. Even though she turned me down that day, I thought that she would be happy to know that I was okay and not lying in a ditch somewhere with a missing kidney. I thought that everyone would be happy to see me again. I thought that when I went back I should tell everyone about what I can do, and that I was okay with what was happening.

The problem was that I didn't believe that myself.

These people were going to use me to bring down an enemy that I hadn't even known existed until this week. Plus, I had no idea which side was even the right side to be on, and now I was expected to lead retaliation against a group of people that I didn't have proof that they were bad in the first place. Granted, the Clade didn't tase people right away like the man who was going to tase me a week ago, but still.

I pushed all of those selfish thoughts out of my head and told Sarah and Gabe about Trish. I told them about how we had gone to school together in New Haven, and how I had failed at asking her to the dance thus sealing my future to serve the Clade. They listened intently. Half of the time Gabe couldn't keep his head still, he was shaking it up and down so much.

I finished and Sarah said, "You tried to get with *her*? No offense, Zeke, but she looks out of your league."

Gabe gave a little chuckle and then added, "But hey, nice try though. She looks like a keeper to me," then he gave me a little wink. I chuckled a little when I saw that Gabe didn't wink like most people. He couldn't push just his eyelid down. He scrunched a whole half of his face, so I laughed and Sarah did too. That made me relieved. Even though we were faced with being locked up in a hospital and taken away from our families, families that were never really ours to begin with, we can still act like normal kids. I wished Thomas was here too though.

"Hey!" I shouted, "I tried at least. It's better to get shot down than to never try at all."

"Are you sure?" Sarah added smiling a little.

All three of us laughed, and then we got down to the important issues on everybody's mind. How was the mission going to play out?

I was sure it would go fairly smoothly with Nathaniel covering my butt, but still, what if one of those Agent guys showed up and tried to waste me right in front of Trish. That would just make me look weak in front of her. Also, I guess it would be bad because I would be dead. I didn't really know which one was worse. I guess if I could survive getting rejected by her, dying wouldn't be a big deal. Maybe then she would run and get help and take down the Clade.

In a mellower and more serious tone, Gabe asked, "What time do you head out tomorrow?"

"Tomorrow at first light."

Sarah added, "About six o' clock."

"Yes. I don't know where to go to meet up with Nathaniel. All I know is to be ready by, what Sarah said, six o' clock," I said.

After saying that out loud, I realized I had no idea where to be when that time came. I thought about asking Marcus, but I didn't want to piss him off anymore than what I had already caused that morning.

Then I had an idea. "How about I ask Juliette? She seems to know what is going on around here," I said.

"Ooof," Gabe replied, "She is my instructor, and I am even afraid of her."

"That sounds like a great idea, Zeke. Where do you think she would be?" Sarah asked.

I looked around the cafeteria and didn't see her, not even by the instructor table. Marcus was sitting at the head with Nathaniel in the middle. There were only five of the instructors, and you could see Marcus was in charge just by looking at the table. At the table was Marcus, at the head of the table, Nathaniel, in the middle, and Betsy's instructor, Gregory, at the other end. Gregory was a younger guy compared to the rest of the instructors. He had blonde spiky hair and a skinny face. I wished that I could've had him for an instructor instead of Marcus. He seemed like the kind of guy you could have fun with and he seemed much less intimidating.

Marcus had started off as a reasonable guy right up until he tased me. After that, he had become one big mystery. I would ask a question about who we were, and then he would change the subject. Also, he was using me. I hated that. Either way, he was making me mad.

"I don't see her. Maybe she is down in the training area," I said.

"Alright," Sarah replied, "We can all go together after lunch."

"I'll be there," Gabe added.

"Okay, let's hurry up and eat," I finished.

We finished eating quickly and rushed out of the cafeteria. We had about twenty minutes before our next training session began, so we ran quickly to the training area in the basement.

The doors to the elevator opened up, and we stepped into the long hallway to the training area. In the process of walking to the training room, Gabe and I walked past the area where we had been kept until we had woken up from our deep, electricity induced, coma when we had first arrived. It seemed odd that we had been in there only a week ago.

We entered the training room and found Juliette throwing her air spears at dummies. It was amazing to watcher her tranquil build-up and powerful release. Anything in the air's path was destroyed. I was glad she wasn't mad at me like Marcus was. All he could do was move through the air, and still the thought of him stalking me in the air gave me the chills.

Juliette turned around and saw us watching her. "What do you three want?" she asked sounding a bit annoyed.

"We want to ask you a question," Sarah said.

"Yeah," she replied, "And what might this question be."

I stepped forward towards her and said, "I have a mission tomorrow to retrieve a...freshy. I have no idea where to go at sunrise to meet Nathaniel."

She gave me a weird look; A look that said, "What? You on a mission?" She pushed her hands out of the sleeves of her dark cloak. She turned back towards another dummy and said, "Don't worry, with Nathaniel, you will know."

All three of us looked at each other confused until Gabe finally asked, "Uh, ma'am, what does that mean?"

Juliette turned around and noticed that Gabe was slightly shaking, "Gabe, I am your instructor. You do not need to fear me," she stared at Gabe for a second and then turned to me and said, "You, Zeke, will find out tomorrow. Now leave, you still have ten minutes before I must start pushing you to your physical limits."

After that encouraging comment, the three of us turned and left. We were all silent until we reached the elevator.

Gabe and I turned to Sarah at the same time and asked, "Hey, what is Nathaniel's ability anyways?" We looked at each other and laughed but then looked back to Sarah.

The elevator rang, and Sarah stepped inside. "Nathaniel has an ability that deals with the earth, but even I don't know what it is."

Wow, if Sarah, Nathaniel's own student, didn't even know, then the only ones who probably knew were the other four instructors. The elevator doors closed at that thought. When we reached the 3rd level, we all stepped out and went back to our rooms to get ready for training. I thought about how much I had pleased Marcus this morning, and thought that the next training session would go perfectly.

Not.

After a brutal training session, sleep came quickly. I dreamt about life with Gabe and Sarah growing up in a regular world, a normal world. We would go to school together, and we would hang out after school and talk about video games and movies. Unfortunately, it was only a dream, and I woke up soon.

I thought about Trish and how I was going to have to ruin her life. I thought of how Marcus had ruined my life. Actually, he really hadn't ruined mine. I had only had Thomas and Brandon. My life had been very basic. I wasn't athletic or popular. My own mom had even given me up when I was born. I had nothing but the Clade. Trish, on the other hand, had everything. People would miss her. She was popular and athletic. She probably was dating Mikey by then, and he would miss her. I felt terrible that I was going to be the one to end everything she had going for her in just a few hours.

The alarm started blaring, so I got up quietly and shuffled to the desk near the boarded up window. I turned it off, hoping Gabe hadn't woken up. He didn't have to be awake for another hour yet, the lucky guy. I put on a cloak and... waited.

I didn't know where to go from there. Nobody had told me where to go. I sat back down on the bed and waited. I still felt drowsy, so I placed my head back on my soft pillow. I was sure no one would blame me if I lay down on my bed for just a minute, especially considering I didn't know where to go.

My eyes were just about to close when I felt my bed shake a little. I looked down to the floor and noticed there were a few cracks in the floor. I figured it was just Betsy walking by or something, so I just ignored it. I was about to go fall asleep again when the same rumble passed again. I looked to the floor this time and saw that the cracks were getting larger, much larger. I got up from bed and looked at the inch wide cracks in the floor. I peered at them and they suddenly were pushed back together. I jumped back and was amazed. This was not Betsy's work. This was someone else.

While I was still standing there wondering how that happened, the door flung open, and the piece of floor I was standing on moved like a conveyor belt. I fell on my butt and watched as the floor pulled me towards the elevator that had just opened up. I sat in the elevator and waited until it opened on the 1st level.

This was the first time I had ever been on the 1st level. There were hardly any differences between the 1st and the 3rd levels. It was the same layout with the registration desk right in front of the elevator in view of the revolving doors. The hallways stretched in the same direction but then continued out around a corner. It looked exactly the same as the 3rd level.

The floor continued to pull me along; however, this time I was on my feet instead of my butt. I looked around at some of the strange posters placed on the walls. A few described the hospitals processes, and a few described immediate death by instructors if you were caught leaving the hospital without permission.

Wow, the place really was a prison. I guessed that was why they didn't want anybody on the 1st level; they were paranoid that someone would run and then the Agents would find the Clade. That solved the 1st floor mystery, now the 2nd...

The floor stopped right in front of the revolving doors. I peered through the glass and saw Nathaniel standing out near the edge of the long driveway to the parking lot about a half-mile out. He stared at the revolving door. His black cloak absorbed the light from the rising sun behind him. He looked as if he was not just wearing black, but also shrouded in darkness.

Nathaniel waved his hand. I walked through the revolving door and starting walking up towards him. Before I knew it, I was already standing right in front of him.

"Ahh!" I yelled, "How did I get here so fast?"

"Being able to slide the earth is a pretty good ability when you look at how often you can use it," he said smiling.

"If you can move the earth," I asked, "How could you move the floor up in the hospital? It's not made of ground."

"I will tell you," he said, "but first we should get to the truck, so let's start walking."

We began walking down the narrow driveway through a forest of trees. It looked as if the forest surrounded the entire hospital for many miles. I saw that it was a perfect hiding spot from the Agents.

Nathaniel began his story, "When the Clade began inhabiting this hospital almost forty years ago, we placed ground from the forest on top of the insulation and in the floor to be able to collapse the building in case we were ever overrun. I have found a good use for this accessory until that day comes."

"Do you really think the Agents will overrun the hospital?" I asked timidly.

Nathaniel waited a few moments. We kept walking until the truck finally came into view. It was a camouflaged pick-up truck. It was dark enough to be hardly noticeable in the dense trees covering it. We walked over to it. Nathaniel stopped right in front of the truck and said, "Yes, I do believe that they will be here sooner than later. How did you know that the Agents were so close?"

I stuttered a bit trying to think of a reasonable answer so that I wouldn't get busted for listening in on Marcus and him on the 2nd level, "I... uh... I just thought-" he cut me off.

"I know. You were sneaking around on the 2nd level and hid outside the door to room 241F haven't you?" he said in an almost uplifting tone.

"No," I stammered, "I was... uh..."

"It's okay, Zeke. I knew you were out there to begin with. You, Gabe, and Sarah were snooping around the 2nd level three days ago when Marcus and I discussed... things about you. I understand. I would feel like I had to know what people were saying too if they were talking about me."

Nathaniel was a cool guy. He knew what all of us was going through. I asked, "Really? I heard some things in there. Things that I shouldn't know about and if Marcus found out..."

"Don't worry, Zeke." Nathaniel said soothingly, "I won't tell Marcus, and yes, I'm sorry you are being used in his own outrageous attempt to save this place. You see, Marcus was with the original three who found this place. This has been his only home since he was just eighteen. He just doesn't want to let go. I am sorry if you are being thrown into something that is beyond your control."

"Thank you, sir," I said back to him.

"No problem. Zeke be careful though, you have a great gift. You are more powerful than anyone else here. I think Marcus fears you too."

"Yes, sir," I said feeling a bit more encouraged.

He opened the driver's door and stepped in. I followed him on the passenger side. I belted myself in, and he started to drive. I felt better about myself after what Nathaniel had said and wondered if I was really that powerful that even Marcus worried? I didn't know but at least a few questions were being answered.

Our mission began, and I would be heading back to the place that was once my home. New Haven awaited, and I was about to tell the girl I had feelings for that she was in danger for her life.

I just hoped she wouldn't kill me.

Chapter 10

The drive lasted about two hours before I started to know where I was. We passed by my favorite McDonald's which was proven to be better than the one around the corner, and we passed my old apartment. I wished that I could still look at that apartment window and picture myself still living in there; however, that was not the case. I would never be able to return there again. My home was at the hospital. Well, for now it would be. The Agents would be coming soon.

I looked at the clock in the truck and noticed that it was 11 A.M. "Excuse me, Nathaniel, but won't everyone still be in school?" I asked.

"Yes," he said, "You are going to go in and get her out. I'm sure you remember Marcus appearing out of "thin air" in your cafeteria almost two weeks ago?"

"Yeah, but, I can't evaporate into the air. How am I supposed to get her?" I asked with a slight whine which annoyed even me.

"This is where we find out if you have what it takes to do this on a regular basis. Let's see what you are worth, and don't worry, if anything bad happens, like if she rejects you again, then I'll be here," he said with a small laugh.

I, on the other hand, wasn't laughing, "How did you hear that!?" I yelled.

"Doesn't matter. Just don't worry about it."

I was mentally preparing myself for the next ten minutes. I saw the school in the distance, and my heart started pumping like crazy. I had the terrible urge to go and see Thomas right when I walked in, but I knew that I couldn't do that. I had to stick to the mission and that was to get Trish.

We parked about a mile from the school doors. The school seemed like a faraway place; although, it felt like only a week and a half ago that I was sitting in its classrooms. Then I remembered it had been only a week and a half ago.

I got out of the truck, and Nathaniel said, "Good luck soldier."

Yeah, good luck. I had to convince the girl to run away with me to a place where no one would find us, but she would have to leave everything behind. When I thought about it, it didn't sound half bad, but I knew that it was that bad. I knew she would probably hate me forever for doing this, but it was for her own good, right?

I walked up to the building and stood in front of its glass doors. I should be at lunch which meant so would Trish. Instead of using the front doors, I walked around to the back of the school and entered there.

The halls were empty. Not a soul was pacing the halls. Not even Mrs. Johnson and she usually had the place on lock down 24/7. I turned left and walked down the stairs near my old locker.

I stepped down the flight of stairs slowly hoping no one would be around a corner waiting for me. After ten or so steps, I reached the cafeteria. I peered slowly through the glass in the doors. Everyone was still sitting at their lunch tables. I looked for Thomas and Brandon at our old table and, yes, there were still sitting there.

I slowly stepped through the doors and walked quickly, but yet inconspicuously, down the hall the other way and stopped short in front of the girl's bathroom around the corner of the hall. I opened it slowly and found no one in there. I took a deep breath, knowing what I was about to do, and slipped into the girl's bathroom.

I looked around and noticed that it was the same as the boy's except they had no urinals which, I figured, was a good thing. I snuck into the far stall and locked the door. I felt awkward sitting on top of a toilet in the girl's bathroom, but I had to do it.

I knew that Trish used the bathroom everyday during lunch. I know what you are thinking, and no, I am not a stalker, but you seem to notice more about someone when you have special feelings for them. I also knew that

Trish would be the last one out. I just had to wait until she came in.

Time passed slowly. I heard different groups of people enter the bathroom and talk. I tensed up when anyone came near my stall, but thankfully, no one tried to come in. I wondered how long it would take until Trish would come in. Lunch had to be almost over and then I would be trapped down in the girl's bathroom until class began.

When I thought about leaving and trying something else, she came in. I felt like a pervert watching her wash her hands in the sink. I shook that thought out of my head and put on my hood. I opened the stall door behind her and stepped out.

"Trish..." I said slowly, "You have to come with me before it is too late."

She stopped washing her hands and turned around to look at me. We were practically the same height so her eyes would be looking straight into mine, if the hood hadn't been concealing them. "Who... who are you?" she asked sounding frightened.

"Trish," I said again, "Please come with me before it's too late. They are probably on their way right now to get you."

"Who? What is going on?"

I decided to lift off my hood and show her who I was. Now perhaps she would listen to me.

"It's me, Trish," I said, "Zeke Laufor. You need to come with me now."

"Zeke," she said like she was in shock, "What happened to you? You disappeared, and then we got a letter saying that you moved away. Where did you go?"

This was news to me. Maybe the Clade sent letters to everyone I knew so that no one would think anything about my disappearance. "I'm fine," I said, "There is no need to worry, but if you don't come soon, then you'll probably need to start worrying."

"Zeke, I don't know what you are talking about, but I can't go with you anywhere. I am... a freak."

"What do you mean a freak, you're the most popular girl in school, everyone likes you, and you're great at sports. What else do you need? "

"I mean this," she said. She held out her hand, and it lit into a flame. The flame spread up her arm until it reached her shirt. Then, her leg began to do the same up until the bottom of her shorts. Before I knew it, all of the skin on her body was on fire. It appeared to be the exact opposite of what Gabe could do. Gabe could think of things, and they would be engulfed in flames. Trish could turn her own body into fire.

The room began to heat up, and then it slowly died down. She seemed to have complete control of it. I thought about my lack of control when I had first found out and decided I liked Trish even more. "I'm a freak, Zeke," she said to me in a mournful tone, "Mikey found out and he dumped me after the dance, and now my friends aren't speaking to me. I don't know what to do."

My heart felt like it was about to be torn apart. "I know this looks bad, Trish. But if you come with me, then you can get help. You're not alone, it's happened to me too."

I decided to show her what I could do. I had been practicing using my ability when I was not afraid, but I could only get it a few times. This time, thankfully, it worked. Tiny bolts of lightning zipped between my fingertips. Soon, my body began to illuminate in a blue glow. Electricity bolted up my arms and up my back. Trish's face looked awestruck. I thought that I had finally gotten through to her. I slowed it down until it eventually faded. Trish stared at me, perplexed.

"Trish, you're not alone," I said slowly, "There is a group of people that call themselves the Clade. They help anyone who is like us, who has an ability."

"Those letters," she stammered a bit, "Those weren't real?"

"No, they weren't. And trust me Trish; I wouldn't be doing this to you if I knew it was bad. I've got to warn you, it'll get worse before it gets better, but I've made some friends where I am now. We have fun and go to school. Granted, it's a bit different than it is here, but you could still be valedictorian," I said with a small smile.

"Zeke, have you forgotten about Thomas and about all of us here? Thomas misses you every day, and we can tell that he's mad at you moving without him even knowing."

"I know, and I will tell him eventually, but now, you have to come with me."

The bell rang, and Trish said, "I'm sorry, Zeke, but I have to get to class."

She turned and opened the door. I sprinted and shut her in by pulling the handle out of her hand, causing a small bruise to form. "Ouch!" she yelled, "Zeke, move now!"

"Trish, this is your last chance," I said feeling a tear form in my eye, "You have to come with me, or… I'll have to make you."

She stared at me intensely. It felt like fire was emanating from her dark eyes. "Fine," she said, "I'll go." She held out her hand to me.

Yes, I thought. Finally, she will listen to me. I reached over to her and held her hand. I looked into her eyes and said to her, "Don't worry, Trish. This is for the better. You will see in time."

I was about to open the door when she said, "I think you're wrong, Zeke. I wish you had actually moved away." I opened the door and turned to face her. She squeezed my hand tightly and blew up into flames.

I wriggled and twisted my hand free from her intense flames. "AAAAHHHH!" I yelled at the top of my lungs. The fire burned deep into my skin. I looked at my hand, and it was covered in deep blisters and burns. I looked back at her, and she started walking towards me.

Her whole body was engulfed in flames now. "I'm sorry, Zeke. I'm sorry this is how it had to be. I won't go with you anywhere."

I was pushed into the back of the door. She was only a few feet away when I knew what I had to do. "I'm sorry too, Trish. I'm sorry you wouldn't come peacefully."

I let all of my power go. Lightning arched up and down my body. The whole room lit up into a fluorescent blue. Trish stopped and stared at me and began to run for me. I stuck out my hands, and she ran into them with her fiery body. Lightning arched from my arms up her arms. I tried to contain some of it, so it wouldn't kill her. I needed her to be alive.

She screamed an agonizing shriek and then collapsed on the bathroom floor. Trish lay unconscious at my feet. I felt terrible in so many ways. I was burned, wished I didn't have to ruin her life, and I had just had to shoot the girl I had feelings for with huge amounts of electricity, enough to knock down an elephant. It was definitely not my day.

I checked my hands and noticed that the deep and painful blisters had electricity coursing through them. I looked a little bit closer and noticed that the electricity was stimulating the cells in my body to grow. My skin stretched across the deep blisters that were now bleeding out and covered them completely. It was the same with the burns. I touched my hands a few times and noticed there was no pain. "No way…" I said to myself, or, at least, I thought because standing behind me was Nathaniel.

"Wow," he said looking at my hands and then Trish, "What happened here?"

I have never been a bad person, at least, in my own opinion.

However, after the incident with Trish, I felt like a bad person. I had snuck into my old school and kidnapped a girl whose world had been turned upside-down by things out of her control. My heart had sunk the whole time I was in New Haven and while I was at the hospital for some time. The girl that I liked had attacked me by lighting herself on fire. That was incredible. What was even more incredible was the fact that I stopped her by using electricity coursing through my veins. Plus, my burns had been healed by my own electricity. Things couldn't get any more bizarre than this.

Nathaniel had helped me carry Trish to the truck outside of the school. I carried her arms, and we walked out the back entrance. Everyone was in class right now so there was no need to worry about kids finding us. We did, however, have to worry about the threat of Ms. Johnson sneaking up on us, and being caught carrying away their valedictorian would definitely look bad.

We took our time and peered around every corner. Slowly, but surely, we stepped out of the back entrance and onto the pavement where the camouflaged pick-up was waiting for us. We put her in the back seat behind me and left the school.

We didn't say a single word to each other until we left New Haven's city line. Nathaniel spoke first, "I'm sorry for what had to happen back there. You did your best to convince her. Since she decided to attack you, I think it was wise to defend yourself," he paused before speaking again, "Don't worry. I know I say this a lot, but she will thank you for this some day."

I turned around and stared at her unconscious face. Even when she was asleep she looked beautiful. Her face had a soft glow from the sunlight shining through the rear window. She looked as though she couldn't hurt a fly, like she was too delicate to. I couldn't believe that though because underneath that beautiful exterior was a fiery core just waiting to be released. She had attacked me and had almost killed me if it hadn't been for my ability, but the sad thing was, I still had feelings for her, if not even more.

I turned back around and faced Nathaniel, "Are you sure?" I asked him.

"Am I sure of what?" he said.

"Are you sure this is for her best interest?"

He turned off of the highway and continued for a bit concentrating on the outstretched country highway in front of him. "To be honest with you, Zeke," he said to me as though he was in a trance, "I don't know. People take the change differently. Some love it at the hospital and, some… well… some hate it so much that they try to leave, but find themselves unsuccessful and disposed of."

I quickly looked at him and said, "You mean," I stammered, "Th-they get killed?"

"Yes," Nathaniel said sadly, "If one violates the important rules that must be obeyed, that must happen. I am sure you noticed the posters on the way out of the hospital?"

"Yes, but they actually kil people for that? For leaving?"

"I'm afraid so. Marcus wants to keep everyone on a tight leash. He believes that if he can keep everyone in a confined area then they will be easier to control."

"Is that why we are not allowed on the 2nd level?" I asked.

He paused thinking over how he should answer and then said, "Yes. There is another reason, but I think you have already stumbled upon it."

I thought about the 2nd level, and my ghastly night there and immediately knew the answer, "What is in room 241F?"

"I am afraid, Zeke, I am not at liberty to tell you. I wish I could but some things are better left unsaid. I will tell you that what lies behind it concerns you greatly, but it will be horrifying to you."

I let that answer sink in and then slouched in my chair and said, "Okay, thanks for your honesty. I wish everyone gave answers like you then I wouldn't be so confused."

Nathaniel laughed and said, "But isn't being confused exciting? You have no idea what to think then. I mean, just look at us. We are not normal, and I'm pretty confused about it. I'm still living," he gave another small laugh and then remained silent for the rest of the trip.

I began to drift off to sleep. We still had another hour until we would arrive back at the hospital, so getting a little sleep wouldn't hurt me.

Gabe was pacing around the training room waiting for Juliette. Zeke wasn't scheduled to be back until three o' clock, so he would have to face Juliette on his own. His nerves caused him to shake slightly at the thought of him alone with Juliette.

Today was not going to be one of Gabe's days. He had woken up this morning and stepped on a nice sized crack in his bedroom. "How did that get there?" he asked no one.

Gabe found Sarah eating in the cafeteria, and then they hung out until Gabe had to go to training. Nathaniel was gone with Zeke, so Sarah got a day off. Even though Gabe and Sarah had become good friends over the past week, Gabe was still uncomfortable talking to girls by himself. He had never had a girlfriend, and when he tried to talk to a girl, he got sweaty. It was beginning to get better with Sarah though.

Gabe paced around the training room until Juliette walked in. She wore her dark, hooded cloak, like every other day, but it looked as though she was in a better mood than the day before. Gabe couldn't figure out why, but she just did.

Juliette began, "Hi, Gabe, and how are you today?"

Gabe began to stutter both out of fear and the fact that Juliette was another female, "I am... uh…good, yeah, good."

"Are you feeling alright Gabe? You keep stammering. What's wrong?"

"Uh...I uh… nothing, I'm fine."

"Really? You don't sound fine."

"Well," Gabe confessed, "I get nervous around females when I'm by myself. That's why I let Zeke talk more when we are with you or with Sarah."

Juliette gazed at Gabe and gave a small smile, "Aww, someone's a little shy?" she chuckled a little. "You don't have to worry about girls. They're people just like you. I am a person just like you."

"Not actually, you could probably kill me without breaking a sweat."

Juliette laughed. This made Gabe laugh too mainly because he had never witnessed Juliette as a "normal" person. When she wasn't under stress trying to show the freshys how to be powerful to the Clade, she must actually have fun.

Juliette quieted down and began to take the dummies out of the large closet. Gabe walked up behind her and peered into the closet and noticed that it was extremely large. It was bigger than any walk-in closet he had ever seen. Anything needed for training was in there either on the shelves or just standing around in the middle. Juliette turned around while holding a dummy and then waved him to come inside the closet.

Gabe stepped in and turned slowly. The closet was as large as all of the rooms he had seen in the hospital. Tiny devices like tasers and little tubes that looked like blow darts sat on the shelves. All of the objects, Gabe noticed, were weapons. Gabe remembered when Zeke had been tased during training to bring out his powers. Gabe had also been tased and sent here when Juliette had arrived at his house a week and a half ago. He was glad he hadn't been blow-darted.

"This is where we store our weapons," Juliette said. "We keep these underground where, if the Agents ever did find us, they would be safe until another division came in to take the hospital back."

Gabe listened to Juliette intently. He believed Juliette, but Gabe thought she was hiding something from him. Tasers, blow-darts, and a few bow-and-arrows? These were all weak weapons. They couldn't help take down an army of Agents. No, there had to be weapons hidden somewhere else here. He was sure they didn't rely on their powers that much. Half of them didn't even have full control over their abilities yet.

Juliette took one of the dummies and went back into the training room. Gabe turned around and followed her. Gabe asked, "Is this all you have for defense against the Agents? You have to have more than this, like guns or something."

Juliette held a gaze with Gabe that he felt pierce right through him. "No, our abilities will be more than enough to defeat the Agents. Now," she said changing the subject. "Let's start training. I want to see what your "spontaneous" combustion ability can really do.

Chapter 11

Nathaniel and I pulled up and parked near the beginning of the driveway in the trees where the truck had been parked earlier. I got out and thought about the length of the driveway. "Nathaniel," I asked. "This driveway is a quarter-mile long at least. How are we supposed to carry Trish back to the hospital?"

Nathaniel just smiled at me then opened the back door. He gently put Trish, who was still unconscious, over his shoulder and then walked to me. "Easy," he said smiling. "Same way I got you to come out here."

I realized what he was talking about when Nathaniel outstretched his arm. The ground began to slide under our feet again and we began to move.

"What are we going to do with Trish when we get back?" I asked him.

"We will put her in the same room as you were in with Gabe when you first arrived here. It is a scary place, but then we know that they won't try to escape and try to kill us. Especially this one, she could burn down the whole place."

"Okay, but that won't keep her from using her ability. She would only be strapped to a table."

"Well, we have developed a way that will suppress someone's ability for a few hours."

I thought it over, and I realized that I hadn't been able to use my powers while I had been strapped to the table. I had been afraid and worried, but yet nothing had happened. That is usually when my ability would work too. I asked Nathaniel, "How would you suppress someone's ability? Is that room made of kryptonite or something?"

Nathaniel laughed loudly, "No no, we actually created a sort of vaccine. It is an injection that targets wherever it is your ability develops and numbs it for a short while. I assure you it is not kryptonite," he laughed again.

"Wait, you injected *me* with it?"

I hadn't noticed that we had already reached the hospital doors. I had been so caught up in the conversation that everything around me had become invisible. Nathaniel remained quiet and entered through the revolving glass doors.

I ran in front of him and then stopped. "Hey, I asked you something important. Did you inject me with that stuff when I was here? It's really no big deal. My ability is back now, and the past is history."

"Yes," Nathaniel answered. "We did inject you with the vaccine."

I looked at him for a little bit longer and then moved to the side. Nathaniel kept on walking, and I moved my legs a little bit faster to keep up. He got into the elevator first and pushed the button to the basement floor. We went down and down until we reached the basement, and the doors opened. Nathaniel remained silent until we finally placed Trish down on the table and strapped her in.

My heart began to ache again seeing her lying there with the bright light swinging over her face. I knew I had hurt her in a terrible way. This place was a living hell. Rules and regulations are enforced by death, no one gets any privacy, and everyone has to train and eat and sleep and bathe with someone. And what was the point again? We train and help protect the Clade from Agents we know nothing about in a place we know nothing about with people we know nothing about. Everything was a secret, even our real parents.

That's probably the toughest part of this whole experience too. Finding out that you never had real parents, or that they had to give you up for someone who was working for the Clade. I just hoped that Trish's parents were dead. I knew it was morbid to think about, but if her parents were dead, then she wouldn't have to think about the thought of her parents just giving her up. Like mine had.

Nathaniel walked over to the table and pulled out a small syringe. Inside the syringe was a foggy yellow solution. He walked back over to the table and stood next to me. He pushed the spring in causing the solution to squirt out the end. "You may want to look away from this. It is only a shot, but you might not want to see what happens after."

I didn't respond, but I knew I had to watch. I wanted to see what was so wrong with this that Nathaniel hadn't even responded when I had asked him about my injection.

He stepped over to Trish's shoulder and put the needle just outside of her bare arm. He looked over to me, and I just shook my head. He looked back down and pushed the needle into her arm. Quickly, he pushed the spring on the top of the syringe, and he pulled the needle out. He put the syringe in the discard slot on the wall and walked behind me. He put his hands on my shoulders and then said, "I would look away now."

"What?" I asked.

He didn't have to answer. Trish began to squirm and convulse in her restraints. Her face shook and scrunched in on itself. It was as though she was having a seizure. Foam began to emit from her mouth. I quickly turned around, but that didn't stop the sounds. I could hear the foam sizzling out of her mouth. The straps rattled on the side of the table holding tight against her wrath.

I couldn't take it anymore. I ran out of the room and ran straight to the reception desk in front of the elevator. I took deep breaths and tried to get the thought of Trish out of my mind. It was impossible. I grabbed the wastebasket and threw up in it. I was disgusted with this place and with what I had seen. This had to be the last straw.

After what seemed like years, Nathaniel walked out of the room and stopped in front of the desk. "I'm sorry," he said apologetically. "It is just one of the side effects of the vaccine."

I took a few deep breaths in and out hoping not to puke again. "Is that why you wouldn't respond before?" I asked.

He stared at me for a bit longer and then said, "I'm sorry Zeke. I really am."

After saying that, he headed for the elevator and pushed the button. I would've stopped him if it wasn't for my now empty stomach.

After all of that, I knew that we had to do something; we had to get out of there. But first I had to get some questions answered. The only problem was that the only place in this whole hospital that I knew would answer my questions was forbidden.

Room 241F on the 2nd level.

Before I got up, Gabe walked in front of me heading to the elevator. He turned and smiled brightly. "How was it? I just got done with training, and I found something out. They have a huge closet filled with tasers and other weapons, but I am sure that is not all of them."

"Really? That's great. Wait till you hear this though."

And I told him everything.

We sat in our room after dinner and waited for Sarah to show up so that we could sneak down to the next level. In the meantime, I told Gabe about what had happened on my mission to retrieve Trish and about the injection. He stared with his mouth open, nodding at the interesting parts. Although, by the look on his face, I guessed that it was all pretty interesting.

Sarah walked in right as I finished. She wanted to hear about my day too, so I told her. After I had gone through my story yet another time, she straightened up and asked, "Are we ready to go? It's now or never. I think it's time to find out what they are hiding in Room 241F."

Gabe and I answered with a not-so-resounding 'yes.' We put our hoods over our heads and opened the door to the dark hallway. It was a little after midnight, so we were sure no one was walking the halls. We crouched low and scuttled along the walls to the door that would take us down to the 2nd level. We found the door with the small window and continued on.

We ran down the four flights of steps until we reached the sign that said level 2. We all glanced at each other and nodded showing that we were ready to go. Sarah grabbed the handle and pulled it open.

The halls were as dark as they were last time. Luckily, I was sure that we all remembered the way to Room 241F from our last adventure. Nathaniel had known that we had been there last time, so we had to be extra careful this time to make sure no one spotted us, especially Marcus.

We took a few steps into the dark halls. It was almost impossible to see. Sarah pulled out her flashlight and gave it a click into the "on" position. Nothing happened. She tried again but nothing. "Oh crap!" she said whispering.

"What's wrong?" I asked.

"The flashlight died. We have no light anymore, and it's not like we can see anything. I guess we'll have to try again tomorrow night once I find some new batteries," Sarah stated disappointed.

Gabe and Sarah turned around and started heading for the door back to the stairwell. Almost instantly, I had an idea. "Hold on, wait, I have an idea."

Gabe responded, "What's that. Do you have a flashlight?"

"No, I have something that won't run out of juice. Me."

If I could've seen their faces, I was sure they would be in some sort of shape that would resemble the international sign of "WTF are you talking about?" I planned to show them.

"Watch," I said quietly. I concentrated on focusing my ability to run into my hand. After a few seconds of concentration, my hand began to spark and emit its warm, blue glow. I held out my hand in front of Sarah and Gabe. They looked as surprised as me to see that this had worked.

"Well," Sarah said, "Aren't you full of surprises."

Gabe just replied with a "Yeah, nice."

I smiled and turned around and continued into the not so dark anymore hall.

We walked in a single file line remaining silent until we reached the intersection. We turned left and went towards the laboratories. Gabe asked, "So, what do you guys think is in that room anyways?"

I replied, "Nathaniel told me that I didn't want to know, so it must be something good."

"Maybe it's the actual fighting weapons, like guns and stuff, that weren't in the closet Juliette showed Gabe?" Sarah said.

"Why do you think that?" I asked her.

"Well, if the other Clade members found out about these kinds of weapons. They could steal them and then escape." She had a valid thought.

We continued down the hall giving our own theories of what might be in the room ranging from food to extraterrestrials. Even though I highly doubted that extraterrestrials were locked in a hospital room in the middle of nowhere, it sure gave us something to calm our nerves as we continued down the hallway.

We reached Room 241F just before 1 a.m. We sat just behind the door waiting for someone to try it. I turned off my hand (that sounds weird) and grabbed the handle. We all took a few deep breaths, and I turned the handle. The suspense was killing all of us as the doorknob slowly turned downwards. I could've just opened it quickly and got over with it, but something was holding me back. I didn't know what it was. Maybe it was the thought that maybe I really didn't want to see what's beyond the door. What if there was information on our parents on the other side? I mean our *real* parents. Maybe we really didn't want to go back there. "No," I told myself. "I have to see what they are hiding back here."

The door opened. I peered into the dark room and heard no movement at all. I lit my hand up again and waved to Sarah and Gabe, who were now shaking in anticipation behind me, to go in. They took the signal and entered the room. I walked in behind them and shut the door.

"Zeke," Sarah whispered. "Turn on the light."

I put my hand against the concrete wall and felt around for the light switch. I couldn't find one anywhere. I waved my hand through the air hoping the light had a chain that you could pull on, but there was no switch to be found.

"I can't find one. What about you guys?" I whispered.

I heard Gabe and Sarah shuffle along the walls looking for the light switch that appears to be non-existent. After all of the walls were checked, we stopped.

Gabe said, "There has to be a light source somewhere. They wouldn't use this room only in the day, so they could use sunlight. No, they have got to have another means of turning on the lights. I mean we saw them a few nights ago down here and the light was on then."

Gabe was starting to impress me with his intelligence. If I ever had to take a math test here, I had to make sure I cheated off of him.

"Yeah," Sarah said. "Maybe there is a special password or something that turns on the lights."

"Like what?" I asked her.

"I don't know. How would I?" she had a point on that one. "Wait, Zeke, turn your… hand on again and lets see where a switch could be."

I listened to her and my hand re-electrified itself emitting its blue glow. The light was not powerful enough to even see all of the walls of the room at once, but it was enough to maybe find a light switch.

We walked around the room and saw that it contained small lab tables with beakers and flasks. It looked as though the laboratory was still in use even after the hospital had been shut down for over fifty years. Something didn't make sense. Nathaniel warned me not to come in here, but why? It was a normal looking laboratory.

After ten minutes of searching, we halted and walked towards the center of the room. "I don't get it," Sarah said sounding frustrated.

I did a quick three-sixty to take a look at the room. It was a little larger than the training room with a dry-erase board behind me on the wall to the right of the door. There were cabinets in front of me, and another boarded up window to my right. Nothing seemed to be out of the ordinary. Something smelled fishy.

I said, "No, Nathaniel knew I was down here a few nights ago. What if there's a special password to turn on the lights, you know, like the clap-on light?"

"Well," Gabe said agreeing with me, "What do you think we have to say?"

"Zeke," Sarah said, "Think of Marcus and Nathaniel the last time you were down here. What did they say before they left? Maybe they said it when they left the room."

"Good idea," Gabe said.

"Okay," I said. I thought about the conversation Marcus and Nathaniel were having of me in this very room only a few nights ago. It seemed like an eternity because I had learned so much about this place since then.

I kept thinking and remembered the last thing Nathaniel and Marcus said, "*If Zeke's father finds out about what you are going to do to his son, you will be no more.*"

That was Nathaniel speaking; then Marcus had replied, "*Zeke's father? I do not fear him and his ability, and, for Zeke, I am sure he would appreciate the opportunity I am giving him once he becomes loyal to the Clade. Zeke Laufor is our key to freedom.*"

After that, they left the room. I really didn't want to remember what happened after that. That had been a long night.

"Well?" Sarah asked. "What do you remember?"

I looked down at the floor. The blue glow was illuminating the tiles and the tiny specs of dirt in between them. I looked up and answered, "I know Nathaniel said something about my father being alive."

"Yeah," Gabe said. "I remember when you told us that during lunch break. That was really heavy."

"Anything else?" Sarah asked.

She was determined to figure out the mysteries of this room. I replied, "Yeah. Marcus said something about how I am their key to freedom."

We looked around the room and nothing happened. "What specifically did Marcus say?" Sarah asked grudgingly.

I was getting agitated with her fast, "All he said was, '*Zeke Laufor is our key to freedom!*'" I yelled.

That was all it took. Immediately the lights began to flicker and a soft yellow glow came out of them. When the lights turned on, we could see that the room was the same as it had been in the dark. This didn't make sense. I had expected some large computer monitor with beeping red lights or something. Even the alien idea was a good one at this point.

We were about to leave disappointed when we heard a small generator kick in. It buzzed and hummed quietly. At first, it just sounded like the light bulbs, but it stood out too much. If there was a small generator in there, it must be giving power to *something* in the room.

We turned around and waited to find out what the generator powered. We heard the clicking of gears and the air from pneumatic pistons. Then, almost immediately after, the chalkboard stuck out from the wall. It was incredible! The chalkboard slid out a few feet and then it flipped around revealing, and who would've thought, a large computer monitor with beeping red lights. After that, the tables turned over through the floor revealing little gizmos to operate the computer. The cabinets also flipped around through the wall and an armory of guns, rockets, and bulletproof vests popped out.

The generator whined down until it was almost inaudible. All three of us looked at each other with dumbfounded expressions. "I guess that worked," Gabe said.

Neither Sarah nor I could reply to Gabe. We were too stunned, and it wasn't over yet. The lights darkened into some color that resembled black lights. Anything white in the room turned purple and glowed.

We all walked around the room taking in the new surroundings when Sarah said, "Zeke…you have to come here."

I walked over to her and replied, "Yeah?"

She didn't say anything in return. She just raised her hand and pointed at the computer monitor because on the monitor was a picture of a person. A person that looked familiar to me.

It was me.

Along with my picture, it said Operation: Zeke Laufor.

Chapter 12

We all stared at the screen dumbfounded by the image flashing on the blue tinted screen. None of us knew what this meant, but we all had the same idea. I was being used by the Clade to help them break free from the Agents, or so all the clues were pointing towards. For all I knew, they may've just wanted me to shovel the snow off of the hospital driveway in the winter. The word "Operation" flashing on the screen next to my picture, however, suggested it was a little more serious than shoveling snow.

Gabe spoke the phrase to turn off the lights, and we left. I was angry at everything that was happening. Nothing, up until that point, had been the truth. No one had ever told me about some "operation" where I was the main point of interest. I held out my hand into the darkness and quickly walked down the dark halls.

Sarah spoke to me in a whisper, "Maybe…" she paused. "Maybe it's not so bad. Maybe it was just the plan to get you to come here, and they forgot to delete that program."

Gabe answered, "No, I don't think that is it. I am sure that with a computer that high-tech that they would keep it up-to-date with whatever this place is planning. That wasn't some desktop computer that was a super computer. I wonder where they got it?"

I didn't respond to any of those ideas. I just kept moving forward grudgingly. We reached the stairs and walked up to the 3rd level. I let my hand go out and then peered around the corner checking to see if anyone was out on patrol. We kept moving quietly until we reached our room.

I quietly shut the door once everyone was back in and then began to talk. "I am sick of this! I am tired of them using me in some sick plan for them taking over the Agents. I heard what they said a few nights ago down there. There is a pretty big chance I will not even make it out of the war between us and the Agents alive."

Gabe and Sarah remained quiet. I added, "I…I just can't be manipulated and lied to anymore." It was true. I had been lied to since I had arrived here. It wasn't a question anymore of whether or not I was special to them. I knew I was, but I was afraid that I wasn't so important that they wouldn't let me die.

Sarah responded, "Well, what do you think we should do?"

I could tell Gabe was thinking about the same plan as I was. We couldn't stay here. Well, I couldn't stay here. I needed to escape, and if that means risking my life, so be it.

Gabe answered for me, "We run away. Escape. We run and don't stop."

"No," I replied quickly. "I am going by myself. You are not a part of this. I am. I will not put you guys into unnecessary danger anymore."

"Zeke," Gabe replied. "If you go and we stay, Marcus will know that something happened, and that we were probably involved. He's not dumb, in fact, he has been watching us, I'm sure, for the past few days. He knows who your friends are, and I bet once you left, he would find us and then *make* us tell them where you are."

"It's true, Zeke," Sarah said. "Marcus will torture us until he gets what he wants. He is a ruthless and evil being. We *are* going with you, so don't think you are so special that you've got to play the hero."

Ouch, that last bit hurt, but she did have a point. I loved my friends. They're so smart, and they'd risk their lives to help me… to help *us*. "Okay," I said. "What's the plan?"

Gabe answered, "We leave sometime this week. Either tomorrow or Saturday night, that way there would be a minimum chance of anyone finding out."

Sarah agreed with Gabe's plan. I agreed also but said, "We should go on Saturday night."

"Why wait?" Sarah asked.

"I want to get Trish out of here before she is thrown into this mess." I answered hesitantly.

"Zeke!" Gabe exclaimed in a whisper. "She tried to kill you last time you had a run-in with her. Why don't you just take the hint?"

"It's not fair to her. If I can save her, I will, so there is no point in arguing," I said.

Sarah put her hand on Gabe's shoulder and that calmed him down. If I didn't know any better, I would say that Gabe had a slight crush on Sarah. Good for him.

"Gabe, it is fine," Sarah said as she looked over at me. "She better be worth it though, Zeke. Tomorrow she'll be put in a room somewhere on this floor. We won't have much time to try to convince her. Marcus and a few of the other instructors will be watching us."

"Don't worry," I said assuringly. "I'll get her to come."

Gabe shrugged Sarah's hand off of his shoulder, "And what if she doesn't want to? Then what?"

I thought over the idea of having to leave Trish behind quietly. Yeah, she had tried to burn me into a Zekeburger, but I had been like that too when Marcus had tried (and succeeded) capturing me. I remembered when my lightning bolts had arched across the room and down the hall leaving scorch marks. She had had a little more control over her ability though.

I responded after a few moments of complete silence. "Then, we will leave without her." It hurt saying that out loud, but that was the way it had to be. Maybe if I was gone, she wouldn't have any problems adjusting here. Trish was a quick learner, and I was sure Marcus would not do anything to her. She would be loyal to the Clade.

The clock read 3 A.M. Sarah said goodnight and tiptoed down the hall to her room. Gabe took off his cloak just leaving his boxers and a white t-shirt on and climbed into bed. I was right behind him and crawled into my bed. I hadn't realized how tired I was, and I was going to be even more tired tomorrow if I was only getting four hours to sleep.

I let out a big yawn and began to drift into sleep. I thought about the flashing computer screen with my face next to the words "Operation: Zeke Laufor." I pulled up the covers a little more and then fell asleep. I needed as much rest as possible; tomorrow would be the day I had to start convincing the girl I had just captured to escape with me, Gabe, and Sarah.

It sounded like tomorrow would be a rough day.

My dreams were not ready to take a break. I dreamt about Gabe, Sarah, Trish, and I after we had successfully escaped the Clade. We were back in New Haven living in my apartment where my mom and I used to live. We were all attending New Haven High School and were living normal lives. Thomas forgave me for leaving after I told him what had happened. Unfortunately, it was only a dream, and I woke to the wake-up call over the P.A. system.

I sat up and rubbed the crispy particles from my eyes. My mom used to call the crusty things "sleep" because you get it when you sleep. I really missed my mom. Maybe, when we got out of here, she would take me back; although, she probably had never wanted me. Perhaps I could find my real mom. I would take her away from the Agents control, and we could live together. It would be awkward for the first few weeks, or months, but I would forget about it because I would be with my real mom and nothing would take her away from me again.

Gabe dropped down from the top bunk and grabbed his clothes. "Good morning, Zeke," he said to me. He grabbed his toothbrush and was about to open the door when he said, "Good luck with Trish today. I'm sorry I was so opposed to that last night. I just don't want to see you get hurt."

"Thanks man," I replied genuinely. "I'll do my best, but no matter what happens, I'll be right behind you tomorrow night. You better be ready to run."

Gabe smiled and then left the room to take a shower. I stood up, grabbed my hooded cloak and hygiene products, and left for the bathroom myself.

I shut the door behind me and entered a hallway filled with the hustle and bustle of people. There were shouts from one end of the hallway to the other end with the sound of panic in them. An alarm blared over the loudspeakers making almost every sound inaudible without screaming. I pushed past a few people running around like chickens with their heads cut off and found Marcus standing near the reception desk. He was talking to Juliette about something serious. I just hoped it wasn't me again and that it had to do with something that was going on now.

I set my stuff down on the desk and shouted to them, "What is going on here!"

Marcus yelled back, "The newbie girl you captured yesterday woke up and had an outburst! The entire basement level is engulfed in flames!"

"WHAT!" I yelled at the top of my lungs to the point it was painful. "Is she okay?"

Juliette replied, "She will be fine! Her body can handle the heat, of course, you should know all about this! I heard she used her ability on you!"

Then Marcus said, "Don't worry! We have the recruits that have control over the water element working on that right now!"

That made me feel a little bit better. The water would put out Trish's flames, and then she would calm down, hopefully. I felt like I needed to help because I had brought her here after I had tased her; then again, I had been ordered to, so maybe she would listen to me over the others here.

I thought of something and then asked Marcus, "What about the solution to keep her powers in control!? Did that not work!?"

I realized I wasn't supposed to know about that, and he just looked at me with an angry yet surprised expression on his face, "How do you know about that!?"

I didn't answer. I just ran away from there, and fast. I left my stuff lying on the reception counter. I didn't care if I was still only in my pajamas, I had to help Trish. I headed for the stairs and ran down to the basement level passing the 2nd and 1st floor doors. I noticed that the first floor doors were boarded up. Maybe that was to help keep people from leaving? They would have to use the elevator, and then Marcus could just turn that off and trap them. I would have to remember to tell Gabe and Sarah about that.

I opened the basement door and found myself on the far side of the hallway, just to the left of the elevator. I could see black smoke bellowing from the main hall going down to the training rooms, so I expected the water recruits to be down there. I ran down to the reception desk in front of the elevator and watched as about thirty trainees used whatever water-like ability they had against the raging flames. Some of the recruits were turning their limbs into water and then whipping tiny droplets at the flames, and others were just melting in front of it to slow the fire down. I would've been afraid of getting stepped on.

Covering my mouth with my sleeve, I walked into the group of water recruits. Sarah had to be somewhere down here. She would help me get to Trish. My eyes began to sting from the ash and chemicals in the smoke, but I knew I had to keep moving.

Sarah was towards the front of the group near the bathroom. She pulled water out of the toilets and sinks using swift hand motions and then threw it on the flames. It was probably the most affective method, besides the guy who could literally vomit water in a huge stream, but it still had hardly any affect. Trish was just too overwhelmed.

I tapped Sarah on the shoulder, and she looked back at me and said, "Zeke!? What are you doing here? Can't you see I'm busy trying to save our butts at the moment?"

"I can tell, but I have to get to Trish. I could help."

"Zeke, the last time you tried to help her, you were almost cooked into a black crisp. Do you really think you can help?"

"Yes," I said pleadingly. "Just get me into the holding room. I can take care of myself there. If I have to, I'll shock her."

"Okay, but it's your funeral."

I didn't care what the possible outcomes were. I had to help. I felt responsible. I had no idea where this courage was coming from, but I was starting not to like it. I just kept putting myself in more and more danger.

"What's the plan?" Sarah asked still throwing water at the fire.

"Would it be possible for you to take the water and make a bubble around yourself?" I asked her.

"Zeke, that is asking a lot. I can barely even control ice in training. How am I supposed to do that?"

"You just have to try. You never know until you do, and, besides, we only have to go thirty feet. Could you do that?"

She kept throwing water at the raging fire. Sarah had to make up her mind because the flames weren't going to stop coming. "Okay," she said. "I'll give it a try."

I stepped away from Sarah, and I let her do what she does best. It really is an art form, water control. The way your hands flow like a stream through the air is really mystifying. I would have been excited if it wasn't for the huge wall of fire coming our way.

Sarah willed the water to her. She kept swirling her hands in a circular motion, but it was no use. The water wouldn't stay put. It kept falling to the ground or spraying people around her. "I can't do it!" she said frustrated.

"Don't talk like that!" I replied. "Just relax and focus. I know you can do this, Sarah."

She listened, took in a few deep breaths, and tried again. The water swirled around her as it had before. It kept spraying in all directions, and it just would not stay put. Finally, I came up with an idea.

"Sarah!" I yelled to her. "Stop. I have an idea."

She stopped and the water fell to the ground and formed a puddle around her. I walked toward her and pressed myself up against her. "Zeke?" she said sounding confused. "What are you doing?"

"Listen. Try the water thing again. I'm going to zap it with my electricity then the water molecules will be stimulated and be more sensitive to your movements," I said sounding a heck of a lot more intelligent than I had thought. I didn't even know if the plan would work, but it was worth a shot.

"Alright, get ready," Sarah agreed.

She began to manipulate the water around herself again. It churned and twisted through the air like a rhythmic dance. Sarah began to pull it around us when I held my arms out at full stretch. The water was only a few inches from my hands on both sides. All I had to do was stimulate the water so that Sarah could hopefully pull it up over our heads and hold it there.

I focused on what I wanted my body to do. I felt small tingling sensations at the tips of my fingers as the electricity arched from them to the almost sphere of water. The water shimmered with each small bolt that hit it.

"There," I said to Sarah. "Is that working?"

"I'll try," she said.

She moved her arms up over her head, and, amazingly, the water followed. I kept stimulating the water with my electricity while she moved it up around us. Before you knew it, Sarah had created a sphere of water with us on the inside. "Great job," I told her excitedly.

"This is… awesome!" she replied happily.

"Alright, don't forget why we did this. The hard part starts now. Can you hold it?"

"Yeah, no problem."

"Okay then," I said. "Let's go through."

I followed just behind Sarah close enough so that our bodies touched. I tiptoed behind her as she made her way toward the bellowing wall of fire. We stopped just short of the flames when Sarah asked, "Are you sure about this?"

I replied with a straight forward, "No."

"Okay, me either." After those last few words, which could have very well been our last few words, we pushed through the wall and into the fire.

Chapter 13

I didn't know how long the bubble of water would last against the inferno, so we had to move quickly. The bubble sizzled and steamed making the inside of the bubble feel like a sauna. Sarah and I were sweating to the point of collapsing, but we had to keep moving because we still had about twenty feet to go.

The water and the fire created glowing images around the sphere. They were really eerie, but we didn't have time to get distracted looking at them. Not now. Instead we were forced to look out at the burning halls. Everything was black. Ashes were all over the floor. So much so in fact that I was worried that they would burn us, but the water sphere cooled them down. The walls were black and peeling and falling to the ground. It was a fireman's worst nightmare.

With only ten feet to go, I began to think of what I was going to do to stop Trish. We couldn't push her into the bubble because then we would be as crispy as the walls. We couldn't leave the bubble because then we would end up like the walls again...crispy. If we couldn't calm down Trish, which I highly doubted we could, then I would have to do something drastic. I just hoped it didn't have to come to that.

Sarah said, as we were approaching the door to the holding room, "Okay, we're here, but hurry, I don't know how long I can hold this thing. I'm already getting pretty tired holding it this long."

"Okay," I replied. "You are doing great, Sarah."

The door was just a black smolder on the floor, so that saved us one step. We walked through the doorway and into a firestorm. It felt like wind was actually blowing us away from that room, but it was just the fire stemming from Trish.

Sarah and I kept pushing harder until we saw her. She was on the other end of the room huddled in a corner holding her legs. We stopped just short of her, and I began trying to convince her to stop. "Trish," I yelled over the fire. "It's me, Zeke. You have to stop this or a lot of people will die. You are just overreacting. I'll make this all better, but you've just got to stop!"

Looking up at me, Trish replied, "How can I even trust you, Zeke? You kidnapped me and brought me here. How can I even respect you again?"

"You'll have to. You will learn, over time, that this was for the best. There were people already on their way to kill you when I found you at school, but you're safe here."

Trish began to cry. I think she already had been but now it was definitely noticeable. I looked back at Sarah, and she said, "Zeke, I'm running out of juice. I can't hold this much longer."

I quickly turned back and continued with Trish, "Hey, it's seriously going to be okay. We'll teach you how to keep your ability in-" she cut me off.

"NO! I don't *want* this. Look at me. I'm a human matchstick. Why are you trying so hard to convince me that this place is for my own good? Why didn't you just let me those people kill me?"

"You're too important to me, Trish. I wouldn't let that happen. I'd protect you and stand up for you no matter where we are or what you are."

I turned back to Sarah, and she looked like she was about to faint. "I…I can't do this much more, Zeke. You have…have to stop it before we die."

Trish was looking back at me again. "Do you here that, Trish? If you don't stop, all of us are going to die."

"I can't help it. This just happens when I'm angry. I don't even know why."

Time was almost up, and I was afraid I was going to have to do the drastic idea I had thought of before. "Trish," I said slowly and gently. "I am going to knock you out again. That will stop the flames, but I promise nothing will happen to you when you wake up. You will be safe and sound. Please trust me."

She looked around at the damage she caused. It wasn't her fault. I had been the same way except my power just randomly shot things, and it definitely had not caused the whole basement to burn.

Sarah said something in a very muffled tone sounding like, "I… I'm done, Zeke."

My time was up. I said to Trish, "I'm sorry Trish. I really am." I took a few steps away from Trish, and then, without hesitating, I jumped out of the bubble and grabbed Trish with my electric hands. The fire burned so badly I couldn't help but scream. I had never felt anything like that before in my life, and I hope I never have to again. Trish convulsed and collapsed on the ground. The fire soon faded, and Sarah collapsed to the ground also passed out.

My body felt like a million degrees. I looked at my arms and legs as I lay spread out on the floor. There were deep burns, and I could see a small layer of muscle in my arm. The pain was so unreal that I thought I was asleep, dreaming. Before I could continue to scream, the ground moved underneath my body, and I was pulled out of the room and down the ash filled hallway along with Sarah and Trish.

The floor stopped moving in front of Nathaniel and Marcus. I looked up to Nathaniel, and he just smiled at me showing that he was proud of what I had done. Marcus, on the other hand, couldn't stop staring at my 2nd and almost 3rd degree burns. I looked at them and noticed that tiny filaments of electricity were stretching across the burns telling the cells to form new tissue.

After about two minutes, the burns were gone along with the pain. I looked back up to Marcus and caught a murderous glare from him. All he said was, "Well, well. Look who is full of surprises."

Being not the brightest kid at Middleton High, I had always appreciated the little comments that my teachers or my mom would make about some of the good grades I had gotten. I hadn't gone as far as to hang them on the refrigerator door, but I still smiled when anyone would say anything nice about my hard work. Unfortunately, that wasn't going to happen today.

Immediately after Marcus noticed the extra extension of my "gift," I was rushed into his office on the 3rd level. I sat behind the hardwood desk with my arms folded across my chest. Nathaniel stood next to Marcus like some sort of henchman from a James Bond film.

Marcus stared at me with intensity as he spoke, "When were you going to tell me that your ability was progressing so rapidly?"

I looked up to Nathaniel for support, but he remained unresponsive. "I didn't think it really mattered," I said.

"Didn't matter?" Marcus replied starting out angry, but soon not able to contain his glee. "This is terrific. You'll be able to fight along side me when we begin the war against the Agents."

Marcus sounded like a child on Christmas opening a new toy. I, unfortunately, was the toy. I knew how things would turn out if I fought in this "upcoming war" that Marcus kept talking about. "If I may ask one thing," I said trying to sound as enthusiastic about fighting as he was. "Who are the Agents, and where are Trish and Sarah?"

Nathaniel looked at me grimly. Marcus stared down at his desk as if he was storing his anger. "The Agents," Marcus said slowly, "are why we are like this."

I hadn't seen that coming. I had thought that the Agents were people jealous of our abilities or something. Believe me, I wouldn't be jealous, but that was the only logical answer I had really thought of. "How'd they do that?" I was about to ask when Marcus continued, "We have been hunted and tortured for decades for being something *they* created."

"Are you saying they gave us our abilities?" I asked.

"No, they didn't," and Marcus left that conversation there.

The idea that humans have created a way to make super powers was beyond me. I still didn't really believe that someone could create some sort of synthetic chemical or something like that to make someone… beyond human.

I realized Marcus hadn't responded about Sarah and Trish yet, so I asked again, "Sir, where are Trish and Sarah?"

He looked up from his desk as if he had just been snapped out of his weird delusion, "Oh yes, about them, we will have to keep them in a special facility for now until they have recovered from their injuries. Using one's power too much can result in drastic consequences. Remember that."

"Okay, thank you sir," trying to sound politely. "But where is this 'special facility'"

Marcus replied with a simple, "You don't need to know." I knew he wouldn't tell me, but it had been worth a shot. Perhaps it was because I didn't like Marcus one bit, but I was beginning to think he was doing more than just trying to help heal Sarah and Trish. I was worried about them now. Marcus quickly continued, "We just don't want them to push themselves over-the-edge with visitors. Not in the state they are in right now."

I knew he was hiding something; he had to be. I looked up to Nathaniel, but he just kept a blank look on his face. He was no help to me now. I had to find Sarah and Trish before it was too late. Gabe, I was sure, would be in as well. We had a plan to keep on schedule. We had to leave this hell in a day and a half.

I slid back in my chair and asked, "May I leave now? It's lunch time."

Marcus replied, "Oh yes, of course you may leave."

"Thank you," I replied while heading towards the door. Before I got to the door I heard Marcus ask Nathaniel to stay for a moment.

I left the room and waited behind the door. I didn't care what happened to Nathaniel in there. He hadn't been any help to me, so why should I help him. In fact, what if he had wanted me to go down into room 241F. I felt the urge to listen in on them again, but there were too many people walking around for me to even think about trying that. Instead, I left to go have lunch in the cafeteria.

Gabe was already at the table eating his Lean Cuisine type meal when he spotted me walking in. He sat straight up and waved for me to come sit by him before I got my food. I sat down across from him, and he said, "Hey, I heard what you did with Trish and her fiery outburst before. Wow! Oh, and I heard Marcus found out about your healing gift."

Wow, news travels fast in an abandoned hospital. "Yeah, he did. In fact, I was just in his office."

I told Gabe about my talk with Marcus and Nathaniel. I went on about how Nathaniel may not be trustworthy anymore, and that Sarah and Trish were somewhere in the hospital, but Marcus wouldn't tell me where.

"Sarah and Trish are being held somewhere?" Gabe said sounding worried. "Where do you think they could be?"

"I have no idea," I replied honestly. "I really doubt they are in room 241F. Marcus and Nathaniel use that room for secret meetings, so they wouldn't want them in there to get in the way."

"I agree. Do you want to know what I think? I think Marcus is hiding them outside of the hospital."

"What makes you think that?" I asked him.

"Well, if you were threatened to not leave the hospital, or it meant certain death, would you want to leave and try to find them out there?"

He had a strong argument. "That's a great idea, Gabe! We have to make sure that they are there though; otherwise, we would be screwed."

"Yeah, we better, and we need to find them fast because we are escaping tomorrow night," Gabe said.

That made the whole "search-and-rescue mission" even tougher. We had a time limit to find them. Time was a factor, and, with us leaving in thirty-six hours, it was a definite disadvantage. Marcus would also be watching us closely, so we would have to remain hidden while we searched for them. Yikes.

I asked Gabe, "Where should we start?"

Gabe thought over the possible locations and then replied, "Do you think they have a communications room somewhere here?"

"That's random. Why?" I asked.

"Well," he began. "The Clade would need to remain in contact with other divisions across the United States and possibly the world for all we know."

"Yeah," I said sounding confused. "But why do you want to know?"

"Well maybe that is where they are being kept. If I were Marcus, I would hide them there. I'm sure there's security around the perimeter of the room. Also, Instructors from other divisions could keep an eye on them while Marcus paid close attention to us."

"That sounds about right, but why would other divisions agree to watch over two random girls if it had nothing to do with them?"

Gabe was starting to think. It would be great if he could come up with a logical explanation for why the other divisions of the Clade would agree to watch them. To me, it sounded preposterous that two girls, a hydrokinetic and a... a flaming valedictorian, would be a main point of interest across the Clade, but I've been wrong before.

Gabe continued, "Zeke, this is all about you. If Marcus could persuade the Clade to watch over two girls, two girls that are your friends no less, they would be happy to make sure Marcus succeeds in his plan with you."

Could it really be because of me? I didn't do anything wrong; I am in the same boat as every other teenager here.

I hated being the center of attention, even before when I had been at school. Thomas was my only true friend. He would help me out when everything was going downhill for me and would bring me back up. I only went to him and my mom for help. Other people didn't really matter to me at the time. I had all I needed, but now, everyone in this psychotic group of science projects, or super humans for all I know, knows about me.

The whole while Gabe and I were talking, I was paranoid that we were being watched. "Gabe," I said to him slowly and quietly. "Turn slowly around and check to see if the Instructors are watching us."

Gabe listened and turned around. I caught a quick glimpse along the side of Gabe and saw that, for once, I was right. Marcus and Juliette were watching us. They quickly turned back towards each other and began talking in an inaudible from where we were sitting.

Gabe turned back and said, "Well, that can't be a good sign; the Instructors of the Clade watching your every movement. Gosh, you can't even have a peaceful lunch."

"It doesn't matter what they do. We are going to get out of here tomorrow night with Sarah and Trish. They won't stop us," I said definitely.

Gabe gave a small smile of hope and then the bell rang. We got up, left through the double-doors of the cafeteria, and went back down the hall for our last training session of the day. After that, we were going to get Sarah and Trish back.

Chapter 14

A normal day in the Clade would actually be very similar to a school day. We would wake up, take a shower, get dressed, and head off to our first training session. After that, the bell would ring, and we would all go off to eat. Once the hour lunch break is over, we would head back to training for a few more hours until the bell would ring again. Then we would get a three-to-four hour break to do whatever we want until the bell for bed time rings. I don't think I have had a normal day in the Clade yet. Something strange had happened each and every day.

That day's new event was that training was moved from the basement to the few open rooms on the 3rd level until the basement was re-modeled. The re-modeling would take a while too because the walls were literally breaking apart the fire charred them so badly. That was fine by me. I didn't want to be completely alone with Marcus. The way I saw it, the more people who walked by the door to the "new-and-improved" training room, the better.

Only a select few were chosen to continue training until the basement level was fixed. Unfortunately, I was one of them and Gabe wasn't. I found out that only about ten people would have to continue training out of the hundred or so. That was just my luck. My guess was that they wanted to keep Gabe and I separated for as long as possible.

Marcus put out the dummies, and I began to shoot lightning at them. After I was done, all that was left were small pieces of wood and straw lying randomly around the room. I was getting pretty tired from using my power so much. So much so that sweat was beginning to drip off of my face. Marcus said, "Good Job. You can take five if you'd like."

I decided to listen to him for once. I fell down on my butt and leaned against the tile wall. The room we were using used to be, by my guess, a bathroom, but all of the stalls were removed leaving just a few small holes in the walls and a small janitorial closet. I wondered if that closet was as large as the one in the basement and filled with as many weapons.

Marcus walked up to me, and I began to tense up. He sat beside me, his cloak up on top of mine, and began to talk. "You have shown a lot of promise. I am sure you are tired of hearing that, but it is true. Therefore, I think you deserve to know something."

I perked up and listened closely to what he was about to say. "What?" I asked.

He waited a few moments to build up the suspense, I guess. I really wanted to know what he was going to say. Maybe he was going to tell me where my dad was; although, I wasn't supposed to know he was alive, or, perhaps, he would tell me where Sarah and Trish were.

"Your father is alive, Zeke," He said slowly. I knew that already, but I let him continue. "Actually, your father was the creator of this whole thing we have going on here."

I think I knew what he was talking about, but I didn't believe him. It didn't make any sense. "Zeke, your father is the leader of the Clade. Not just this one, that is me, but the *entire* Clade." I let the words hang in the air for a bit as I thought about how that was at all possible. An organization like this would need time to create, a lot of time actually, how would he have even met my mom in college. I was starting to get a headache and decided to worry about it later.

"So," I began to reply. "Was my father the first person to have an ability?"

"No, but he was in the first group of individuals that had an ability. Your five minutes is up. Let's start practicing again."

I let out a sigh and pushed myself up. Why would Marcus be telling me all of this if he just wanted me dead after the war? There was more to be figured out, but for now, I didn't have time to think about that. I needed to find Sarah and Trish and then get the hell out of there. I guess it really didn't matter what he was hiding anymore.

Marcus pushed out a few more dummies and placed them in a line, one in front of the other, and then said, "Focus all of your power into one powerful bolt and obliterate all of these dummies in the line."

I began to focus my energy. I thought about tiny lightning bolts moving through my blood and nerves. All of the bolts were moving towards the same area, the palm of my right hand. I kept concentrating on this thought for a few minutes, and then I unleashed a bolt so powerful the lights hanging from the ceiling shattered.

Gabe was waiting for me in our room after training. I wondered what he had been doing all day since he didn't have to train. He looked like he was in planning mode, so I sat down on my bed and watched Gabe paced in the gap between the bunks.

"Alright," Gabe said. "The lights will be out in a few hours, and then we will start searching. Where do you think we should start first? I mean they could be hidden anywhere in this hospital."

"I have no idea. Maybe, we should start searching the rooms on the far side of the hall up this level and then keep going down the levels until we find them."

"Okay. That sounds fine by me. We need to move fast up here then. Level 2 is huge. Searching all of the rooms will take a long time."

"Alright, we have a few hours to get ready before "lights out. I think we should look around the rooms that we haven't been in on this floor now so that we can search the 2nd level sooner," I said.

"Okay," Gabe said hesitantly. "We should be separated in order to look less obvious of what we are doing."

"Right, let's go," I said, and we stepped out into the hall. I walked down to the reception desk near the elevator and turned left toward the new training rooms and Marcus' office. I have only been in two of the twenty rooms down here, so there is a possibility that Sarah and Trish would be hidden up on this level. Gabe swept through the rooms on our side of the 3rd level.

I opened a few of the doors a crack and peeked in. Nothing unusual about any of those rooms. Well, except one of the rooms that had an operating table in it with some sort of drill that I knew was made to cut into your head. I quickly shut the door, shook off my chills, and continued again.

Some of the doors I didn't have to open. Small windows were installed in the door to look inside. They were the same kind of windows at a common doctor's office.

That made me remember my trip to the doctor's office when I got the chicken pox in second grade. I remembered licking my lollipop after leaving the doctor's office in the car and I asked my mom, well my "mom", "Why don't we come here more? Thomas comes here almost once a year to get a check up."

My mom replied, "Because honey, you are too special. They might notice something odd and get jealous." I had just pushed her thought to the back of my mind at that point because I was young and she made me feel great. Me, special, I would always tell myself after that. Now that I thought about it, could a doctor have been able to notice a person with an ability like mine? My mom had known I had an ability, so is that why she kept me away? There were so many questions floating around my head, but I had to stop thinking about that and stay focused on finding Sarah and Trish.

After searching all of the rooms and not finding Trish or Sarah, I headed back to my room. I laid on my bed for what seemed like an eternity waiting for Gabe. When the dinner bell went off, I got up and looked around the halls for him while I walked to the cafeteria. Gabe was nowhere to be found. I grabbed some food, sat down at our usual table, and began to eat.

I finished eating and waited at the table for Gabe to show up. This wasn't like him, in fact, Gabe was usually the first one to show up at lunch. He had a big stomach and liked food quite a bit. He would make jokes at lunch about his eating problems and Sarah and I would just go, "Yeah, uh-huh, you are *so* big."

I was starting to worry as I headed back to our room. I had been waiting in our room for ten minutes when Gabe walked in. His looked as if he had just seen a ghost.

"Gabe," I said jumping up. "Where were you? You missed dinner and everything."

Gabe replied spooked, "He... he knows what we trying to do."

"What," I asked. "Who knows what we are doing? What happened, Gabe"

He replied with a simple, "Nathaniel knows what we are trying to do."

It was, once again, hard for me to fall asleep. I was sure Gabe was finding sleep troublesome too because he was up all night rolling around on his bed. Either that or he was having a nightmare. The clock read 1 A.M. In a half-hour, Gabe and I would wake up and start searching the 2nd level for Sarah and Trish, but with Nathaniel watching us, as well as Marcus and Juliette, it would be tough to even get a drink of water let alone sneak out in the middle of the night to find our captured friends without them knowing about it.

I rolled back over and tried to at least get a little bit of sleep before Gabe and I had to get up. I shut my eyes and let my thoughts wander. I didn't know if I was dreaming or not, but I had a vision of Sarah and Trish locked in room somewhere. The lights were out, and they were handcuffed to a wall. The only light came from a tiny crack above Trish's head. The air had a musty smell which probably came from the mold and mildew growing on the walls. Trish was looking around trying to find some slim chance of escaping while Sarah laid unconscious still from using most of her energy on the water bubble.

I walked around this imaginary room until I found the door shrouded in the darkness. I grabbed the metal knob and tried to turn it. It was locked. I pressed myself up against the door to try to hear someone on the other side coming for help. The door was also metal, but it was freezing cold. I felt the walls around the room and found that they were that cold too.

I tip-toed quietly back to the door and heard footsteps on the outside. I felt around the pitch black room trying to find some place to hide. I kept searching frantically until the door unlocked and a dark silhouette stepped in the room. He walked over to Trish and Sarah not noticing me in the corner of the room. The man stepped right in front of Trish who was now squirming and yelling to try to get out. The man put his hand over Trish's mouth to keep her quiet.

"Ssshhhh," the man said. "We can't have your friends find you. If they were to know what we are doing to you, they wouldn't trust us."

He looked down at Sarah and then added, "Oh no, she is not looking very well. Did you know that you are the reason she is like this? Oh yes, using too much of your ability can do that to you. It can leave you so drained to the point that your body can't keep itself alive," he said quietly.

The man paused and then looked straight at where I was standing in the corner. I began to shake nervously. I thought for sure the man would kill me then and there, but he just turned back to Trish and said, "I do believe we have a guest. Did you know about this?"

Trish shook her head looking as afraid as ever. The man then said, "Are you sure? How did he even get in here do you suppose? Oh wait!" the man said in a loud whisper. "What if this is some sort of twisted dream. This would just be imaginary to the boy in the corner."

He looked over to me, and I began to sweat and breathe heavily. I didn't know if it was a dream or not, but it sure felt real. The man looked back up at Trish who looked like she was going to faint. "Oh no!" the man said again "She won't faint."

How did he know that I was thinking that? Before I could think any longer, the man said, "It will be much worse than THAT!" Almost instantly, the man grabbed Trish's arms and began to kill her… using electricity. Blue sparks sprouted from the man's hands. Lightning bolts arched through his veins emitting a blue glow. Trish began to convulse heavily.

"NOOO!" I yelled out. I didn't care if the man knew who I was, I was going to kill him!

I jumped at him with my own hands beginning to spark. I was about five feet from him when he took a hand off of Trish and pointed a finger at me. I panicked and tried to move, but it was too late. A bolt of electricity left his finger and shot me in the chest. I fell to the ground and laid there in serious pain while he finished off Trish. I slowly got back up, surprised I didn't die, and noticed that he had stopped shocking Trish… because she was dead.

I was defeated. I couldn't move. I wished that that bolt would've just killed me because that would be better than living in this hell. I couldn't save her. She had died for something she could not control, and it was mainly my fault. I wanted to finish myself off to save this guy's time.

He took a few steps toward me leaving Trish's limp body hanging on the wall. I was still down on my knees as he approached. I wanted to just shoot a bolt so powerful that we would both die, but I couldn't. He was standing over me now. I noticed that he was wearing a black cloak. I didn't care to think about who it could be because I knew I was dead.

He grabbed my cloak and pulled me up by the hood. The force choked me, and I gagged a little bit until I vomited on the floor. The man laughed at me a little and said, "Don't worry. We will just get the janitor to clean that up." Why was he laughing? He probably knew I was going to lose the fight, but the laughing? That was just cruel.

"Why?" I asked weakly. "Why did you do that."

I could tell by the faint light that he tilted his head a little, but I still couldn't see who it was. I was still crouched over and shaking a little. Tears swelled up in my eyes and began to fall on the floor. "WHY!?" I yelled at him.

"Because," he said forcefully. "If you don't save them, that is what will happen to them. The Clade: Marcus, Nathaniel, Juliette, they will kill them. Find them and save them!"

I just realized I hadn't put two-and-two together. No one else in the Clade could use electricity except-

The man stepped forward towards me and let his hand burst with electricity showing me his face. It was ME.

"FIND THEM!" I yelled at myself.

I woke up from the dream to Gabe shaking me. I jumped out of the covers and looked around the room to confirm that it was indeed a dream. I haven't had a dream like that in a long time. That was one of the top ten worst dreams in my life before. I always heard that dreams are your sub-conscious trying to tell you something. If that is the case, then Gabe and I need to find Sarah and Trish now.

"Geez," Gabe said. "Are you okay? You were yelling in your sleep and sweating. You didn't look like you were going to make it."

"Yeah," I said trying to catch my breath. "I just had a bad dream. What time is it?"

"It's 1:30 already. Let's go." Gabe said.

"Yeah," I replied. "And Gabe," I paused, "we have to find them."

"We will," Gabe said finally. "Now let's go."

We headed out of the room quietly and went down the usually path to get to the 2nd level. We opened the door to the staircase and stepped into the 2nd level hall. I filled my hand with concentrated electricity again, and we walked down the hall. We looked into every room we could find to see if Trish or Sarah or both were in there. There were so many rooms that we didn't even get to the intersection for an hour.

Once we reached the intersection, we looked around the reception desk and soon found nothing. Gabe said, "Do you think we should split up?"

"I don't know," I replied. The truth was that I didn't want to be alone down here. Not after what happened last time. I made up an excuse. "Do you have a light? How are you supposed to see down here?"

Gabe thought for a second and then said, "I guess you're right. Where do you want to check first?"

I already knew where I wanted to check, and I was sure that Gabe wanted to go there too. "Let's go down to room 241F. If there is anyone on this floor, they will be there."

"Okay, I'm right behind you," Gabe said.

I headed down the left hallway that, no matter how many times we had already gone down it, always seemed to become longer and longer. We searched every room in the hall down to Room 241F. At times, the door would be locked and then Gabe would have to concentrate on focusing his power to create a small flame in the center of the dark room. His ability came in handy. I was glad he couldn't use it as a flashlight though; otherwise, he would burn the whole hospital down. With no luck, we continued down the hall.

I noticed that Gabe was getting more and more agitated after every room we checked came up empty. I started to think that it might be because of Sarah. I was worried that he would go to any lengths to save Sarah. Even if he had to die so that she might be free. Then again, would I be any different? We both had crushes on the girls that were captured, but Gabe had only known Sarah for two weeks and I had known Trish for like ten years. There was a difference, right?

We finally reached room 241F after an hour of walking. That meant that it was about 3:30 in the morning. I was really wiped out after everything that had happened the day before. I had used a lot of my power, as did Sarah, to get to Trish in that huge fire, and Nathaniel had found out about our escape plan. After remembering that, I was afraid that Nathaniel would have wanted us to be down here. But he would have stopped us by now, right? Gabe tried opening the door to 241F, and it was locked.

I was partly relieved because I wanted to get out of there before one of the instructors came. "Gabe," I said to him. "Let's get out of here before someone comes." Gabe just kept trying to open the door getting more and more frustrated with each passing turn of the handle.

I tried again. "Gabe, you need to stop before someone comes. They are not down here. We will try the basement and then the 1ˢᵗ level if we have to."

My pleading was no use. Gabe just kept pushing up against the door grinding his teeth in anger. Finally, Gabe responded in a harsh tone, "Shut up, Zeke. Just shut it!"

I was taken aback. "Woah, I'm sorry. I know you like her, Gabe, but she is not down here. Listen to reason, please, buddy."

"You don't know what it's like," replied Gabe starting to weep. "You have no idea what it is like to never be liked by anyone."

"What do you mean, Gabe?"

"You know what I mean! I mean that no one has ever liked me. Not *ever*. Do you know how that feels? You tell a girl you like her, and they laugh at you and walk away. That's me, Zeke, but Sarah is different. She's never laughed at me or scoffed in my face. Sarah actually might even like me, so DON'T tell me to stop. I will do anything to find her."

Wow, Gabe really wanted to be liked by someone, a girl. I couldn't argue with him because I did know what it felt like to be liked. Of course, the last girlfriend I had was a few years ago and for a short period of time, but still. The fact that she had given me a chance is what counted, and Gabe had never gotten a chance. I felt really bad for him, but I still had to stop him before something terrible happened.

"Gabe," I said apologetically. "You're right. I don't understand, but we're in the same boat here." He looked up and began to calm down. I continued, "They took Trish too, remember, and *she* doesn't like me. We'll find them, Gabe. I promise, and then we will get the heck out of here."

He slouched down and fell on his butt on the floor, and then he began to cry. I walked up to him slowly and sat next to him. I put my hand on his back and let him finish before we had to go. "I'm sorry," Gabe said with tears rolling down his face and onto the floor.

"It'll be okay, Gabe," I said. "Just let it out, and then we can go. There is no rush." There was a rush, but I couldn't just hurry my best friend's tears.

"I… I don't know what happened to me. My mom and dad, my *real*, mom and dad, are actually dead, and with Sarah gone, I don't know what to do or what to believe anymore."

Gabe needed a little bit of hope and solitude. He needed something that would never change. "I'll always be here for you, Gabe. And once we get out of here, we'll find a place where we can all hide until this blows over, and by all, I mean *all*, you, me, Sarah, and Trish."

Gabe sniffled a little bit and then said, "Promise?"

"Yeah," I said nervously. "Yeah, we will get out of here. All of us."

I didn't know what to say to Gabe. I had to promise him that we were all going to leave here and that everything would be great, but that in itself was a lie. Even if we beat all odds and escaped with everyone, it would be hard to have a normal life for a long time. I mean Sarah had been at the hospital for a few years already, and she had never even thought about escaping. I wasn't going to tell Gabe that though.

"Alright," I told Gabe giving him a little shake. "Let's get out of here and find Sarah and Trish. We only have three hours till the wake-up call."

Gabe stood up, and we began to walk back down the hall with my hand dimly lit. We reached the staircase and headed down until we reached the basement door. "Why are we here? Shouldn't we try the 1st level?" Gabe said.

"I have a feeling that they'll be on this floor. What better place to hide two teenagers than a place we are not allowed to be in, and no one else would even bother to come down here because-" I opened the door and showed Gabe the black, scorched halls. "There is barely anything left down here."

Chapter 15

Gabe looked awestruck as we walked down the long, charred hall towards the reception desk. "You're telling me," Gabe said sounding astounded. "That Trish did all of this?"

"Yeah," I nodded. "Her vaccine ran out of juice, and then she went off the deep end."

"Wow. I wouldn't want to mess with her in a completely wooden house."

Gabe and I both laughed out loud. It felt good to laugh instead of always being serious and worrying about our lives. We kept walking until we reached the reception desk. The hall down to the old training rooms had the most damage. I would be surprised if The Clade could even fix this.

We walked down the dark hallway with my hand guiding the way. With every step we took, black ash crunched underneath our shoes. Most of the rooms we checked were in the same condition as the hall. The walls were charred to black crumbs of ash, and they would periodically fall to the floor. The smell, however, was probably the worst. If you have ever been to a chronic smoker's house, you can imagine what it smelled like except times a thousand. Half of the time I plugged my nose to keep myself from getting a terrible headache.

After half of the hallway was searched, Gabe said, "Do you think we will find them before the wake-up call?"

I didn't know how to respond. I mean I wanted to find them just as badly as he did, but we didn't have much time left. "What's the time?" I asked.

Gabe pulled up his cloak sleeve and read the time from his watch. "It is currently," Gabe pushed a small button, and the watch glowed very brightly compared to the darkness surrounding it. "5:00 A.M." He then pushed another button, and the screen flashed once, and then he said, "And in Hawaii it is midnight, and in Paris it is noon, and in-" I cut him off.

"I think we just need to know what the time is here. I'm fairly confident that if the morning bell rings and we're caught, they wouldn't believe 'but it was noon in Paris?'" It would've been funny if we weren't in such a hurry.

We kept walking down the halls until we reached the beginning of the training rooms. Gabe stopped behind me while I was walking into our old training room. "What's wrong?" I asked him.

"I… I think I know where they are." Gabe said.

"What? How do you know?" I asked him.

"Well, why did you think they could be on this level instead of the 1st or not in this building at all?"

"Well… I… uh… I thought about going on this level because no one else would want to come here. You know, look at this level. It is completely trashed. It looks like someone had a bonfire and forgot to throw a bucket of water on it down here."

"You still had a feeling right?" Gabe asked.

"Fine, whatever. Take the lead." I answered

Gabe flashed a smile as he walked past me. I just shrugged off whatever nonsense he said about 'having a feeling' and followed him. We walked through the main room without even searching for a sign of Trish and Sarah and went into the training room.

The training room looked absolutely terrible. The foam padding around the room looked like a marshmallow that had been roasted over an open fire never taken off of the flame. Like everything else down here, the room and everything in it was charred black. The floor was made of the same material as the walls, and with every step we took, it felt as though we may get stuck to the floor.

Gabe just kept on moving, though, as if the floor had no effect on him. He ran up to the steel door of the large closet that lied behind it. "Gabe, do you really think they are in there?"

He waited a little bit to respond, "I…I don't know. Like I said before, I just have a feeling. Haven't you ever had a feeling about something?"

He turned back to the door and turned the handle. The handle wouldn't budge. Gabe kept pushing on the door hoping that it would somehow fall over. He needed to be 'The Incredible Gabe' in order to do that though. Gabe started to ram his shoulder into the door. I ran up to him and quickly grabbed him. "Gabe! What are you doing? You will dislocate your shoulder and think of how that would go with Juliette at training tomorrow. Not to mention that you would have to convince her that you dislocated it in bed."

He began to break down again. He put his back against the door, and his face became long and mournful. I patted him on the back with my non-lit hand and began to console him. Gabe let out a loud, "Where are they!" I was worried that someone would hear him, but figured that the training rooms were pretty sound proof.

While I was consoling him, I began to think back to training in that room before everything had gotten out of control. That's when I remembered it. "Gabe," I said. "I think you're right. This door is usually unlocked, and if it's locked now, that must mean that someone came back down to lock it. So that must mean they're hiding something. And *that* must mean that Sarah and Trish are in there!" then someone came down here and locked it themselves."

Gabe sniffled and replied with a hopeful, "You really think so?"

"Well yeah, do you have any other thoughts for why the door is locked when nobody is apt to come down here?"

"Well, I guess not." Gabe said. "How do we break in?"

I looked at the imposing door. It was made of solid steel so any force against it would be useless. I thought about asking the guy who could melt to sneak under the door for me, but it wouldn't be smart of us to drag someone we hardly knew into this mess.

I began to think of the possible ways to use our abilities against it. Lightning would have no affect on the door, but maybe fire would. "Gabe, what is the temperature you can burn stuff at?"

"Huh? Why? That's an odd question,"

"Face it, Gabe. We are odd people."

"Um…" Gabe thought. "Juliette never really made me check. But I know it's pretty hot."

I guess pretty hot would have to do. "Do you think you can melt the steel door? It'll take a lot of heat to do it. Do you think you're up for it?"

"Wow, that is a lot of heat," Gabe said sounding dumbfounded at the idea of melting a solid steel door. "I can try right? Step back."

I did. I hadn't been in training with Gabe for a while, so I wasn't going to take any chances with his ability. In fact, I thought about finding a fire suit before I let him begin, but that would've just been silly. Anyway all of the fire suits were on the other side of that steel door.

Gabe began to focus his energy and concentrated on the door. I remembered to back when we had first arrived there two weeks ago. He would've needed about ten minutes to create a small flame, but now, he only needed five for a massive fireball. The door was completely covered with flames. Gabe began to sweat with the heat and the amount of energy and concentration it needed.

"How hot do I need to get it!" he yelled.

"If I recall about 2500 degrees."

"What! That's extremely hot!"

"I know. If you get exhausted just stop. I don't want you to end up like Sarah and pass out on me."

We stopped talking until the room became a sauna. I began to sweat fiercely. Gabe was working hard to get through the door. The thought of melting a steel door seemed impossible, but it wasn't. If anyone could get through that door, it was Gabe. His ambition was too great not to get in. Sarah and Trish had to be back there; otherwise, I don't know what we'd do next.

His will was stronger than the door. I noticed little spots on the door starting to drip and melt away. The plan was working; Gabe was succeeding at melting the door! "Great job, Gabe. It's beginning to melt. Keep it going, but if you are exhausted, stop now. We can probably push it down now."

"No," Gabe said through clenched teeth. "I will finish this."

Over the next ten minutes, the door began to disappear bit-by-bit. It started in the top right corner, and then the space opened wider and wider until it was big enough to fit someone's head in. Over another ten minutes, the door hole was wide enough to fit a person, but they would have to jump through the hole considering it was about three feet off the ground.

"Gabe, stop!" I yelled. He did so and immediately fell to the floor. I jumped over to him and sat by him. He was lying in a heap, breathing heavily. "Gabe, you did amazing. Are you okay?"

"Aaaahh," Gabe said worn out. "I think I need to take five if you don't mind?"

"Don't worry. I'll give you a little break. I'll see what's on the inside of the closet. You can relax here for a little bit. I'll call for you if I need any help with anything."

Gabe yawned, "Okay. Have fun."

I stood up and walked towards the hole. I felt the edges, and found that they had already cooled off enough to allow me to crawl through. I stuck my hand inside the closet and lit up the room with my electricity. I couldn't see much other than the corner of a metal shelf containing tasers and blow-darts. I checked the time and realized we only had an hour left. I looked back at Gabe one more time and jumped through the hole into darkness.

Chapter 16

I pushed my way through the small hole and into the closet. The sharp, steel, edges gave me a few cuts and scratches along my back when I stepped down. The air smelled burnt probably because it was locked shut right after the fire. If Marcus wanted to hide Sarah and Trish quickly, this would be the best place. I lit up the room with my hand and checked it out.

What Gabe told me about the closet when Juliette showed him was true. It was a massive closet about three times larger than our room with a few metal shelves containing useful recruiting equipment like bulletproof vests, tasers, blow darts, and other useful capturing devices. A part of me wished that Nathaniel would've given me some of this stuff when I had to recruit Trish, then maybe I wouldn't have felt so guilty when I had to use force.

I searched the closet from corner-to-corner and found nothing that would have led me to believe that Sarah and Trish were ever in here. Frustrated, I picked up a taser from a shelf and eyed up the far wall. "Aaarrrgg!" I yelled. The taser flew and smashed into a bunch of tiny little bits and pieces.

Gabe must have heard the taser break because he yelled, "Hey, Zeke are you okay? What was that?"

I told Gabe, "I'm fine, Gabe. It was one of the tasers. It fell and smashed on the floor."

"Okay, just be careful in there," Gabe said sounding worried. Gabe was starting to sound a little bit better. I was pretty nervous that if we would have to get back to the room in a short amount of time, and he was exhausted, we probably wouldn't make it, or he would be unable to perform in training tomorrow. That would be a red flag to the instructors.

I walked over to the hole where Gabe was standing on the other side waiting for me to exit. I put my hands on the outside of the hole and began to climb out when I noticed a little bit of light glimmering in the corner of my eye. It could not have been my hand because that was "turned off" a while ago. I stopped and turned around in mid-air and noticed that a little bit of light was escaping from a crack in the wall. "What the-?" I said softly.

"What is it?" Gabe asked. "Do you see something?"

"Yeah," I replied. "Yeah, the taser that fell, well, it didn't really fall. I threw it in frustration at a wall. I made a crack and light is shining out of it. Come in and see."

"Alright, give me a sec."

Gabe crawled in through the hole and found me crouching near the floor by the crack. The light was bright enough to illuminate half of the dark closet. My makeshift hand flashlight was no longer needed. "What do you think is on the other side of this wall?" Gabe asked.

I began to think about the locked door again. Maybe that was just the first defense from keeping intruders out. Perhaps, there is another room or hallway on the other side of this wall. "I think Trish and Sarah are on the other side."

Gabe remained silent. We were both thinking about how to get through the wall. "Maybe there is a secret button we have to push? You know, like in room 241F," Gabe said.

"Maybe, let's hurry up and check. We only have fifteen minutes now until the wake up."

Gabe and I quickly felt along the wall. I took the left side, and Gabe took the right. Our hands moved in smooth but rapid motions hoping to find…something that would allow us to enter whatever was on the other side. While we were busy searching, the clock kept ticking away. Once we reached the seven minute until wake up mark, I said, "Alright, we'll have to check back tomorrow night. Hopefully, Trish and Sarah will be back there, and we'll just have to run away from there."

Gabe wasn't paying attention. He kept looking around hoping that there would be a secret switch that would let him through. I shook him a little bit saying, "Gabe, we will find them, but we are out of time we have to go now!"

Almost immediately after I finished that sentence, a little piece of concrete fell on the floor revealing a small red crank imbedded in the wall. "Woah," Gabe said in shock of what he had uncovered. "This place is full of surprises."

We checked the time and found that we had five minutes. I said, "We'll come back tomorrow night. We will go through there and hopefully find them. Then, we will get the hell out of this crazy place."

"Good plan," Gabe said approvingly. "Let's get out of here."

We headed out of the room through the hole, hoping no one would go in there and find it, and left for the stairs. We made it back to our room just as the sun had risen and the wake up announcements began. "Good morning Clade members. It is currently fifty-five degrees outside with a high today of seventy degrees Fahrenheit. Collin please see your instructor for training today, or there will be consequences. Thank You."

Although I was extremely tired, I had to fit in with the crowd and not sleep at all. If I even look remotely tired, Marcus would suspect something. I looked up at Gabe who was sitting on his bunk looking back down at me. He said, "What are we supposed to do if we find Sarah and Trish exactly? We never even made a plan to escape. How are we supposed to come up with one while we are trying to save them?"

"I don't know, but we have to try. We can wait another day, I mean, once we find them we could come up with a plan and then leave the next night?" I said.

"No, we can't." Gabe said. "If they get out, Marcus, Nathaniel, and Juliette will notice that they are gone, and then they'll find us. Face it, Zeke. We have to get them and leave at the same time. I'm just so sure they are behind that wall though."

"I agree. They must be back there. It all makes perfect sense, and no one even knows that that is back there," I agreed.

"Tonight then, we are getting out of here and going...where exactly? We have no idea where to even go."

"We will just find safety and then find a place to go after that. We will make our own little home somewhere where The Clade will never find us."

There was silence in the room. The thought of a home where we would all be safe from the Clade was great, but it was all in our heads. Deep down we knew that we would never be safe no matter where we ended up. We would have to keep running from one place to another making sure the Clade never got track of us. Gabe jumped down from his bed and said, "Zeke, how are you supposed to tell Trish about her parents."

That was a great question. She hadn't even found out yet about her parents. How was I supposed to tell her that they weren't her biological parents and just hired protectors? I was beginning to kill myself with all of this stress, so I decided to push that thought to the back of my head. I just wanted to make it through the day. We opened the door and stepped into our last day with the Clade.

In high school, I had never taken any drama courses or even gone to any of the plays. Well, I went to one play just because Trish was the lead character, but I wasn't really paying attention to the play. The drama classes had never appealed to me. I wished they would have that morning because I would have to act my way through that day.

Training began at the usual time. I found Marcus waiting for me in the "new" training room at the end of the hall on the 3rd level. I tried my best to not look exhausted, but I think a little showed because he asked, "Good morning, actually, more like good night. Did you sleep okay?"

I stuttered a little bit but then said, "No, I had a dream about my mom. I couldn't sleep after that." I hoped he would buy it and then drop the question.

"Well, I'm sorry. It is tough to get use to the fact that we hired your mom to keep you safe, but believe me, if she hadn't been there to protect you, you may not have lived long enough to even have known you had a power."

A part of me wished that, but I didn't tell him that. Training went on schedule with little talking between us other than what I should try doing next. I hoped Gabe was doing as well as I was. Juliette was a scary individual, and she was smart enough to figure out that Gabe was lying about his state, if she asked that is.

After successfully frying some dummies, I asked Marcus about Trish and Sarah hoping that he would reveal some information about them. "How are Trish and Sarah recovering?"

The question seemed to take him by surprise because he didn't respond right away. When he did, though, he said, "They are recovering, but they are still very weak. We will keep them in care, so don't worry about them. You should focus on your training."

He was beginning to sound like my mom. I knew that he was still lying to me about them. Marcus probably already knew that we had found the secret tunnel in the storage closet. If anyone even caught a glimpse of what Gabe and I were doing, Marcus would be the first to find out. How come he hadn't stopped us yet?

I put all those questions out of my head and continued training. When training was over, I would find Gabe (hopefully okay and hadn't spilled the beans to Juliette) in the lunch room and we would discuss our plans for retrieving Sarah and Trish and where to go from there. The basement, like most that I know about, didn't have too many exits, so we would have to move to the first floor and run from there. Hopefully, no one would see. Although, Gabe had said a while ago that Nathaniel knew what we were up too. If he ended up getting in the way, we would just have to defeat him. I mean, what kind of fighting techniques does a person use when all he can do is slide the ground?

After frying a few more dummies and conversing with Marcus about random small talk topics like "how the weather is," the lunch bell rang. I wiped the sweat off my forehead and opened the door to leave, but Marcus grabbed my shoulder. I spun around to face him. When I looked at him up close, I noticed a few differences in his appearance than the day he had recruited me two weeks and a day before. His eyes were slightly bloodshot with small bags underneath them. His whole look was one of exhaustion, like he hadn't been getting any sleep. I wondered why.

After examining him, Marcus said, "Can you tell, Zeke, by the way I look what I have been going through over the last few days? The Agents are right on top of us, the fire in the basement, and the guilt I feel whenever I think of you keeps me awake at night."

Marcus appeared to be breaking down in front of me. Perhaps this was just a ploy to get me to tell him what I had been doing, but that was never going to happen. Or maybe he was telling the truth. Was he really that guilty for recruiting me? "Why do you feel guilty about recruiting me?"

"I don't feel guilty about that," Marcus said. "I feel guilty about what I have been doing to you."

"What do you mean? You treat me like any other freshy here," I added to comfort him.

"No, I don't. You know what I mean. You've been to room 241F and saw what Nathaniel and I were up too. I shouldn't have put all of that stress on you. You are only a child, and all of our problems are not your responsibility. Someday they may be, but not now. You don't even know the full potential of your powers. That was wrong of me, but I'm not going to do that to you," Marcus confessed.

His apology seemed very real to me. He could just be really great at acting and faking it, but he seemed genuine. "Why are you confessing all of this to me? You could've just let me keep training harder and harder until I am ready to face them, and then you could've told me. Why now?"

Marcus rubbed his bloodshot eyes and then said, "Because I don't want you to hate me. I want you to trust me and allow me to be your friend. I don't know if you know this, but I wouldn't be where I am today if it wasn't for your father."

That struck a chord in me. My dad seemed to have influence everywhere in the Clade. Marcus and Nathaniel had talked about him in room 241F when I had spied on them, and Marcus seemed to talk about how great he was to the Clade all the time. "Why? What has any of this got to do with my dad? First, you tell me he's dead. Second, you tell me he is dead again, but he helped create this whole operation, the Clade. What made him so special?" I didn't want to sound angry, but I was. My dad had never even written me a card, let alone visited me or even introduced himself to me. Why should I care about him if he never even cared about me?

"Your father, Zeke, was the one who recruited me," Marcus said.

"Really?" I added actually interested. "He has been around long enough to do that?"

"Oh yes," Marcus said sounding a bit happier. "He is about fifty now."

"Wait, isn't he dead?" I asked. I knew from listening on his conversation in room 241F that he had to be alive. Where? I didn't have the slightest idea, but they had referred to him as being alive. Maybe he would tell me if I caught him in a trap.

"Huh? Oh yeah, he is dead," Marcus said beginning to squirm. "But I thought I would let you know that he recruited me, and if he was alive today, he would be about fifty years old."

I guessed that Marcus wasn't ready to give up anything about my dad yet. Oh well, whatever. Once I was out of here, it wouldn't even matter. "Oh, okay," I said trying to sound a little reassuring. I was growing tired of Marcus' apology. It may be real, but I was hungry and I wasn't quite ready to trust him. "No offense, Marcus, but Gabe will be worried if I don't show up for lunch soon." I had to get out of there, and lunch was the perfect excuse.

"Oh yes, sorry about that," Marcus said straightening himself up. "If you need anything, anything at all, just look for me."

"Okay, don't worry. I'll find you, and it's fine, really," I said just ready to find Gabe. Marcus let me go and I took that chance to leave for lunch.

I walked quickly down the hall towards the 3rd level cafeteria. I looked into Gabe's usual training room and found that he already was at lunch. I picked up the pace and reached it just as Gabe was throwing away his leftovers. I sat in my usual spot at the lunch table and so did Gabe. There was an empty and still feeling with Sarah missing. Her chair had been taken away by a group of teenage girls two tables down. Sarah had always been so chatty. The silence sent chills down my back.

Gabe sat on his chair and slid into the table quickly. "Where were you? I thought you had disappeared to," he said out of breath.

"Don't worry about me. I won't let them take me," I told Gabe. "I was late because Marcus had a breakdown."

Gabe looked confused and worried at the same time. "A breakdown?" he asked. "He doesn't seem like the kind of guy that would have a breakdown. He is too large and powerful to do that. If anyone here would breakdown, it would be me."

"No, I would to. I felt like breaking down a few times already," I argued. "This place messes with your head. If the idea of having supernatural abilities doesn't drive you nuts, then the people here will."

"Agreed," Gabe said. "So, what did Marcus tell you?"

I told Gabe everything that I had heard from Marcus. I even told him more than that just to make sure he knew everything I did. He listened intently up until I told him about my father recruiting Marcus. "Wow, you guys are like family," Gabe laughed again.

I laughed too. "Yeah," I said. "He is like the "brother" I never wanted."

"Oh, come on," Gabe said accusingly. "You never wanted a brother or sister to bother you and play games with?"

"I never really thought about it. It was always just mom and me. I always thought that that was how it was suppose to be, a boy and his mother. I didn't need anyone else besides Thomas, my friend," I said. "What does this have to do with anything?"

"It doesn't," Gabe said shaking his head. "I just like to know things. Did you know that I was top of my class back in Missouri? I guess I won't be valedictorian after all."

Wow, I had known Gabe was smart, but I hadn't known he was *that* smart. Gabe was a lot like Thomas in many ways. Thomas was smart and relied on me for anything that he couldn't do himself. That is probably why Gabe and I had become such great friends so quickly. Other than our need to survive, of course. I fit with him like Thomas and I used to fit. I still missed Thomas, but, sadly, it was getting lesser and lesser each day.

I finished my explanation of training and Marcus' breakdown when the end of lunch hour bell rang. Unfortunately, I only had had enough time to eat a bagel and cream cheese. The next training session would be brutal with me starving. It wouldn't stop me, however, from pushing through until dinner time because, after that, Gabe and I would be heading to our dorm to finalize our plan for escaping with Sarah and Trish.

Chapter 17

The next training session seemed to take forever. My stomach was aching and grumbling at me with every bolt of energy I unleashed. I felt like I was going to collapse if I didn't eat something really soon. Using an ability so much without any food for energy is a bad idea. I felt sick, and I was pretty sure that the room was starting to spin.

Marcus took it easy on me, thankfully. He only had me take out five dummies in a row at most. My guess was that he felt bad for what he had done before with his outburst of emotion and all, but I still didn't fully believe that he was being completely truthful. After all, he was the reason I was here, he knew where Sarah and Trish were, and he refused to tell me where they were. That makes him the bad guy.

The dinner bell finally rang, and I was finished with, what I was sure of, my last training session. The day had been long, and it sure didn't help that Gabe and I were out of bed all night. My eyelids felt extremely heavy, as if gravity had just decided to become all-powerful.

Gabe and I didn't talk about the Clade or any of its problems at dinner, which was nice. Instead, we talked about things back home. What we missed was a big topic, but that didn't matter anymore because we could never go back to it. Our lives were forever changed because of this place. Sure, you could argue that our abilities were the reason, but they would be easier to control than a group dressed in dark cloaks resembling a cult.

Gabe and I decided that, to look less suspicious, we should go one at a time back to the room. I agreed with his idea, and he left first. I was still hungry anyways. After about ten minutes, I left the cafeteria, after getting stuffed on thirds of roast beef of course. I walked down the hall towards the dorm. After I rounded the corner, I noticed Nathaniel walking quickly towards me. That image quickly made my brain have a flashback to when Gabe had come running towards me saying, '"Nathaniel knows what we are trying to do."'

I turned around and started to sprint down the hall back to the cafeteria. Nathaniel just rounded the corner when I was halfway down the hall. He saw me and yelled, "Stop, Zeke!" I didn't want to stop, but I was forced to. The ground was moving faster than I thought it could because, before I knew it, he was standing over the top of me.

"Ahhh!" I yelled. "What are you doing!?" I tried to remain calm and act natural. I wasn't ready to call it quits on our plan, so I played dumb about what Gabe had said. "Where have you been lately? I haven't seen your face around here very recently."

I guess Nathaniel was smarter than that because he said, "Yeah, you were so happy to see me that you ran away yelling." Ouch, he got me there.

I was stuck, so I rambled on, "Well, what do you want now that I'm here?"

"What I want?" Nathaniel said sounding confused. "Oh yeah, I forgot Gabe ran off before I could finish a few days ago."

"Wait, back when Gabe and I had started searching for Sarah and Trish? Gabe ran back saying that you knew what we were up too?" I said.

"Yeah, I do," Nathaniel said helping me up onto my feet. I turned around and watched as the cracks that the ground made when it slid filled themselves in. I turned back and listened to Nathaniel finish. "I found him looking around Juliette's office. I walked up to him and told him that I knew what he was doing, and he freaked out and ran away from me. I didn't get to the part I needed to though. I don't know why, but I want to help you."

"Help us? Aren't you going to kill us for what we're trying to do?" I asked. The thought of Nathaniel knowing that Gabe and I were trying to escape was causing me to sweat.

"No, I want to help you escape, but on one condition," he said.

"Umm... well, depending on what your request is, I may have to talk to Gabe about it," I said in a frightened tone.

"Don't worry, it's nothing bad," Nathaniel said. He looked left and right checking for something or someone, and then looked back at me and said in a hushed tone, "I want to leave with you."

I almost fell off of my seat. "I thought you liked it here. Why would you want to escape? You and Marcus are like BFF's or something like that."

"No, were not. He may think we are, but I can't stand him. If we don't stop him, we are all dead. The Agents are on their way, you know. They will exterminate all of us without even thinking about it. That's why I need to get out of here. I told him that we should evacuate while we can, but he is so in love with this place that he refuses to leave. Personally, I think he is with the Agents. How else would he know that they are so close? It makes perfect sense."

"But why run now? Why didn't you earlier?" I asked

"I never had a reason, and when I heard that you, Gabe, Sarah, and Trish were going to make a break for the hills, I figured this was the best chance as any and that I could run with you three. I would have company," Nathaniel confessed.

I had never thought that Marcus was working for the Agents, but it did make perfect sense the way Nathaniel had described it. I was glad that I hadn't trusted him before. I knew that he was too strong a guy to break down in front of someone or even break down at all.

Nathaniel had been here longer than anyone else, minus Marcus. Heck, he had become an instructor. If anyone knew where Sarah and Trish were hidden in that tunnel down in the basement it was him. Nathaniel had always seemed trustworthy to me. He had helped me catch and recruit Trish, sort of, but he had always had sympathy for me. I respected that, and now he needed us. I felt like I owed him because of all that he had done for me.

"I'll talk to Gabe. He is probably worried about where I am since I have been gone for so long. Where should I find you?" I asked.

Nathaniel thought about it and said, "Room 241F. I'm assuming you remember where it is. Marcus won't need it anymore because the Agents are already on our doorstep, and he thinks his plan is running perfectly. It should be safe."

"Okay, I'll find you tonight," I finished.

"Alright, I'll see you around one in the morning," Nathaniel added, and then he turned and left down the hall behind me. Now, I had the job of trying to get Gabe to trust Nathaniel and to let him help us out.

That should be fun.

"What! Are you out of your mind!" Gabe yelled at me. I had walked back to the dorm and told Gabe what Nathaniel had requested. He didn't like the idea of Nathaniel coming with us. Can you tell?

"Look, you have to see reason," I argued with him. "Nathaniel knows this place inside and out. He could help us find Sarah and Trish and escape quicker than we thought we could. He probably knows passages that never get walked down. It seems smarter to bring him than to just go it alone."

"Yeah, Zeke?" Gabe said jumping down from his top bunk. "What if he is the one playing with us and not Marcus? Marcus could be telling us the truth, and Nathaniel could make it look like Marcus is the one to blame for all of this."

"Do you know how ridiculous that sounds?" I told him. The idea that Nathaniel was the one that was manipulating us was just as ridiculous as the idea of Juliette being a nice person. Marcus was the one behind all of this. How could Nathaniel be if he had been gone for the last few days? No, for once, I was right.

Gabe wouldn't give up, though. We argued for at least an hour until the bell rang signaling bed time. We crawled into bed and turned off the light. The clock read 9 P.M. Nathaniel wanted us to meet him four hours later in Room 241F, so we would have to leave in three and a half, that is, if I could convince Gabe in the meantime.

I had the same nightmare that night. I was in the concrete room with Sarah passed out, and Trish hanging on the wall. I followed the same paths as I had the last time I had had this dream. As if on cue, I, or the other me, walked into the room and began his accusations to Trish. Once again, I had to face the fear of Trish's death because of me. It was just as terrible as it had been last time. I hoped that I would never see it again.

I woke up with a cold sweat. I was worried that I had missed Nathaniel's meeting. Luckily, the clock read midnight. I stretched and got out of bed. I shook Gabe a little bit, and he groaned and rolled over while opening his eyes. "So, what did you decide to do?" I asked Gabe.

"I really don't want to, but maybe you have a point. I have a bad feeling though. Maybe it's just because he's an instructor. I don't know, but I guess I will go with it and let him help," Gabe said agreeing with me. Yes, finally I was the one who was right.

"Alright," I tried to keep my composure, but I was right! "We have to meet him in 241F at one, so we should get ready to go."

Gabe jumped down and stretched one more time. We grabbed our black cloaks (hopefully for the last time) and put them on stretching them over our heads. We took a glance around the room that was supposed to be our home for the rest of our lives; however, the Agents were coming, so I doubted that it would've been forever anyway.

"Ready?" Gabe asked

"You better believe it."

"Okay, then let's get out of here with our friends," Gabe said confidently.

We opened the door for the last time and walked down the hall towards the staircase. Hopefully, this was the last time we did this too because, if not, the Clade would probably kill us for sneaking out so many times. Just think, a little more than two weeks before (I was beginning beginning to lose count) I had been a normal boy. Now I felt like an undercover soldier or something geeky like that.

We reached the stairwell and descended into, what was hopefully, our final adventure.

Chapter 18

We scampered down the stairwell and bolted through the 2nd level door. We rushed ourselves through the 2nd level until we reached room 241F. I guess we were both anxious to find Sarah and Trish and then leave. We hardly talked on the way to 241F.

We reached 241F with five minutes to spare on the clock. I opened the door and scanned the room with my lit hand and found no one. We were early, so Nathaniel may still be on the way. Gabe and I took a chair and sat down next to a lab table in the dark. Then I had a thought that made a chill go up my spine. Gabe must have thought it too because he asked, "Are we sitting on the floor that flips over when you say... you know?"

"Possibly," I said. We both scooted ourselves towards the door and away from the table that turns when the password is said, "Zeke Laufor is our key to freedom."

We sat in silence waiting impatiently for Nathaniel. I began pacing back and forth across the room after the fifteen minute mark. I knew I was being an impatient person, but he had said 1 A.M. and I assumed he knew how to tell time if he was an instructor in the Clade. The clock now read ten after one, but we had to keep waiting. He would probably know where Sarah and Trish were. I guessed we would just have to deal with it and wait.

Finally, about twenty minutes later, Nathaniel showed up. The door opened, and he looked around inside. "Where were you?" Gabe asked anxiously.

"I wanted to wait to make sure you two would see reason and show up," Nathaniel answered. "Now, are you ready to go?"

"Yeah!" Gabe said cheerfully. He was as pumped as I was about getting out of here.

"Wait one second," I told Nathaniel. He turned around and faced me. My face glowed blue from the electricity flowing into my hand making my face look like I was about to tell a ghost story. "Before we get out of here, we need to find Sarah and Trish. Do you have any idea of where they might be?"

"Yes, I do," he said. "But why get them when freedom is so very close?"

"Because they are our friends," Gabe said.

Nathaniel thought this over for a little bit. I hoped he would say, "Yes, let's go find them," but I couldn't be sure. He was hard to read, and I was nervous about whether or not he would agree to help us first. After a few moments, he finally said, "Okay, but let's hurry."

Gabe and I looked at each other and nodded thinking that everything was going better than we could have imagined. We raced down the long hallways and back to the stairwell. Nathaniel ran down, so we followed close by. We had only one idea where he could be going and that was the tunnel in the closet of the training room in the basement.

He skipped the 1st level and continued downward. That proved that they were in the basement level. "Hey, Nathaniel," I said as we descended down the final flight of stairs. "Do you know anything about a tunnel hidden behind a wall in the closet of mine and Gabe's old training room?"

"You know about that?" he said continuing downward. "That's where Sarah Ubanks and Trish Dawson are being kept by Marcus."

"Really? Zeke we were close then!" Gabe shouted.

"Why is that tunnel there?" I asked Nathaniel as we approached the basement level door.

"That tunnel is an escape route that the Clade built in case recruits were still left in the building if we were ever overrun, and we decided to collapse the building. The basement would remain safe, and then they could escape through the tunnel and meet us about a mile into the forest."

"Why did you hide it behind the wall then?" Gabe asked as we headed towards the training room. The walls were still as crisp as a burnt piece of bacon, and the smell was just the same. The basement was never going to be useable again by the Clade.

"We hid it for many reasons," Nathaniel continued. "We decided that if the Agents were to find the area where we could exit from, they would reach the end and find nothing. The second reason was because we didn't want new recruits to get any ideas about escaping, so we hid it. How did you two find it anyways?"

I didn't have to tell him. We reached the training room, and he saw the door with a large hole in. "Well, you two just love to break our rules and things, don't you?" I explained to him how we got through it, and how we first noticed the tunnel on the other side of the wall when I threw and broke the taser.

Nathaniel sighed and crawled through the hole. He clapped his hands and the lights turned on. The lights burned at first considering we had been traveling in the dark for the last half hour. Gabe said in anguish, "Of course, we would try everything to turn on the lights but clap!" I just laughed and put my hand on Gabe's shoulder in hopes to relax him.

The light was not as noticeable with the closet light on, but it was still there which meant that the lights in the cave were bright. Nathaniel looked at the crack and said, "Again, you like to break our things." After shaking his head disapprovingly, he moved to the crack in the wall with the red crank and began cranking.

The crank pushed hard against Nathaniel. It was small for the size of the thing it was lifting. It was circular with a little handle on it. That was all, and what it was doing was amazing. The middle portion of the wall, with every push of the crank, lifted slowly showing us the cavern. "I don't believe it," I said slowly.

It took Nathaniel only a minute to have the wall completely lifted. The cavern was natural looking. There were no concrete, steel, or brick walls, just dirt. The only things that were not natural were the small lights that glowed brightly in the dim cavern. Even with the bright lights, it looked as if the cave stretched on forever.

Nathaniel waved for us to follow him as he began walking into the start of the cavern. We closed in on Nathaniel, and then I asked, "Where could you hide them in here?"

Nathaniel answered, "This cave contains a small room. It contains a few beds and supplies in case someone is hurt from the building collapsing. We just locked it so that they couldn't get out."

"Why?" Gabe asked. "Why would you hide them? What good would that be to you?"

"That is a question I would ask Marcus," Nathaniel said. "As I told Zeke before, he keeps me out of the loop most of the time. Even though we look as though we are close, we aren't. I believe, though, that he did this to keep Zeke focused on training. He had this crazy mindset that Zeke would save all of us. Ha! That's what I say to that. No offense, Zeke, you're gifted, but to take down the whole Agent division? That will take more than just the Clade, so I'm pretty sure some newbie boy wouldn't be able to do it. That's why I'm getting out of here before the Agents come and kill us all."

We kept moving forward until I noticed a steel door, like the one in the closet, in the wall of the cavern. "This is it," Nathaniel said. He pulled out a key from under a rock near by and said, "If they try to hit me, would you please stop them?"

"Yeah," I said confidently. "Now open it."

He put the key in the lock on the handle and turned it. The sound of the tumblers created an echo down the cave. I hope no one else who decided to wander around tonight heard that. Nathaniel pulled carefully on the steel door, only opening it a crack.

Before he could finish opening it, Sarah came bursting out of the room in rage. Trish was right behind her. They both looked better than ever as if the incident in the basement never occurred. Sarah grabbed Nathaniel and shoved him against the wall with the help of Trish and yelled, "Who do you think you are locking up teenagers for no reason! I should drown you right now, Nathaniel!"

"Hey!" Nathaniel yelled. "I didn't do it! Zeke and Gabe, help!" After they heard our names, Sarah and Trish turned around and beamed. Sarah sprinted and jumped towards Gabe, and they gave each other the biggest hugs I had ever seen. For a second, I thought Gabe's head would pop off.

Trish was different, though. She walked slowly up to me and said, "I'm sorry, Zeke. I'm sorry for all of the crap I caused. I never meant to hurt anyone, but how can you handle this place?" Then, after apologizing, she hugged me. "I'm going to listen to you now, and thank you for saving us. That is very brave especially in here."

"Don't worry about it," I said. That was all I could say. She had hugged me. It was the greatest day of my young life, but we had to stay on track. The first part of the escape plan was over, and now we needed to get out of there.

After a few more hugs with Sarah and the girls thanking us over and over again, I told them the plan. "Alright, Nathaniel wanted to escape with us, so he is going to help us get out of here."

"How can you trust him?" Sarah asked with Nathaniel in the circle.

"Thank you, you know, for everything I helped you with," Nathaniel commented.

"He helped us find you two. I think that is reason enough to trust him. I think Marcus put you both in there. He kept telling Gabe and I that you were both being treated after the incident and that we weren't allowed to see you because it would interfere with training," I explained.

"Do you have any idea who put you both in there?" Gabe asked.

"No," Trish said. "We were both unconscious after my stupid mistake, so we had no idea about anything going on. Where are we even?"

Nathaniel explained to them about the escape tunnel in the basement. After everyone knew everything about what had been happening over the last few days, I said, "Okay, Nathaniel, we have no time to talk anymore. How do we get out of here?"

"The best way," he thought for a few moments. "The best way would be to leave going out the front driveway. It may be open so that people may see us, but it's the closest way to a city. If we go out of the back through this tunnel, it would be about an extra two miles."

"I'm not a fan of running three miles, thank you very much," Gabe said.

We all laughed for a few seconds and then got back on track. "The front will be our exit then," I said. "What is the easiest way to get out there?"

"The best way would be to go to the first floor and find a way out there. The revolving door has a security system, so if anyone starts it, an alarm will go off," Nathaniel said.

"Okay," I said. "Let's get to the first floor, and then we will find an exit." We all then ran to the beginning of the cave, and Nathaniel sealed it back up. I thought that the hole in the steel door was a giveaway that people had been in there, though.

We continued running up the flight of stairs to the very next level. We opened the door and quickly moved to the front revolving doors. We all stopped and looked out at the tall trees surrounding the very curvy and long driveway to freedom.

Everyone's dreams were about to come true. I kept thinking about how Gabe and I couldn't stand to be here for more than two weeks, and Sarah had been here for a few years. Nathaniel had been here for upwards of twenty. My mind would have been lost long ago. The only challenge left was to find, or make, an exit. A feat Gabe and I had already done.

My all-time favorite games had always been the ones on the video game websites that you had to escape a room or a car or something else. You kept searching around the room until you collected items that would help you break out of an almost impossible to escape area. This made me feel like I was in one of those games. Hopefully, I could get out like I had then.

Sarah was constantly looking around every corner and behind every desk in every room. "What are you doing?" Gabe asked.

"I'm trying to find stuff that will help us get out of here," Sarah said as she kept moving from room to room. "Until we have an idea, we might as well collect whatever we can find that could help us."

She had a great idea there. Finding stuff that would help us would save time and give us an idea of what we had at our disposal. Nathaniel and Trish agreed to go help look for stuff, so they went off in different directions.

Gabe and I were the only ones left standing in front of the revolving door. "What do you think about this?" Gabe asked.

"About what?" I replied.

"What do you think about just breaking down the wall. I'm getting sick of all of this breaking and entering crap. I say we just bash a hole in the wall, like the door in the basement, and run before they find us," Gabe said.

Gabe was beginning to get restless and destructive. He reminded me of the times when I played red light-green light. Once you were so close, you just wanted to run no matter what and get there even if there was a slim chance of you making it. Unfortunately, that was a game and this was real life.

Looking around the room for stuff, I came up with a mini-plan. "Where is the security system for the door, Nathaniel?" I asked.

"I believe it is mounted on the ceiling of the room behind the reception desk. Why?" he asked in reply.

I started to make my way over to the reception desk. My idea was simple. Anything with a security system must run on electricity. If it ran on electricity, I would use my own electricity and fry its circuits (or something like that) hopefully disabling the security system. We all reached the room, and I told everyone my idea.

"It's risky," Sarah said. "If your plan doesn't work, the alarm will sound, and we will be screwed."

"Yeah, Zeke," Trish said. "It is a huge risk. Are you sure it is even possible to overload a security system?"

To be honest, I didn't. The only time I had ever heard of someone overloading anything was in my comic books or in cartoons like Static Shock. Thomas would come over every Saturday morning to watch those cartoons. It was what I looked forward to all week because I wasn't old enough to walk to Thomas' by myself, so Thomas would come over to my apartment because his mom didn't care.

Fact of the matter was that I still had no idea if my plan would even work. Gabe said to me, "I believe in you. Heck, if I can melt a hole in a steel door, over 2500 degrees, then you can definitely fry that security control box."

"What do you think Nathaniel?" I asked him. Nathaniel was leaning up against the wall next to the door. He had been quiet most of the time. It must've been weird for him to be working with a bunch of teenagers when he was like forty or fifty.

"I think," Nathaniel said. "That the limits of our abilities are immeasurable. I know because The Clade tried to measure the power an average fire member can create, and they found that it was enormous. You, Zeke, are incredibly powerful, so I believe that you can destroy that box before the alarm goes off."

"That settles it. Three-to-two. I'll give it a try," I said. I asked everyone to back away from me and up against the wall in case my lightning went wacky again. I shook off my nerves and stared at the small, square, gray, box with colorful wires emanating out of it. I focused all of my energy into the palm of my hand. Lightning sparks erupted followed by massive bolts that arched between my two hands. I never had done that before, not even in training. I looked back up again and threw a ferocious bolt of pure energy and power into the box. I held the bolt for about ten seconds. The room was brighter than if the lights were actually on. Everyone was covering their eyes, either from the light or from not wanting to know what was going to happen.

I stopped the bolt and looked up at the box. Actually, there was no box left to look at. It was gone. All that was left were a few wires hanging on the ceiling and a black scorched stain. It reminded me of the basement except that this was caused by electricity and not flame.

"Woohoo!" Gabe cheered as he approached me. Everyone else did the same. We all circled together and cheered quietly so that no one would hear us. We had succeeded. There was nothing left in our way to get out of here.

"We don't have any more time for cheering," I said taking charge. "Let's go, and we can celebrate in the real world."

Nathaniel led us out of the room and down the hallway to the revolving door. We looked up at the wires on the door that led up into the ceiling. If my plan worked, we should be able to move the door without any alarm signaling our escape. "I'll go first," Nathaniel said. He moved slowly into the first open area of the revolving door and, after a moment to think about what he was doing, he pushed the door. He pushed slowly hoping that no alarm would ring.

Nathaniel made it halfway with no problems when the next open slot came around and Sarah jumped in with Gabe. "We'll see you outside," she said as Gabe began to push. They were cute together. That just left Trish and me for the next open space. Nathaniel pushed a little more and finally made it outside. Nathaniel gave us a friendly wave of support on the outside as Trish and I stepped in.

We pushed at the same speed of Gabe and Sarah who had just made it outside too. It seemed as though we would be in there forever pushing slowly and thinking that an alarm would start signaling our imminent death.

While we were in the revolving door, Trish said, "Zeke, I'm so terribly sorry for everything that I've done. I should've listened to you. I burned you for goodness sake, and you repeatedly risked your life to save me. I can't say I'm sorry enough."

"Don't worry about it," I told her. "We are all safe now, but if you feel that badly about it, you can apologize as much as you want on the outside. I do have a question for you, though."

"Yeah? What is it?" Trish replied.

"Well, about two and a half weeks ago, I was recruited. On my birthday remember?"

"Yeah, I remember," she said. "One day you didn't show up for school and that was your birthday. The next day you still didn't show up, but in the mail, all of your friends and anyone who knew you had received a letter saying that you had moved away because your mom was transferred to a different hospital. You should've seen Thomas. He was really upset.

Oh god. I felt terrible. Is that what had happened to everyone here? How does the Clade even do all of that so quickly? It must've been set up before hand. I needed to find Thomas and tell him everything. Maybe he could even help all of us. This part of the escape felt like it was taking forever.

We kept pushing the door very slowly. After a few seconds that felt like minutes, we were all out of the revolving door of death and into the open forest air. "Finally!" Nathaniel said. "After all of this time of being locked up in that place of tyranny, I'm free."

"Not yet," Sarah said. "We still need to go down the mile long driveway, and then we are pretty much safe because we will be in public."

"Sarah's right," I agreed. "Let's go now so we can celebrate sooner."

We all began to walk together down the long driveway. It swerved through the forest making it almost impossible to even see the hospital anymore after the second turn. The thoughts of everyone around me were all the same, "We are going to do it!" I was just as confident as they were. I wanted to believe that we were going to do it, but something kept nagging me in the back of my mind that said we weren't home free yet.

Sarah must have noticed this because she said, "Zeke, what's on your mind?"

"I don't know," I answered truthfully. "I feel like I'm forgetting something. Something very important."

Nathaniel overheard us and replied, "Nothing, there is nothing left. We will just keep going until we reach-" he was cut off because standing in front of him, marching forward, getting closer step-by-step, was an army.

An army of large men wearing business suits.

It was the Agents.

They had found us.

Chapter 19

This couldn't be happening. Marcus had been right, but he hadn't known how right he was. The Agents were only two turns away from reaching the entrance to the hospital. We all hid behind some trees and crouched low so that we wouldn't be seen. There was no way to get around them without getting tased or shot by the large shotguns and rifles they were now carrying. They were done with the capturing. Now, they wanted to kill us all.

"Zeke," Gabe whispered from the tree next to me. "What are we going to do?"

I looked around for Nathaniel. Maybe he would know a way to help us get around this armada, but he was nowhere to be found. I wasn't worried about Nathaniel though; I was worried about our safety. "I don't know," I replied to Gabe. "To be honest, I think the best idea would be to get back to the hospital and wake up everyone to tell them about the Agents."

"Really?" Trish asked. "We just got out of there. Why do you want to go back?"

The Agents were almost on top of us, so we had to move. "Let's just go back, and I'll explain it to you. Hurry!" I whispered urgently. We crept quickly through the trees with the army marching behind us.

We reached the hospital just as the army was approaching the final turn. They would be there in less than five minutes, so I quickly told everyone why I wanted to go back. "Marcus won't let the Agents win without a fight, so while everyone is fighting, we get out of there."

My plan sounded good. Everyone would be busy keeping the Agents away, so we would be able to just walk away from there. The army would be a great, big diversion, but if Marcus was lying the whole time, then it may get scary.

Gabe must've read my mind because he asked, "What if Marcus is lying about not using the plan anymore?" I was afraid to answer because I knew they would disapprove, but it had to happen. They would be safe then.

"Then I will fight, and I will give you a diversion to run," I explained. All three of them gasped.

"Zeke," Sarah said. "Don't be stupid. You are coming with us. Don't try acting like a hero and being all tough."

I didn't know where all of this bravery was coming from, but I guess after losing my mom, my home, my friends, pretty much everything, it had just sparked somewhere inside me. Ha, 'sparked somewhere inside me.' Now that was funny. I got that thought out of my head and said, "No, it's the only way. If we can't all go, then at least most of us will."

The marching was getting louder. The Agents were rounding the final turn, and we were standing in front of the revolving door. "Go, get inside now. We need to wake them up," I said. They looked at the road and ran inside.

We didn't care about the alarm anymore. We quickly pushed through the door and ran down the halls. We were extremely loud. Our footsteps and huffing and puffing could have woken up an entire city block. We were making loud noises hoping that everyone would be waking up upstairs, so that it would be quicker to notify them of the attack. The door to the staircase didn't stand a chance. We rushed through it and ran up the stairs.

When we finally reached the 3rd level, no one was awake. I realized that I had never known where the Instructors slept. I turned to Sarah and asked, "Sarah, do you know where Marcus and Juliette sleep?"

She replied, "Down on the other end, by the new training rooms and Marcus' office."

"Show us and hurry!" I yelled.

We ran down the halls. Our yelling must've been working because I could hear a few people starting to wake up. We just kept running and didn't worry about the thought of being tased from behind by someone who saw us running down the halls at night. We passed the reception desk, and I turned around. Two teenagers were out of their rooms and starting to look at who was making the noise. I could tell they were afraid to step into the hall at night because they just peeked their heads through the doorway.

Sarah finally reached the door to Marcus' dorm. I pounded on the door and yelled, "Marcus! Marcus! Wake up! The Agents are here!" I felt a little like Paul Revere. I just hoped that I didn't end up like him.

Now the Agents marching was audible from the 3rd level of the hospital. Marcus grabbed the door handle and violently ripped it open. "What is going on out here! Why aren't you in your dorms! I could have you all locked up for-" he stopped when he saw who it was. "Zeke? Gabe? What are you two doing-" He then noticed Sarah and Trish behind us. "Where did you two come from? Nathaniel put you two in a hospital dorm to get better. You weren't supposed to be out for another few days."

"Marcus listen," I pleaded. "The Agents are here. You were right. We need to fight or run."

"What? They can't be. They were still a few weeks out and had no idea where we were exactly located," Marcus said.

"Trust us," Sarah stepped in. "They are probably ringing the doorbell now."

"How do you know this?" He paused waiting for us to answer, but he didn't need any answer. He knew why we knew.

"We were out of our dorms. We have been for the past few nights trying to find Sarah and Trish because you wouldn't tell us where they were," Gabe said.

"I know," Marcus said. "Nathaniel told me about you two sneaking around. He went to room 241F two nights ago and waited for you two to show up. I don't know how he knew you were going to be there, but he did."

Gabe and I knew why. Nathaniel had found Gabe looking for Sarah and Trish on the third floor. I guessed that he had assumed we would continue looking for them, and room 241F would be a perfect location because he had known we would look there.

Marcus finally wrapped is mind around the fact that the Agents were here, and he began to take action. "Zeke, go to the reception desk. Underneath the counter is a small button that activates the alarm. Hurry and pull that!" I listened to him, and I took off.

I ran to the desk and felt underneath the counter top. I couldn't find it right away, so I felt from the left to the right. I got to the far right side and found the small button. I pushed it and a red light began to flash everywhere. It flashed in every hall and every room. The Clade was really serious about the Agents if they had installed a high tech alarm. Recruits began to step into the hallway rubbing their eyes and putting on their cloaks. I ran back to Marcus and the others to find out what we do next.

I got back just as Juliette arrived to meet the group. "What's going on!?" She yelled. We informed her about the impending attack. "Oh no," she responded.

"Juliette," Marcus began. "Go tell everyone to get ready. The Agents are here and are about to attack. We need soldiers." She listened and ran off to tell everyone in The Clade. "Now," Marcus switched subjects focusing on us four. "While they get in formation, we are going to get some weapons from room 241-" Marcus was cut off by the sound of bombs blowing up the front entrance of the hospital.

We were out of time. Everyone else had heard the bangs and were beginning to run down the stairwell to face their impending demise. Any member of the Clade that could harm another person with their ability ran off.

Marcus grabbed me and Gabe and said, "Go to room 241F and grab whatever you can for weapons. I'm assuming you know the pass code to activate the power."

"What about Sarah and Trish?" Gabe asked.

"They will stay with me and help me organize all of the recruits while we still have some left to fight with," Marcus said.

I didn't want to leave Trish and Sarah alone with Marcus again. Gabe, by the look on his face, didn't like it either, but Sarah came up to me and whispered, "Don't worry. We girls can handle ourselves." I smiled, grabbed Gabe, and took off for the staircase.

We descended the staircase quickly while avoiding running into Clade members going to fight. They didn't seem too happy about having to fight right away. Other recruits were hanging back waiting for more instructions. I guess if your ability wasn't all that great, you were second string.

Gabe and I stopped short of the others and entered the 2nd level. We sprinted all the way to room 241F without talking at all. The only sounds in the hall were the gasps of air from Gabe and me. Once we reached 241F, however, that's when a new sound was heard.

The sound of gunshots and screams.

People were dying.

Room 241F was just the same as it had been we had left it a few hours ago. Was that really only a few hours ago? "Zeke, hurry up and activate the power."

"Zeke Laufor is our key to freedom," I said aloud to no one. It didn't happen right away, as it usually did, but after a few moments, you could hear the generator springing to life and providing huge amounts of energy to the room. Just after, the table sank into the floor and spun around revealing a table full of chemicals. Next, the cabinets flipped through the wall revealing open gun cabinets, and, lastly, the super computer was revealed to us by the sliding wall.

Gabe said, "After doing that a few times, I still don't believe that this is possible."

"Well, you better start believing in something because we are about to be thrown into a war that revolves around superpowers," I responded.

We grabbed whatever weapons we could carry, like pistols, shotguns, and rifles, even a few bow and arrows with a quiver, and ran back to Marcus in no time flat. The sounds of guns and cries of pain rang through the building as if the hospital was some kind of haunted house.

Marcus was standing in the middle of ten or eleven teenagers, some of which I recognized, and began giving orders. Sarah and Trish were a ways behind him helping another instructor give orders. We dropped the weapons in front of Marcus and all of the teens eyes lit up in fear. "Thank you," he said.

Sarah and Trish noticed us and signaled us to go over by them. Gabe and I crossed through the chaos of kids and adults getting ready to fight to get over to the girls. The cries of the kids and the orders from the adults were brutal. Their lives were on the line. I bet none of them actually believed they would die here. I hadn't believed that that would ever happen either.

The girls were trying to comfort an instructor who had to command teenagers to fight. The group of teens was very resilient to the idea of fighting against a trained army. I asked Sarah, "Who is that?"

"That is Jacob Schuman. He was promoted to be an instructor just a few months ago, so he doesn't have much experience in warfare. We are just trying to tell him that everything will be okay. He is actually freaking out more than some of the other kids," Sarah said.

The instructor was about twenty-five give or take. He had darker skin and short, black hair which made him hardly noticeable without light. When the red light did flash, however, I could tell that he was shaking from the danger of becoming a corpse tonight.

The kids soon became disgusted with his orders and his uncertainty. One of the older boys said, "I have been here for four years, and I think I am more stable than you are," he insulted. "C'mon guys, might as well die together."The group then left and walked down the stairwell.

Sarah said to Gabe and me, "I really like the confidence level in these recruits."

"Well, their hopes are slim," Gabe said. "I'm starting to feel like them to. How are we supposed to escape when the war is happening right outside the front door?" All three of them turned to me.

"Why are you asking me?"I complained.

"You are the one who came up with the last few plans. We are just following what you say," Trish said.

"Yeah, you are a born leader, Zeke. Maybe Marcus was right," Sarah said.

"Right about what," I said starting to get annoyed by all of the attention.

Gabe said, "Sarah maybe you are-" he was cut off by her.

"No, you have all of the traits of being a leader, and with your electric ability, you could very well help take down the Agents," Sarah said.

"No way!" I yelled louder than I intended. I looked around and found Marcus with Juliette at the other end of the hall comforting recruits. "I am getting out of here with you guys unless Marcus makes me fight, and then you are all getting out of here."

"You have to think realistically, Zeke. Yes, we can escape and live on our own moving from one spot to the next, but can we really live like that? In the end, the Clade will be our true home. There is no way of getting around that, but I will try to stay with you guys. I promise you," Sarah confessed.

I was going to keep complaining and arguing with her until I made her believe that she was going to be safe on the other side of this forest, but Marcus and Juliette showed up. I looked back at the other group of recruits to see what had happened to them and found no one. Nobody was left. Everyone had gone to go fight against the almost impossible armada that was the Agents. The enemies that none of us had any clue of who they were even are or why they were fighting us. I felt like a sixteen year old boy with amnesia. Nothing made sense and everything was happening way too quickly for me to even think about keeping up. Whatever Marcus was about to tell us would have to be what I went off of.

Marcus said in a torn tone, "We are losing heavily. Reports of casualties are coming in left and right. I don't know how long we will be able to stay inside waiting. We are going to have to go out and fight," he frowned.

Suddenly, the threat of actually dying was very real. The choice was an impossible one to make, but we had to choose. We were going to have to kill to live, or we would die. I wasn't the only one with that feeling. Sarah, Gabe, and Trish all had the threat of dying in their heads. They stared at the floor through hopeless eyes. That wasn't going to be their problem, though. Not if I could help it. Hopefully, I could provide enough of a distraction that the others could get out.

Juliette then continued after the silence, "Out of the three hundred recruits that were based here, about one hundred and fifty are left. If we don't go fight soon, we are going to be over run in here."

After a little longer silence, I looked over to the other three and shook my head telling them that Marcus, Juliette, and I will fight while they escape. I scanned over their faces making sure they understood. Trish had tears forming in her eyes, and Gabe looked as if he was going to pass out. Sarah was strong just as she always was. If I didn't make it back to them, she would have to provide hope for the other two.

"Why are we waiting here?" I asked. "Our friends are out there fighting while we are staying in here talking about them dying. We need to help!" I yelled to them.

"So, I'm assuming you are up for it?" Marcus asked.

I inhaled deeply before what I was about to say. "If you won't die for freedom, what will you die for?"

We all began walking towards the stairwell as the bombs and gunshots became louder and more threatening. I guess we were just more tuned into that now that we were soldiers in the supernatural war.

As all six of us descended the stairs, I stopped and took one last look at the place that had been my home for the past two and a half weeks. Even though living here was total hell, the people were not. I had made a great friend, Gabe, and a smart and stubborn one, Sarah. I shut the door and continued down the staircase after everyone else to a war that would either free us or kill us.

The descent down the staircase was one that everyone savored. It reminded me of how a person who was scheduled to be executed walks down the long hallway until they reach the place where they will be killed.

I finally reached the 1st level door and walked through it to find Sarah, Gabe, Trish, Marcus, and Juliette waiting for me by the reception desk. "What took you so long?" Trish asked.

"Nothing," I replied. "It doesn't matter anymore. Not after what we're going into."

More gunshots and explosions rang through the building. Dust and debris crumbled from the walls exposing electrical wiring and the wooden framing of the hospital. I was afraid that the building would collapse, and Sarah, Trish, and Gabe wouldn't be able to escape out of the underground tunnel in the basement. They would have to move quickly.

I looked through the glass in the revolving door and saw blood stains on the black top. Bodies were strewn on the driveway. My stomach flipped and my head felt throbbed, but I had to remain focused.

Marcus regained my focus on him by saying, "When we head out through the door, we have to stay low and slowly work ourselves up behind the first or second lines to provide support. The Agents have positioned themselves in the forest and tree line, so it will be hard for us to hit them. If we wait it out though, we may be able to get a few good blasts on them. Then, hopefully, they will retreat."

Marcus was hoping for a lot, in fact, I think it would qualify as a miracle. We had already lost over half of our three hundred recruits in the division, and he just wants to keep fighting. I would've tried escaping after the first hundred. I mean, these were human lives, and not just any human lives, but teenage human lives. Some of them were not even old enough to drive, let alone fight in a war.

We all began to march, one behind the other, to the revolving door. Marcus took the lead followed by Juliette, me, Gabe, Sarah, and then Trish. The wall was filled with holes big enough to fit bowling balls through, and the foundation was slowly cracking. As we approached the entrance to the war, the cries for help became unbearably loud. I wished that it was pretend like on T.V. and that I could just turn it down, but I couldn't because everything going on was real.

Marcus reached for the glass door and crouched low to the ground. "Hopefully," he said. "I will have the honor of training you all again someday. He began to tear up as he pushed the door around.

Juliette jumped in right behind him followed by Gabe and me, and then Trish and Sarah in the next one. The revolving door stuck out a little ways from the building, so the war was taking place right in front of us. Flashes of light came from the lining of the trees about one hundred yards out. After the flashes, we would see one or maybe even two recruits drop to the ground holding a bloody arm or leg where they had been shot. Some didn't even wiggle after being hit. It was sad and disgusting. There was no mercy with the Agents. All they wanted was blood.

We kept pushing, and as Gabe and I got further around, I noticed that the Clade wasn't just being pushovers. Some of the recruits were hiding behind old vehicles still left in the parking lot and used guns to shoot at the Agents. Others used their abilities. However, their abilities seemed useless because if someone used a fire ability on an exposed Agent, the Agent would merely take the blast and not be affected. That was the same with water and some of air. Earth recruits were a little more effective but barely.

I saw what Marcus meant about me being the key to defeating the Agents. They could handle the elements, but they had never seen my ability before. Not even the Agent who was thrown from my window on the night before my birthday. I was a free-radical to them. That would give me an advantage.

Gabe and I reached the end of what felt like a decade walking around the revolving door witnessing the brutal murders of our Clade friends and companions. Even though I was afraid to kill more than anything else, I was going to have to. I was a soldier, and I would save whoever was left to save.

Chapter 20

As Gabe and I made our final push, a memory emerged from the back of my mind. I was seven or eight, and I was asked a question by my teacher, "What do you want to be when you grow up?" I remembered answering, "A soldier because that was what my daddy was, and he was a hero."

It had all been a lie though. He wasn't dead, and he wasn't a soldier for the U.S. Army like I had thought. I guess being in the Clade would count as being a soldier, but I had always been told that he had crashed in a helicopter overseas. I wondered if it was too late to change my career choice and run back inside.

"Gabe," I looked at him as we were about to exit the door. "Once you escape, don't wait for me. You have to get yourselves out of here."

"No way, Zeke. We wouldn't be here without you. You are coming with us no matter what," Gabe said.

I didn't want to tell him that that was probably not going to happen. As we completed our last push, the thought of not making it out of there with my friends was becoming more and more real. I had to make sure that they got out at least which meant I would have to make sure that they didn't get hurt in the fight. I would protect them with everything I had at my disposal.

The door was now open, and we were exposed. The parking lot stretched out in front of us for about one hundred yards. In the parking lot abandoned cars sat, some of them overturned and being used as shields from the Agents gunfire. We had a little more than one hundred Clade recruits alive. All of the others were scattered across the ground. I felt like I was going to pass out, and I was sure that Gabe felt the same.

"Remember the plan," I told Gabe. "We will go up behind the Clade members in front and provide support. Don't do anything crazy!" I yelled to him.

"You don't have to tell me that," Gabe said. We both crouched low and sprinted into the battlefield. We hurdled over dead recruits as we ran. There were a few dead Agents scattered around, but there were definitely more Clade members which meant they were winning.

The frontline felt like a mile away. At any moment, Gabe and I could be shot and killed. That thought only made me run faster. I caught a few flashes of light coming from the trees about fifty yards in front of the cars. Gabe and I just kept low and hoped that we would stay safe.

We jetted towards a car that was lying on its side hoping it would provide protection. There were three other recruits including Sarah. "Sarah!" Gabe yelled in relief. "You are okay."

"For now maybe. These Agents don't mess around. I heard a grenade go off before towards the east side of the building."

"The east?" I asked.

"The left side of the building when you exit it," she said in frustration. Sarah was handing some of the older recruits magazines for their guns. It was a smart way to stay safe and help the other recruits.

The boy she was giving the magazines to ducked back behind the car. He pulled out the magazine from the rifle and said, "It's jammed. Can one of you three keep them distracted while I un-jam this gun." He began to pound on it.

The boy had black hair that fell down to his eyes. His face was round, and he looked as if he had played football before he had been recruited. He looked calm in the face of danger, almost as though war was normal to him. I wondered if staying in that place could do that to you, make you so cold to anything. It was beginning to sink into my system too if that was the case.

Gabe, Sarah, and I all looked at each other. I had already decided that I would provide cover for this boy, whoever he was. "I'm going up," I said. Gabe was about to jump up, but I put my hand on his shoulder and pushed him down forcefully. "Don't try to stop me. I told you I would get you guys out of here safely, and I will." I looked over to the boy and then back saying, "Just help… whoever this guy is to un-jam his gun. I'll be fine."

I stayed low, walked behind the boy, and walked to the front of the car where the other two recruits were. I poked my head slightly over the car and looked into the dark woods. I scanned the tree line from left to right and saw a few flashes of light directed at other cars, other recruits.

I reached the driveway and saw an Agent running through. He stopped and spotted us. I held my breath and cringed in fear hoping that he wasn't aiming for me. I heard the shots ring from across the parking lot, but they didn't hit me. Instead, they hit the girl that was shooting next to me. She dropped to the ground and held her neck. Blood spewed from the wound as she tried to keep pressure on it.

She was about to die, and there was nothing I could do to help her. I felt so angry and sad at the same time. Then I remembered that I can heal with my electricity. I knelt down beside her and brushed her blonde hair out of her wound.

I charged electricity in my hand when I heard Sarah shout, "Zeke, NO! You'll fry her. You can only heal yourself. If you try it on anyone else, they will get shocked!"

I looked down, but it was too late. Her eyes became empty. She was dead. Fear filled my body, but that fear quickly became anger and rage against the Agents, the one who had killed this girl in particular. This would be my only chance to stop him. My head poked over the overturned car. I closed my eyes and held out my hand. I focused all of my energy into my fingertips and launched it across the large gap between us. I opened my eyes slowly and saw a smoldering crisp of a man wearing a suit lying on the driveway. He was dead, I had killed him.

My breath became short. The man didn't move which confirmed that I was correct, he was dead. My face became damp with beads of sweat and tears. I couldn't believe what I had done. What seemed like ages went by and the man still wasn't moving. I knew that, in my mind, that image of the man lying on the ground with smoke and blood spewing from him would stick with me forever.

I finally snapped out of my haunting day dream and realized that I had been exposed for the last few minutes. The area around me had become silent during that time. Gunshots were no longer being fired and the explosions had ceased. I looked down to find Sarah, Gabe, and that other guy looking up at me in a state of shock. I realized that everyone else was doing the same. All of the Clade recruits had stopped and stared at me. I was afraid that they would be shot and killed, but that didn't happen because the Agents had also stopped firing. The forest no longer had bursts of light attacking and killing recruits. Instead, the Agents stood in the open, vulnerable to attack. Everyone was shocked about what they had just seen. It was then that I felt a tugging on my cloak and looked over to see it was the shaggy hair boy.

He pulled me back behind the car and to safety. Once we were back behind, he said, "You're him, the one that can use electricity and turn it into lightning."

"Yeah, I am," I said to him as I ducked back below the car realizing what the effects of my murder had caused.

"The whole Clade has heard a lot about you," he said. "My name is Trevor Gibbs."

I didn't know why he was telling me all of this now. It was a bad time for that, but he still seemed so relaxed. "Um… hi Trevor. I'm Zeke, Zeke Laufor." I shook his hand hoping that he would drop or at least change the subject. "No offense, Trevor, but what do you want?"

He looked around first and then whispered, "I heard what you said to Sarah and that other new boy before. You are going to escape from this war and this place."

"Yeah, why?" I asked him.

"I want to go with you."

Trevor Gibbs, a person I hadn't met since, let's see, a whole minute before, wanted to get in with mine, Gabe's, and Sarah's plan to escape. I didn't know if it was a good idea, or even if now was the time to be making this idea. All I knew was that he could crush me if I denied him, and he *had* been taking all of the shots so far. Literally.

"I'll ask Sarah and Gabe," I told him as I heard the first gunshot break out again followed by a tiny scream.

"Okay," he said gravely. "Thanks for giving me the chance to get out of this shit."

"No problem," I said.

I went back below the car and went over to Sarah. A voice shouted over the beginning of the new fight. It yelled, "It's the boy! The one who can use electricity! Don't let him get away!"

The fighting then raged on even more deadly than before. Agents actually began to come out of the trees and run towards our car. I grabbed Sarah and said, "We have to go soon. That boy wanted to come with us, Trevor. What do you think?"

"I really don't care. He is pretty trustworthy. Trevor has been here as long as me. A little dimwitted at times but a good guy," Sarah said.

Gabe heard our conversation and joined in as he watched for stray bullets. "Someone else is coming now? Gosh, we already have us three, Nathaniel, wherever he went, and Trish."

Trish. I had totally forgotten about her. She wasn't anywhere near us. I quickly scanned the parking lot hoping she would be with another group of recruits. I finally saw her by Marcus and Juliette, shooting a gun at the Agents. She was beginning to adapt to the Clade, and I was afraid that she wouldn't be the same once we got out of there.

"We have to get Trish away from Marcus and Juliette, and then we have to get out of here," I said to the other two. The Agents kept coming from the sides of the forest lining trying to get to our car, but the other recruits would stop them before they even came close. We were making a comeback, and maybe Marcus would get that miracle he wanted.

That miracle quickly vanished when the sounds of marching echoed through the parking lot from the long driveway. All of the remaining Agents retreated from the hospital grounds and went deeper into the forest to regroup with their reinforcements. The tides had turned.

This would be our small window for escape. I grabbed Trevor and yelled, "If you're with us, we are going now!"

"Alright! Let's get out of here before we're toast!"" he exclaimed.

I grabbed Sarah and Gabe and told them that it was time to escape while the army was a few seconds away. "What about Trish?" Sarah asked as we began to run towards Marcus and Trish.

"We are going to tell Marcus our plan. Maybe he will listen, and we can escape with whoever is left alive. He just has to see reason," I said to her.

"Alright, Zeke, whatever you say," she said in a sarcastic tone. I just rolled my eyes as we kept moving towards Marcus and Trish on the other side of the parking lot.

We were running out of time. The Agents were almost there, and the other recruits, the fifty of them left, weren't leaving from their positions. I knew that we wouldn't make it in time to everyone, so I yelled, "Everyone listen!" The recruits all moved out of their stance and looked at me, Gabe, Sarah, and Trevor standing in the middle of the parking lot. "We have to retreat now! There is a tunnel in the basement level of the hospital! I will show you, but we have to go now; otherwise, it will be too late!"

Marcus began running at me with Juliette right behind him. I wasn't afraid of what he could do anymore. If we didn't run now, then the Agents would just kill us anyway. Whatever he had to say would be ignored. "Zeke! What do you think you're doing?" he asked me.

"Marcus, you have to see reason," I said trying to remain calm with the approaching army almost visible. "If we don't leave now, we will all be killed. For crying out loud, you already lost more than half of your recruits."

Marcus listened as I explained to him what we were going to do. I didn't have to worry about Juliette's opinion because she'd do whatever Marcus did. Then he said, "But if we leave, then we lose the fight against the Agents."

"No, we don't Marcus," I explained to him. "We live to fight another day, and someday, we may even be able to take the attack to them. You're right," I said trying to amuse him. "They were stunned by my power, so let's regroup and fight another day."

He stared at me through his dark eyes. Gabe was beginning to shake from the army about to come and kill us all. "Marcus!" I yelled, and finally he snapped out of it.

"You're right, Zeke," He then turned to the other recruits. "Everyone follow Zeke and me! We are retreating! We will take you through the tunnel and out into the forest a mile away! That should give us enough time to make a run for it!"

Finally, Marcus was listening to us, but we couldn't celebrate yet because our death was literally right around the corner. We didn't take one look back as we began to run for the hospital.

The hospital doors were fifty yards away and even further for the others. We all sprinted as if our lives depended on it because they did. Marcus reached the revolving door before the rest of us and began to push it. Trish and I reached the door next and filled in our slot. It was heavier than it had felt before when Gabe and I were walking towards our death.

The other recruits were right behind. I looked through the glass of the revolving door and noticed that most of the remaining recruits were almost to the door. However, they weren't fast enough. The reinforcements had arrived and began shooting at the rear of the group of recruits. Bodies dropped to the ground leaving me stiff. Trish hit me and yelled nervously with tears forming in her eyes, "Zeke, keep moving!" That snapped me out of it, and I kept going.

Sarah, Gabe, and Trevor kept pushing behind us. I don't think they stopped to look at the blood bath occurring behind us. They were a lot smarter than I was.

Even though a lot of recruits were dying, there were still a lot making it into the revolving door. They helped push us along the track. It was a lot easier now than it had been when we first entered the war. We all worked together until Juliette and Marcus made it into the hospital. Soon after, Trish and I made it in followed by Sarah, Gabe, and Trevor.

We kept encouraging the other recruits to push although time was running short. The Agents had already made their way through half of the parking lot. They didn't even have to aim. All they had to do was shoot, and they would hit some recruit. Finally, everyone that was still alive made it inside. Out of the fifty or so that had made it through the fighting, only twenty had made it into the building. We couldn't stop and mourn for the all of the dead lives that were ruined because of their so called "gifts," or we would be just like them.

"We can't stop!" Marcus yelled. "We have to keep moving! Go to the stairwell!"

The recruits listened to his orders and followed. I stayed near the front of the group with Trish as we ran through the hospital. I couldn't let the others fall behind. I wouldn't let that happen. I was determined to get them out of here.

The door to the stairwell was nearing. We pushed through and continued down the stairs to the basement. The other recruits stayed close together in a tight group. By the time we reached the bottom of the staircase, the last Clade member had made it through the 1st level door.

As we ran through the scorched, black, halls to the training room, I remembered what Nathaniel had said about why the tunnel had been constructed. The whole hospital could be collapsed if the Agents ever infiltrated it. I didn't know where he was now, but I figured that would be a good strategy.

Marcus kept on running, and we kept on following. The Agents could be heard on the 1st level marching down the halls towards the stairwell. I decided to tell Marcus about the fail safe plan as we ran. "Marcus, did Nathaniel ever tell you why the tunnel was built?"

"Yeah, I actually told him. Do you really think we should do it?" he asked.

"To be honest, yes," I told him. I took a few deep breaths, gasping for air, as we ran. "They are entering the building now. We could take out almost all of their reinforcements or maybe even all of them."

We finally reached the training room, and we stopped. He responded, "That would be nice but I can't risk another person's life to save our own."

Trevor must have overheard our conversation because he stepped up from behind Trish and Gabe and said, "What about collapsing the hospital?" We told him what the original idea for the tunnel was for. He then said, "So you need someone who can control the earth element?"

"Yeah," I told him. I forgot that his power dealt with the earth. I didn't know if he was going to volunteer, but it would definitely help.

"No!" Marcus exclaimed at us. "Another life will not be lost because of my mistakes. I knew they were coming. If anyone should die here, it should be me."

"No," Trevor said to him. "The Clade needs you to lead, and you can't control the earth. I will go, and I will be fine." He turned and started pushing his way through the crowd back into the hallway. I decided to follow him and stop him for a second.

"What are you doing? How are you supposed to get out of here alive if you do something stupid like this?" I asked.

I hoped he wouldn't crush me for calling him stupid, but instead he just said, "Look, I will be fine. My own element won't kill me. I won't let it. After I do this, I will just follow behind you and be free."

If Trevor did this, no one would look for him because he would be assumed dead. It was a brilliant idea but incredibly risky. "Well, good luck. I hope to see you on the other side," I said.

He patted me on the back and gave me a quick hug and said, "Take care, dude. This isn't the end of me. I promise you." He then backed away and ran toward the staircase.

I didn't think he would make it to the staircase before the Agents did, but I tried not to worry as I made my way back towards the rest of my friends and Marcus. I just hoped that he knew what he was doing.

Marcus noticed me making my way through, and he asked, "You stopped him, right?"

"No, he was too persistent. I couldn't stop him. We don't have a lot of time so let's get everyone into the tunnel before this place collapses on our heads," I said.

Gabe pulled me back and asked, "Did he really go to protect the Clade?" I told him why he went to collapse the hospital. "Oh, not a bad plan. Well, unless he crushes himself," he said.

Sarah hit him in the ribs with her elbow and said, "That's a little disrespectful to the person who is trying to save your life so that you can possibly live free from the Clade," she said quietly.

"Sorry," he apologized sheepishly.

The rest of the recruits were beginning to get restless after waiting a few minutes. Their fear was stronger than their patience, I guessed. I left my friends and found Marcus and Juliette. "We have to go into the tunnel soon. Are you ready?" Juliette asked.

"Yeah, and, in fact," I looked back at the other twenty restless recruits. "I think everyone is ready. What are we waiting for anyway?" I asked.

Marcus replied instead of Juliette, "I'm waiting to see if that boy, Trevor Gibbs I believe, succeeds in collapsing the hospital."

"Why would we wait? Why can't we just go now?" I asked.

Marcus said, "If Trevor fails, then the Agents will be right behind us, and it wouldn't matter if we went down the tunnel because they would catch us." Marcus was finally starting to sound like a thinking leader.

I was worried that Trevor would fail, and then we would be sitting ducks for the Agents. I hoped that Marcus wasn't going to wait too long. "That sounds like a good idea, but…" I was cut off by a loud rumble.

The rumble was loud, about a thousand times louder than a tree falling down. The cracking and the creaking shook everyone. All of the recruits went down on their hands and knees to cope with the earthquake-like shaking. Cracks began to form slightly below the ceiling. Trevor was doing it. He was collapsing the hospital which meant we had better get out of there before it did collapse just in case the basement wasn't a safe sanctuary after all.

"Marcus!" I yelled through the loud cracking of the hospital.

"I know!" I watched as he pulled keys out from a chain around his neck and went to the steel door. He inserted one of the bronze keys into the lock and turned it. The door swung open (which looked a lot easier than all of us crawling through the hole, I might add) revealing a dark storage closet on the other side.

"Everyone!" Juliette yelled as Marcus went to turn the hidden, red, wheel. "This is our cue to move! Go into the tunnel Marcus is opening now and find the safe haven on the other side!"

The recruits tried to stand back up, but the shaking was so intense that they had to crawl. My friends and I were right up in the front of the group crawling our way into the dark storage closet and then the rock and dirt tunnel.

The lights weren't working as well as they were originally planned for. They kept flickering and a few shattered as soon as the shaking began to intensify when the actually building above us began to fall.

I could hear Juliette yell from the doorway, "Go inside, Marcus! We're all safe inside! Shut it!"

Marcus leapt into the tunnel and turned another hidden, red, wheel to lower the wall. As Marcus lowered the wall, the shaking dissipated to nothingness little by little as the wall descended. Once the wall crashed down with a booming sound, sealing us in, the shaking stopped, and the hospital was fully crushed. Trevor had done it. I hoped that he was still alive and could find freedom. We, on the other hand, were beginning our mile long trek through a dark, underground, tunnel to safety.

Chapter 21

No sounds were heard from either the hospital or the Agents. We were safe, at least for now. If anything the tough part was just beginning. Our goal now was to escape with Marcus twenty feet away from us the whole time.

All of the recruits, including Sarah, Trish, Gabe, and me, looked around in the darkness trying to find some guidance. The lights had gone completely out leaving us in darkness, and we had to find our way out. Nathaniel would have known how to guide us out of there since he had known so much about the tunnel. Fear began to rise up in me again when I started to wonder where he had ended up.

Our group found each other somewhere in the middle of the recruits. Gabe said, "Is everyone okay?"

We all said at the same time, "I'm okay."

"Good," Gabe said. "Now, any ideas on how we get out of here without Marcus or Juliette finding out?"

It was dark and that made it hard to see everyone's expressions, but I think we were all just looking at everyone else hoping they had a plan. For a while, I had had a good run of plans that would've helped us, but now, I had nothing. Hopefully, someone else could think of something before we reached the end of the tunnel.

We could all hear Marcus yell over the group, "Okay! If anyone has an ability that would make a good light, please step forward now!"

I looked around at the dark bodies of my friends. I had just realized that I could, once again, light our way out of here. Part of me knew I had to go up and lead the way out, but I knew that I needed to stay with my friends, so I could help them develop a plan. I decided to play the hero and shouted to Marcus, "Yeah! Marcus, I do! It's me, Zeke!"

"Come up to the front then!" He yelled back. I listened and weaved my way through the group of recruits and up to the front where Marcus stood. As I moved through the group, I could hear Sarah, Gabe, and Trish also weaving their way through the group. They were following me to the front. I turned around and whispered, "What are you guys doing? Stay back and formulate a plan."

"No way, Zeke," Sarah whispered back. "We're a team and we could use your help with the plan formulating." It was dark but I could tell she smiled at me.

We kept moving until the group thinned and that's where I used my hand as a light. This part of my ability came in handy quite a bit.

We looked around and found Marcus right by us. "Wow," he said as he walked up to us. "That ability of yours sure can do a lot."

"Yeah, everything but transport us all out of here," I said back.

He noticed the rest of my friends behind me and said, "What are they all doing up here?" The light from my hand created shadows across Marcus' face that made him look as if he were evil.

I said with supreme determination for them to stay, "They are my friends, and they go where I go." Gabe then patted me on the back in support for our group.

We all waited to hear what Marcus would say in reply. There wasn't much he could say. I was the only source of light in this mile-long cave, so he would have to fulfill my wishes of keeping my friends close by. Finally, he said, "Okay, that's fine by me. Lead the way would you please?" Marcus said as he held out his hand to the rest of the tunnel.

I held out my hand in the cave's bowels and began to walk. The rest of the Clade followed behind me in loud shuffling steps hoping that they didn't run into anybody. Gabe, Sarah, and Trish stayed close behind me, even closer than Juliette and Marcus which surprised me. Even with the help of my light, the cave was still dark.

We all walked in silence for about five or ten minutes until a few of the recruits began chatting about their dead comrades. I could hear a few say something like, "He was only twelve," and "That was my best friend." All of these people had had lives in the Clade. Their lives were now distraught thanks to Marcus and his stubbornness. What he had done could be considered murder. Nothing could be done anymore to mend the surviving few recruits spirits.

Marcus walked rudely between my friends behind me. I didn't know if he was just trying to eavesdrop or was just being a jerk, but my friends and I were mad. He continued to lie low behind me for quite a while until he asked my friends, "May I speak with Zeke alone please?"

I held my hand behind me and walked blindly into the darkness to see my friend's expressions. They looked worried, but I mouthed that I would be okay and let Marcus walk by me. He was really beginning to annoy me; although, he had since I had been recruited. He always wanted to be close by to keep an eye on me. I just wanted to run blindly into the darkness ahead of me and never stop if it meant never seeing Marcus again.

"What's up, Marcus?" I asked trying not to sound annoyed by his rudeness.

"Listen," he told me. "I know you have been thinking a lot about your mother recentl-" I cut him off.

"She's not my mother, I thought?" I retorted. Anytime anyone brought up the thought of my "fake" mother, a rush of anger flew over me. I didn't mean it to, but it was just a sore spot considering the Clade had lied to me about my own mom just to keep an eye on me.

"She isn't your real mother. That is true. I just wanted to say that I'm sorry," Marcus apologized. He had been saying sorry a lot recently. He either wanted to dupe me into his twisted plan or he was really worried about something.

"You're sorry?" I asked sarcastically. For once, I decided that I wasn't going to be nice. He had lied to me about something very serious. I continued, "Sorry doesn't even begin to make up for what you have done to me. To all of us here. I don't know who decides to give us all "fake" parents, but you don't have to agree to do it. My life is never going to be the same,"

I began to jump subjects and just vent all of my anger out at him. I began to shout, "You bring people here after taking them away from their normal lives! Have you ever even been out of the Clade? There is a world out there full of wonders and happiness! This place is the complete opposite! You think you are helping save people, but really all you are doing is hurting them! You take them away from their loved ones, and not just their "fake" parents, but their friends, and then you inject them with a chemical to numb their powers before you even say "hello" to them. Have you ever even had a *real* friend?!"

I was beginning to calm down because I thought that everyone in the Clade was now afraid of me. "You just have no idea."

Marcus was quiet for the longest time. In fact, everyone was quiet. The nerve I had struck must have been deep enough to cause Marcus to feel really upset about this. He should. He has done terrible things. The Clade just kept moving on with me in the lead. The tunnel was supposed to be a mile long, and we must have been about half-way through at that point.

I kept thinking about what I had said to Marcus. I felt he needed to hear this. Of course, I didn't think before I shouted at him. The truth was I didn't want to hear another thing about my parents, real or fake. It felt better if I kept thinking I was alone. That no one back home even cared that I was gone, and then I wouldn't be hurting them.

While I thought about forgetting my friends and family, another thought popped in my head. I had never told Trish about her parents yet. A part of me never wanted to tell her, but I thought that she probably already knew after what I had just said. I decided that I should probably explain it, and what better a time than walking through a dark tunnel. I looked back and said, "Trish, can you come here?"

"Sure," she said as she walked a bit quicker to reach me.

I didn't know how I was going to explain it to her. I wished that I had never remembered about telling her, but I had to now. "What's going on?" she asked me.

"Trish, you probably just heard what I said to Marcus..." I began.

"Of course I did. In fact, I think everyone down here did," she said.

"Yeah," I laughed a little bit, but stayed in my mournful tone. "I uh... have something to tell you." Trish remained quiet and stared at my face as I explained, "Your parents... are uh... not really your parents." I pushed out.

Trish looked down at the cave floor. I knew that it hurt her. Her parents had always cared for her like my mom had cared for me, but she had to know. What if she tried to find them back in New Haven when we escaped? She would be heartbroken. It hurt, but I had to tell her.

She was still unresponsive. I looked back at Gabe and Sarah, and they were just as depressed as I was.

"Trish," I said. "Are you okay?" I knew that was a dumb question, but what else could I say.

Her face finally shifted from one of shock and disbelief to acceptance. She lifted her head and looked at me saying, "I had a feeling. If my parents were actually my parents, then they would be here saving me right now. Instead, it's you."

I gleamed. That was one of the greatest compliments I'd ever received, and it was from Trish. How could she just drop the pain, though? When I found out, I had been crushed. I still was. "I don't know if you heard me, but your parents aren't real. How're you able to just shrug off the pain?"

Trish kept staring forward as she walked and said, "I don't really know. I guess, when you really think about it, it doesn't matter."

"What do you mean 'it doesn't matter? They are your parents. They are the ones that gave you life and are supposed to tuck you into bed and read you stories," I paused for a few seconds. "They are the ones who are supposed to love you and protect you."

Trish contemplated what I had just said to her. It didn't make sense. How could she smile and take away the pain of finding out her parents weren't really her parents. She answered, "It doesn't matter because, in the end, the people who impersonated our parents really did love us and protect us."

That hit me hard. I didn't realize that before because I was so angry at the Clade, my father, and partly my "fake" mother. Trish was right, as she usually was, again. Trish said, "Think about it, Zeke. Sure, your mother may have lied to you about who she really was, but that didn't mean she didn't love you, care for you and protect you."

"You're right, Trish," I said to her. "How come you are always right?"

Trish laughed a little and then said, "Well, I'm not always right. Look at yourself here. You are the leader of a four person escape operation, and you are one of the most powerful recruits in the Clade. Sometimes, you don't give yourself enough credit."

I smiled. She did that to me. "Thanks," I replied smiling. Even though over two hundred recruits laid dead one floor up and three quarters of a mile back, and our futures looked bleak, I was the happiest I had been for a long time.

I invited Sarah and Gabe, who were probably flirting the whole time behind us, back up to the front. For a while, we talked about what our plan would be when we got out of the tunnel. We decided that we would just make it up when we got out there which was fine by me as long as I didn't have to think anymore. Plus Marcus was listening in the whole time. Afterwards, the four of us chatted about random things like normal teenagers.

It was fun while it lasted, but once we began talking about random things, we reached the end. Gabe found out first because he ran into the wall. "Ow!" he yelled. His voice echoed down the mile long tunnel back to the ruins of the hospital.

"Marcus!" I yelled into the darkness behind me. I held out my hand, and some of the recruits that were barely visible backed off as if they feared my hand. "I think we reached the end, but I can't find the exit!"

Marcus pushed through the crowed and up to the front by me. He put his hand up against the wall and felt his way along the width of the wall. He came back and said, "There is no door or way out in the wall." He looked up and then said, "Oh, there it is."

All of us looked up and saw two metal doors lying over the circular hole in the ground. The hinges were bolted into the side of the hole which was about five feet thick. That meant we were five feet underground. Sarah said, "We are going to need a ladder or some sort of human chain to get up there."

Marcus yelled to all of the recruits, "Everyone, look around for a way to get out of this cave! We need a ladder or maybe even a rope!" The recruits began feeling their way along the floor and the wall, but without light, it would be almost impossible to find something that could get us out of here.

The search continued for another ten minutes. My back was getting sore after bending over for so long. Sarah found me by the glowing beacon which was my hand and asked, "Couldn't we just ask if someone could use an earth ability to get us out of here?"

"That would just be too easy," I lied. She was right and I couldn't believe that Marcus hadn't thought of that sooner.

We looked around for Marcus and instead found Juliette looking in the front left corner of the cavern wall. "Hey, where is Marcus?" I asked her.

She did a quick three-sixty looking for Marcus and then said, "I don't know. I thought he was right beside me helping me look."

"Don't worry. We will keep looking for him. He has to be down here somewhere," Sarah added.

"Okay," Juliette looked around for a little bit more and then turned back. She asked, "Why do you need to see him?"

I said, "We thought that, since we couldn't find a ladder or rope in this cavern, we could use someone with an earth ability to get out." Juliette could be mean at times, but she sure could listen to others better than Marcus.

She said, "Perhaps, but earth abilities are tricky to come by."

We made a funny face at her after she said that. "What do you mean 'hard to come by?' There are still almost thirty recruits down here and only four elements that a person can use. How can someone down here not have an earth ability?" Sarah asked. She was bright and had the most experience with Clade issues.

Juliette just stopped looking and faced us. "Well, you see, you both know, even as young recruits, that a human like us can only control one of the four elements and in a specific way, unless you're Zeke here, of course," Juliette said. They both looked at me, but I just shrugged and let her continue. "I, for instance, have an air ability, and I can use it only to make sharp arrows that can pierce anything." She used her ability to give us an example on the near wall to our right.

Sarah and I were quiet the whole time she used her ability and while she talked. After she finished with the first part, I said, "Yeah, we know this already, but how come you think that nobody has an earth ability down here?"

"Let me finish," Juliette said. We remained quiet. "The appearance of a water ability, like you Sarah, varies from someone with a fire ability, like Gabriel."

Gabe heard his name being called in the tunnel somewhere and said, "Who is calling me?"

I said, "It's nothing, Gabe." Gabe maintained quiet after that as Juliette resumed.

"As I was saying," she began slowly. "An ability, first of all, is genetic, so the odds of a person even having one is much less than one percent. Next, the ratio between what element a person may be able to command also varies. The odds of a person with an ability being able to control water in some way are about fifty percent. A person being able to control water is around twenty percent. A person being able to control fire is about fifteen percent, and a person being able to control the earth in some way is less than five."

"And electricity?" I added.

"Electricity is definitely less than one percent. In fact, it's just you," Juliette said with a raised eyebrow. It still hadn't hit me yet that I was different from anyone else; in reality, I was alone. I couldn't ask anyone to help me with my ability because they had never even heard of someone controlling electricity before. They would probably just laugh in my face.

"We can still look for someone though, can't we?" I said as Sarah and I turned around and started to walk to the other side of the cave with the guidance of my hand.

We ended up back by Gabe and Trish who were sitting on the floor of the cavern. Trish was holding a little napkin on his nose to keep blood from rushing out. "What'd you do to your nose, Gabe?" Sarah asked.

"I hit the wall with my nose when I walked into it. It still hurts pretty badly. I think I painted the wall with my blood pretty nicely though," he laughed. "It could use a little brighter paint."

"Oh," Sarah said as she knelt down by Gabe. She took Trish's hand and moved it aside as she kissed Gabe's nose.

"Does it feel any better?" Sarah asked.

"It uh… it ahh…" Gabe couldn't say yes. Everyone except for Gabe laughed as he began to turn red.

"Trish," I began. "Where did you get the napkin?"

"I had it on me at the time," she said. We all just stared at her, and then she said, "What? Don't a lot of people carry around napkins in their pockets just in case?" We all laughed at her.

All of a sudden, a loud pounding noise rang out on the metal doors above us. We all feared it was the Agents, and we backed away from the doors and back towards the center of the cave. Marcus stepped up from the group and took the lead looking directly up at the doors while everyone else was back away from them.

"Marcus," Juliette whispered from the group of recruits, "get back here. Where were you before?"

"I was in the middle of the group looking for some slim hope that we could get out. And no I will not move," Marcus said sounding determined.

"Are you crazy?" Juliette asked. "There is no need to be a hero. What if it is the Agents? How are you supposed to stop them?"

"To be honest with you Juliette, I'm still working on it, but I won't let another recruit get hurt because of my foolishness. We just lost another back at the hospital if you don't remember?" Marcus said. I was shocked. I truly believed that Marcus was shaken up by all of this and that he truly felt sorry.

I couldn't take it anymore. If Marcus got hurt or worse, I would feel terrible for the rest of my life because I could have done something. "Mar-" I pushed out before getting cut off by the doors opening up to the moonlit surface. Marcus' face was glowing by the light. We all waited in anticipation to see who it was, hoping that Marcus would live to see who it was too.

But it wasn't like that at all. Marcus looked up at the mysterious figure and said, "Long time no see. I was wondering when you would show up." We were all very confused, but when a rope ladder dropped down, we knew it was good news.

"Who is it?" Juliette asked.

The figure jumped down into the hole, about a five foot drop. The figure wore a hooded black cloak that fell to the ground, and immediately, I knew who it was. He took down his hood and said, "This is all that is left of the Clade?"

It was Nathaniel. I was never happier to see an Instructor. We were going to be okay.

Chapter 22

All of the recruits stared in silence at Nathaniel as he talked to Marcus. I'm sure we were all thinking that we were going to be the ten percent of the Clade that survived the massacre at the hospital. I kept thinking that to.

Gabe grabbed my back and said, "He sure does show up at the right times."

"Yeah, he does," I agreed. "This is great. We will get out now and escape into the forest away from the Agents." I couldn't go any further with our "go- with- the- flow" plan because Juliette was standing so close to us.

I had a rush of calmness go through my veins when the thought of safety became a reality. Since Nathaniel was out in the forest, that must've meant that no Agents were around, or he took them all out by himself which would be hard to believe considering he could only slide the ground. He saved us from being trapped down here.

Sarah, Trish, Gabe, and I all circled up as Marcus continued to talk with Nathaniel about the Agent problem probably. I didn't really care anymore. I felt safe. Trish spoke first, "Alright, Nathaniel is here, so we should be okay, right?"

Gabe said, "Of course, we will be okay. Nathaniel helped us get out remember. In fact, he probably already came up with a plan for us to escape this time." Gabe sounded like the kind of person I would vote for for president. Not because he sounded right, but because he wanted the same things as me. I wanted to believe that Nathaniel was on our side and that he probably already had a plan on how to get us out. In fact, I was sure of it.

As long as I had known Nathaniel, which was only like seventeen days, he had always known what he was doing or had had a plan formulated for the upcoming mission or escape. I wouldn't have been surprised if he already had a plan to get us out. We would just have to wait and find out. We still had time to think though, since Marcus was still chatting up a storm with Nathaniel.

Sarah said, "I don't know. If this tunnel was created as an escape route for people trapped in the basement like we were, how come we couldn't get out. We were all just sitting here waiting until he showed up. This all seems a bit fishy to me."

It didn't matter what we thought anymore though. Marcus and Nathaniel were done talking. Marcus faced the group of recruits and said, "Nathaniel escaped into the forest when he heard that the Agents were coming. He knew that we would use the tunnel, and he waited for us to arrive at the end. Let's start heading up the ladder and get out of this cave."

Recruits began rushing to get in line so that they could be one of the first to get out of the tunnel. Trish, Sarah, Gabe, and I were all in the back of the group and had to wait until the other twenty or thirty got up. The line moved slowly, considering only one person could go up a rope ladder at a time.

The dim moon light that had been casted upon Marcus was now gone and replaced with small amounts of sunlight as we moved along in the line. I felt safer in the light compared to the dark. Darkness was always a frightening place or state. It's the unknown that hides in the dark which scares people. The light, even a little, brought me comfort, and I felt that I we couldn't be surprised by any attacks while we were in the light.

We were close to the ladder now with only five people in front of us. Juliette had left us a while ago to talk with Nathaniel and Marcus. We all looked up through the doors at the daytime sky and became lost in it. Sarah began to choke up as she said, "It's been so long since I've looked at the sky. The clouds, the sun, I swear I forgot what color the sky even was." We knew exactly what she was saying. We had been cooped up for so long, not seen daylight. Sarah had been there even longer than us. I couldn't imagine not being able to see the sky for as long as she hadn't.

Gabe said, "I can't believe that we actually are going to do it. We are going to get out of here. This place was hell, and the nightmare is finally over." I felt the same sense of hope and freedom that Gabe was feeling. All we had to do now was get to the top of that hole. We were now next in line, and Trish was going up first.

"Wait for us up on top," I said to Trish from behind Sarah and Gabe.

"No problem," she said with a smile as she began to climb up the ladder.

The rope ladder swung from left to right as Trish climbed to the safety of the surface. Once the ladder hit Nathaniel in the back of the head, but he just shrugged it off, and he held onto the ladder better for Trish to finish her ascent. Gabe was next, and then Sarah quickly followed him and reached the top in no time.

I looked up the hole as I held onto the bottom of the ladder. The sun was now high enough over the horizon to cast shadows on the other three. I began to climb, but Nathaniel grabbed me. The three instructors stared at me like I was a felon. "What?" I finally said after swinging back and forth.

"We would like to say thank you," Juliette said.

"Yes," Marcus agreed. "We had all made mistakes. In fact, if it wasn't for your smart idea about using the tunnel and our luck that Nathaniel would be right on top of the door, we probably wouldn't be going up to safety right now."

"We all discussed this," Nathaniel added. "And we decided that if you train yourself properly until you're eighteen, and, of course, you stop playing your little games like sneaking out at night, we would be honored to promote you to an instructor."

Nathaniel winked at me, so that no one else would see but me. I took this as a sign to just agree, so I did,

"Thank you," I said enthusiastically. "I will do, and be, my best."

"We know you will," Marcus finished. "Now, go up there with your friends," Marcus said pointing up towards the surface. "And we will be right behind you." Nathaniel let go of me, and I climbed up quickly to the surface.

The sunlight felt glorious as I moved my way to the surface. The last time I had felt the sun's rays was when I had gone on the mission to recruit Trish, and I hadn't really been thinking about the sun at the time. When you are locked up in a hospital from hell, you really do miss the little things in life that you wouldn't ordinarily miss. I was glad to be out of there and to be with my new friends that I had made on this crazy journey. Many lives were lost, but those wounds would hopefully heal with time.

"Finally!" I shouted as I took my last step on land. Just then, Trish, Sarah, and Gabe, all circled around me and wrapped me up tight in their arms. "Ahh!" I yelled in joy and a little agony. "I get it! You are all very happy!" They all laughed, and I joined in with them.

"What's going on up here?" Nathaniel said as he climbed pushed himself up on land.

We all quickly let go and straightened ourselves out. Nathaniel walked over to our group looking confident in himself. That, and the wink in his eye, had to mean that he had a plan for us to get out of there, and now would be the perfect time, since Marcus and Juliette were still down in the cave.

"Nathaniel," I said quickly and quietly in the hopes that Marcus and Juliette wouldn't hear. "Where were you before when we first saw the Agents?"

"Well," he began. "I was with you when the Agents were marching down the road to the hospital. Instead of running back to the hospital, which is what you four did anyways, I decided to run into the forest near the exit of the tunnel. If I know anything, it is that you kids are quite intelligent. I assumed you would use the tunnel as an escape route from the Agents, so I waited until I heard you underneath the doors or some other sign."

"I guess the hospital collapsing was a sure-fire sign," Gabe said.

"Nathaniel replied, "Yes, it was, fortunately. So, I waited until I decided to check to see if you were at the end yet, and you were. I'm sorry if you had to wait for a while."

"It's no big deal. Now, what is the plan? I noticed your wink, so I assume you have a plan," I said.

"Yes, I do," Nathaniel said. The ladder started to shake in the hole to the cave. Marcus and Juliette were on their way up. We were almost out of time to escape. Nathaniel turned around and saw this. He turned back to us and said, "I'll be quick. There is a helicopter kept by the Clade in the forest north east of here." He pointed to the left. "Go, now. I'll meet you there once I've ditched Marcus and Juliette."

We didn't even think if we should or not. All of us sprinted into the trees to where Nathaniel pointed and escaped from Marcus and Juliette.

Even when we were out of sight of Marcus and Juliette, we kept running deeper into the forest. The forest grew thicker as we moved causing more and more light to be blocked by the trees creating a twilight effect.

"I think...we should...take a break," Gabe said as he took large gasps. We had been sprinting for the last ten minutes away from the instructors. We stopped in a small clearing with foot tall grass and little insects jumping around everywhere you looked. I was worried that we had taken a wrong turn or something along those lines because the helicopter was nowhere to be found.

"What time do you think it is?" Trish asked.

Sarah tried to squint at the sun between the trees, but the trees were too thick to see through. "Sorry, I can't see the sun, but I would guess around six or seven in the morning," she said.

The morning was cool for April. I was glad that the Clade's choice in a uniform also doubled as a sweatshirt. I got cozy with it as I sat down on a fallen tree listening to the others talk. They chatted about one thing the whole time, Nathaniel.

"Something just doesn't seem right?" Gabe said. "Don't you think he would tell us if he was running off into the woods? We could have followed him and not even had worried about the Agents killing us, or the rest of the recruits."

"Yeah, I don't get it? Also, where did the other recruits go when we crawled out of the tunnel?" Sarah asked the group as she sat down next to Gabe on a stump across from me. "You're right, Gabe. Something fishy is going on here. I don't think we should trust him. Did you see what Marcus said about where we were? He thought we were in a hospital dorm. Some dorm that was."

Anger swelled inside me as they talked about Nathaniel that way. He had been the one who had gotten us away from Marcus and Juliette and now we were free. Why would they even question his loyalty? I said in reply, "Hey, why are you all asking useless questions?"

"They're not useless, Zeke. C'mon, it seems pretty strange that Nathaniel would just leave us and assume we would use the tunnel and tell the entire Clade," Sarah said.

"Well, I don't see why you are discussing this when he has already gotten us away from Marcus and Juliette. Everything you're asking about him can be explained." I said starting to get angry.

"Prove it, then," Sarah argued.

"Okay, fine," I began. "He didn't tell us about him going into the forest because he was too far away, or the Agents would've heard us and killed us. Next, Nathaniel probably told Marcus to get the recruits to go in a different way than we were going, so that we wouldn't have to sneak away from them too, and lastly, Marcus is the master mind behind everything in the Clade, so he put you in the room in the cave and acted surprise when he found out you were out and blamed it on Nathaniel who put you in a "hospital room".

"We were just asking questions," Trish said as she sat down next to me. She put her hand on my lap, and I immediately became relaxed as if a wave of warmth had just rushed over me.

"I'm sorry," I apologized. "I just feel like we owe him for what he did for us."

"Zeke," Sarah said across the clearing from me. "It wasn't him that got us out of there. It was you. You and Gabe worked together and did something no other recruit has ever done. You two are the real heroes and shouldn't owe anyone anything."

My stern face broke into a gleaming smile. Now that I thought about it, Gabe and I had done everything. We had found the tunnel and Sarah and Trish. Granted, Nathaniel had helped, but we were the ones who had trusted him enough to let him in on the plan we had already created. We, as in Gabe and I.

We sat there for what seemed like an hour. The sun was still not visible in the sky, so it was still morning. I guessed that it was about seven o' clock and that it was time to keep moving. "We better get moving. We can't sit here all day," I said. For all we knew, Nathaniel was waiting for us at the helicopter a little deeper into the woods.

As we moved through the forest, a patch of light became more clear through the trees. We hurried towards the light as if it was a sanctuary from the darkness we came from. We were about twenty yards away when a solid gray structure became noticeable. It was the helicopter.

"I see the copter!" Trish yelled.

We were all about to sprint for the helicopter when Gabe said, "Guys, don't. What if we alert someone? We don't know for sure if we are alone out here."

We all looked at him funny. "What are you talking about?" Trish said anxious to escape from this place. "There is no one around. Just take a look."

"Well, what about Marcus? He can travel through the air and become invisible. For all we know, he was stalking us the whole time to try to get the helicopter before us."

The thought of Marcus just walking behind us close enough to be able to breath down my neck was giving me chills. I wanted to get on the helicopter as fast as possible and fly away from this place for good. "Gabe, for once, let's just not think about it and go," I pleaded.

He thought about it as we kept walking towards the helicopter quietly. Gabe didn't have enough time to decide because the helicopter suddenly began by itself.

"What the-?" Trish said under the roaring of the helicopter blades.

We couldn't stay and think anymore. We had to move for the helicopter before it left without us. Nathaniel was probably on it thinking that we had died or something. I bolted through the trees towards the clearing faster than I had ever thought I could possibly run. I looked back and saw Trish, Gabe, and Sarah behind me.

I was just about to break into the clearing with the others right behind me when a large "BAAAANNNNGG!" rang out through the forest. I stopped, Sarah and Trish toppled over me, and we fell into the dirt. We wiped ourselves off and stood up slowly wondering what had just happened.

"What was that?" Sarah asked shaking nervously.

"I don't know. I think it was a gun firing off," I said. Whatever that sound was though, it was close. The birds that sat on the treetops all flew away from their perches in fear. I wished that I could fly.

"A gun?" Trish asked. "Then they must know we are here. They have too. We should run now!" She yelled.

Sarah and I put our hands over Trish's mouth to keep her from yelling. I wanted to yell to and I was sure

Sarah did too, but it was not the time, not when we were so close to freedom. All we had to do was make it another twenty yards and across the clearing to the helicopter.

I had a sudden realization come over me. My adrenaline levels spiked as I asked, "Where is Gabe?" Sarah and Trish must have just realized this too as they looked out into the forest all around us. We looked in front of us and back the way we came, but Gabe couldn't be found.

The thought of Gabe getting caught by the Agents or Marcus was dreadful. We kept looking but couldn't find him. "Where is he!" Sarah yelled painstakingly through her tears. "He was just here a few minutes ago!"

We kept looking until we heard another sound. It wasn't a gunshot or a bomb, but instead it was a groan. I jumped up and ran towards the sound with the two girls behind me. The groan was getting louder as we approached whatever was making that horrible sound. The sound eventually said something. It said, "Help! (cough cough) It's me, Gabe!"

Chapter 23

We looked around urgently trying to find Gabe. He had been behind us just a little bit ago. Finally, we found him. There was Gabe, lying in the grass. He had a small bullet- sized hole right below the center of his ribcage. Blood spurted out of the hole and ran down his body. He had been shot.

"Gabe!" Sarah yelled with tear filled eyes as she kneeled down next to his bloody body. His face was pale and eyes were beginning to fade of life. I wanted to scream out and tear the head off whoever had done this. They had better hope I didn't find them.

I just couldn't handle the fact that Gabe as dying. My brain was refusing to accept it; we were on our way to safety, he couldn't die now. "We are going to help you,

Gabe. We'll find anyone, Marcus or Nathaniel. It doesn't matter," I said angrily.

"Aaahh, it hurts," Gabe said with blood still coming out of the wound creating a blood stained spot on his cloak. "I," he said coughing up blood. "I am starting to lose feeling."

"Hold on, Gabe," Sarah pushed out through her crying. "We are going to help you. You are going to be fine. I promise." Sarah began to really bawl now.

If he was going to make it, Gabe had to get out of the forest and onto the helicopter right away. I rushed behind his head and took his arms in my hands. "Trish, grab Gabe's legs. We will bring him to the helicopter and fly him to some help."

"What?" Trish said really freaking out now. "We can't fly a helicopter."

"Well, we are going to have to if we want to save Gabe," I said. I turned to Sarah, her eyes puffy and red from crying. "Sarah," I said softly. "You need to apply pressure to Gabe's wound." She nodded and moved towards his body on the ground.

She looked him over quickly and said, "I need a rag or something."

Gabe was still groaning in agonizing pain as the blood constantly flooded from his body. I lifted him up carefully and started walking to the helicopter. I had told myself that I was going to keep everyone alive, and I planned on keeping that. I looked around trying to figure out what I could do to save him. I let go of one of Gabe's hands and used it to electrify a piece of my cloak sleeve. It charred and burned off to the ground. Sarah picked it up and, without even thinking, she pushed her hand on Gabe's bloody chest. The blood crept around Sarah's hand, but it didn't bother her. She cared about Gabe too much.

"We don't have a lot of time," I began. "Start moving toward the clearing, and we'll get him on the helicopter no matter who is in the way waiting for us." I stated hoping they knew how serious I was.

We all began to shuffle our feet towards the clearing. It was going to be a challenge to get through the rest of the forest and into the clearing without hurting Gabe any more than he already was. I couldn't break down though. The others needed me to be strong, to lead them out of there, and to get Gabe well. I hated to admit it, but with Gabe looking that way, I didn't think the last thing was going to happen.

The clearing was right in front of us. What worried me the most, other than Gabe of course, was that we hadn't heard another gun shot or seen any sign of the person who had shot Gabe. They had either gotten what they wanted or were just setting us up. If the Agents were waiting for us at the helicopter, I'd have to use whatever it took to get my friends out of there. I had already killed today, so there was no point in being fearful anymore.

"Aaahh, stop, stop!" Gabe cried. We set him down gently at the edge of the clearing. We stayed low behind a tree so that whoever was in the helicopter wouldn't see us. Even with Gabe in pain, we wouldn't be able to wait there long. Time was running out. Gabe was coughing out more and more blood.

Sarah comforted Gabe while we let him rest. She put his head on her lap and ran her fingers through his hair. I looked to Trish and said, "I'm going to take a quick look to see who is at the helicopter."

"Are you sure? I wouldn't. What if he is just sitting behind the tree waiting for his chance to shoot us?" She asked.

"Well then we are pretty much dead anyways," I said sarcastically back to her.

I squatted on my heels and slowly looked around the tree. The clearing was, well, clear, but there was someone in the helicopter waiting for us. It was Nathaniel. He was sitting on the edge of the helicopter looking around impatiently.

I turned back around after I realized this and whispered, "Guys, it's Nathaniel. He is waiting for us at the helicopter. I bet he started it up to try and give us a sign of where it was. Gabe, are you okay?"

He began to breath rapidly taking short breaths each time. We were almost out of time to save him, so I decided for him. "We're going, now!" I yelled to Sarah and Trish.

We all moved back into our positions from before and slowly picked up Gabe. The piece of cloak Sarah had been using to keep pressure on the wound was soaked, so she used her hand as a last resort. It didn't help that much though because blood was leaking through the gaps in her fingers.

We broke through the tree line and into the clearing. "Nathaniel!" I yelled. "We need help! Gabe has been shot!" We kept making our way to the helicopter. Nathaniel jumped up and pulled the earth under our feet to help us move faster.

Nathaniel jumped inside the helicopter and turned it off. He then sprinted into the middle of the clearing while also using his ability to slide the earth beneath us to help us move faster. We set Gabe down in front of Nathaniel in the middle of the clearing. "What took you so long? It should have taken you only twenty minutes to get here not an hour," Nathaniel said angrily at us.

"Well, we didn't really have a map," Trish said angrily back at him. "Now, can you help Gabe or not!" We all looked at her surprised. She had never even talked to Nathaniel, much less yelled at him. He seemed impressed.

Nathaniel quickly flew to the ground and checked out Gabe. He looked him up and down. The wound was right in front of him, and it seemed that he was avoiding looking at that. It was kind of hard to miss. He checked him out for longer than necessary to determine that he needed help. I grabbed Nathaniel's shoulder and pulled him up onto his feet and said, "Well, are you going to help?"

He turned his head sideways and looked at me as if I had asked him a stupid question. "Help him? Why should I help him?" He asked.

"Wait, are you going to help him at all!?" Sarah shouted at him fiercely.

"No, I'm not going to help him," he replied. "In fact, I can tell you that someone is going to have to go back to the shooting range and practice."

I was confused, and Nathaniel wasn't going to help with Gabe at all. I grabbed his arms and looked at Trish to tell her to grab his legs. "If you're not going to help, then we will help him ourselves."

I lifted Gabe's arms in the air, but Nathaniel hit my arms causing a stinging pain and a red mark, and he fell to the ground. "Aaaahh!" Gabe cried out in pain.

Why was Nathaniel doing that, and what did he mean by 'someone is going to have to go back to the shooting range and practice?' Something wasn't adding up correctly. He was supposed to be helping us, not letting us die. I had a terrible inkling that Sarah, Trish, and Gabe had been right about Nathaniel before.

"Why would you do that!?" I asked.

What Nathaniel said next confirmed that Sarah, Gabe, and Trish had been right, and it sent a shock through me. "Zeke, he needs to die. Just like you three need to die."

Sarah stopped crying momentarily, and everything else went silent. Nathaniel wasn't there to help us escape. He was there to kill us, but what I didn't get was why. I tensed up and began to send a light charge of energy through my body, just in case. He wasn't going to stop me from getting on that helicopter, so there was no point in him trying to kill us. I'd kill him if I had to.

"What…what are you talking about?" Sarah asked.

Nathaniel began to back away from us and towards the helicopter as he explained himself. "I'm sorry, kids. You have to die, and it's a shame because you came so close to escaping, something no other recruit has ever managed to do."

The forest began to rumble with the footsteps of approaching people. I didn't know if they were recruits or worse, Agents. Nothing made sense anymore. I thought Nathaniel was the only person, besides my three friends, that I could trust, but I had been wrong. He was going to have to die. Gabe was getting in worse and worse condition. It was probably already too late, but I refused to accept that.

"I have no idea what is going on, Zeke," Trish said quietly to me. "But we have to get on that helicopter if we are ever going to save Gabe."

"Yeah, I-" I stopped because so had the rustling in the forest. I looked around the clearing and witnessed about twenty Agents forming a circle around the circumference of the clearing. Nathaniel was somehow an Agent, and, even worse than that, we were trapped in the middle of them.

The Agents didn't wear the business suits when they fought. Instead, they were wearing black military uniforms. They looked thick and heavy on the soldiers, like backpacks that you would wear all around yourself.

One of the Agents stepped forward carrying a letter, opened it and began reading, "Zeke Laufor, Sarah Ubancs, and Trish Dawson, you are under arrest for having an alliance with terrorists. How do you plead?"

We were screwed. The last Agent I had seen, the one that had showed up at my house, had asked me a similar question. It didn't matter what I was going to say because they didn't really care. So I just said, "Um… is it too late to plead the fifth?"

Trish elbowed me in the ribs, but Sarah smiled a little bit. That smile immediately went away when she realized that Gabe was unconscious. "Gabe!" she yelled and began to bend to where Gabe was on the ground.

"Freeze!" the Agents yelled to Sarah. Sarah stopped halfway down and froze. She slowly rose back up onto her feet and obeyed the Agents commands. If she was to die, I would never forgive myself. First Gabe and then her? No, we were getting out of this. We all kept our hands raised in hope that we could delay our deaths and think of a new plan.

Nathaniel broke into the scene by asking, "Robert? Robert were you the one who tried killing Gabriel Mason?"

This took us all by surprise, but the Agent said, "Yes, Nathaniel."

"I see," Nathaniel said, "I would recommend that you go back and work on your accuracy a little bit more."

"Yes, sir," the Agent obeyed.

Something still didn't seem right. "Nathaniel!" I yelled. He stopped right in front of the helicopter and listened. "What's going on? How do you know the Agents?" It was worth a shot. If I was going to die, at least I wouldn't have to die confused.

"Why should I let you even know anything about my plan?" he asked back.

Sarah spoke before me. "Think of it as a last request," she said.

Nathaniel let out a sigh and then said, "Okay, now try to keep up with what I am saying." We all nodded our heads and listened. While he was talking; however, I was thinking of a plan out of this mess. With Gabe. I was sure Sarah was doing the same.

He began explaining. "Quite a while ago, I believe twenty-five years, I was a new recruit, or what you would now call, a freshy. At first, I was just like you. I hated this place, and I would've done anything to escape, but when I heard that whoever tried to escape died, I immediately pushed that thought out of my head. I truly believed that I wouldn't be in that hospital, going through training sessions and listening to idiotic instructors, for the rest of my life." Nathaniel scratched his beard and then continued, "I obeyed the Clade's rules for about fifteen years. That is when Marcus showed up. He became my new roommate after my old one killed himself, and then shortly after, a best friend."

My arms were getting sore from keeping my hands up for so long. It was hard to concentrate on formulating a plan because Nathaniel's story was so interesting. "You and Marcus were best friends?" I asked sounding surprised.

"We used to be," Nathaniel started again. "It was nice to have someone you could trust in the Clade. I was the first generation of people with abilities, and he was the second generation. The age difference was unnoticed though because we were in the same boat."

"So, you were alive when the first people received abilities," Trish stated.

"Yes," Nathaniel said impatiently. He was getting annoyed with us. We had to stay on his good side. "Everyone who was, or still is, a first generation recruit was given their abilities right after birth. We were experiments, but that's not the story you want to hear."

I was interested in that actually. How we came to have our abilities was the most hidden thing about this Clade. My father had had an ability, and I had gotten one too because of him.

He began, "I was promoted to an Instructor by the main division of the Clade, which contains the leaders who created the Clade, about eight years ago. At first, I was pretty excited. The thoughts about trying to escape had been long forgotten. I had a life in the Clade. I even had friends whom I considered family. About three years later, Marcus was promoted to lead instructor, and I was happy for him."

Nathaniel used to be a happy man. "Then why did you turn to the Agents?" I looked around to the group.

"Patience!" He snapped at me. "I'm getting to that. I soon realized that the Clade might be corrupted when Marcus was elected to lead instructor. He was far too young to lead three hundred recruits against an army of trained Agents and recruit young people with abilities. So, I decided that I wouldn't be a part of the corrupt idea of a sanctuary for people with abilities. My thoughts of breaking free soon returned but they mixed with thoughts of taking down the entire Clade operation. I had to recruit a young boy with an air ability in New York, but before I revealed myself to him, I waited until the Agents showed up. They always do, and I was right. I stopped them from killing the boy by joining them secretly. I would be a spy in the Clade. I laid low for another five years until I was ready for them to attack, and they waited patiently. That is when you, Zeke, showed up with Gabriel, and your ability truly amazed me. I wanted control over your ability, so I notified the Agents that the time was here and revealed the location of the hospital to them. The reason all of those other recruits are dead is because of me," he laughed gruesomely.

I couldn't believe what I was hearing. He had murdered over two hundred recruits, but not just recruits, other instructors. They had been his friends, and he hadn't even cared about them at all. "Okay," I said trying to push away my anger. "What about when the Agents actually did show up? What did you do then?" I looked over to Sarah and saw that she was about to bawl again as Gabe's face became ghost white. I couldn't tell if he was even breathing.

For once in my life, I couldn't think up a plan. We were down to possibly our final minutes of life, and I hadn't thought up a plan yet Sarah wasn't going to be able to help this time either because her eyes were so filled with tears that she could barely even see. "Where were you when Gabe and I were looking for Sarah and Trish?" I stalled.

I could tell that Nathaniel was getting frustrated with all of the questions. He said, "You are a curious one. Well, since there is no hope for your survival I'll tell you. I was hiding in room 241F. You already know about the computer in that room. That isn't Marcus'; it is mine. I designed it after I first allied with the Agents to communicate with them. At that time, the 2nd level was also off limits, so I knew that no one would go down there. A few years later, however, Marcus was snooping around in the night and caught me. 'What are you doing down here, Nathaniel?' he asked me. I told him about the computer I found, but I didn't tell him about the communications program for it. He then used it to create his own plan for you, Zeke, once he learned about it. But, to answer your question, I was in room 241F to communicate with the Agents to formulate a plan on attacking the hospital."

Trish shook dreadfully back and forth. The Agents kept their guns held high on their shoulders to make sure that once our conversation was over so were we. The Agents fully surrounded us. NO plan would get us all out of here alive, much less Gabe in his state. Nathaniel interrupted my thinking by saying, "I'm done now. Robert," he nodded to the Agent. "Execute them."

"Yes, sir," the Agent replied.

Robert and two other Agents approached us and circled around to our backs. One went behind each of us and grabbed our collars and kicked us in the back of the knees to bring us on the ground kneeling. They grabbed our wrists in their large hand and held the gun at the back of our head in the other. This was the end. After all we had worked for and done to escape this horrible fate.

My life flashed before my eyes and I realized that everything I had known had died a long time ago. It was idiotic of me to think I could go home and hang out with Thomas like nothing had ever happened. It was too late. I would never get the chance to even see anyone again. I wouldn't even know what my real mother or father looked like. We needed a miracle.

The lead Agent, Robert, was behind me and started a countdown to our executions. "5...4..." he counted.

I was finished with crying or anything that resembled weeping. If I was going to die, I was going to look Nathaniel straight in the eyes so that he could see the pain.

I quickly glanced over to Trish. She looked so strong, even in a situation like this. I couldn't imagine how much she was breaking inside. I wanted to help her and kill all of these jerks. It was weird thinking that I had known Trish for almost my whole life, but I hadn't ever seen us dying together. I had wanted to be with her, but when I thought about it, I had thought about dating, having a job with her, and living together. I hadn't expected this. She was so beautiful.

"3…2…" the Agent continued.

I looked to Sarah on the other side of me. She showed no emotion at all. Her thoughts were on Gabe, not us. Gabe was dying slowly and painfully. We would get lucky and die quickly.

We needed a miracle now. The Agent was almost finished, "1…"

I closed my eyes and waited for whatever would happen. I wondered what dying would feel like before the last second ended. I had heard that a bullet is supposed to feel warm and not hurt that much. But tell that to Gabe... I was about to find out right…now.

Nothing happened. I peeked open my eyes to find that the Agent holding on to me was dead. He had a slit throat. I looked over at the Agents that were holding Sarah and Trish and saw that they also had slit throats. I saw a shadow on the ground next to me and looked up. It was Marcus.

We had gotten our miracle.

Chapter 24

There stood Marcus, not five feet behind us, crossing his arms and glaring directly at Nathaniel. He stood in the center of the other twenty or so Agents that circled us. Why would he reveal himself if the other Agents were ready to kill us? Also, why would he help us if we had run away from him? Either way, it really didn't matter. I would be eternally grateful to him.

I jumped up off the ground quickly and pulled up Sarah and Trish. We moved behind Marcus and made a diamond, one of us each facing five or so Agents, and prepared for a battle. "Thank you, Marcus," I said gratefully. "That was close."

"I told you before, Zeke. I am here for you. I'm sorry again for all of the crap I put you through," he replied.

Sarah said, "It is okay. You saved our lives."

"Don't count your chickens before they hatch," Marcus replied staring at all of the Agents around us. "I haven't gotten you out of here alive yet."

It became a standstill. We were trapped in the middle of a twenty man army and one traitor. Why weren't they shooting at us? They could easily take us all out. I was glad they weren't, but something had to be keeping them from shooting us all.

Nathaniel stepped out from behind his army of Agents and yelled, "How did you know where we were, Marcus!?"

Marcus turned his head cautiously to Nathaniel and said, "I used my ability, Nathaniel. You may not know this, but I deserved that lead instructor role because I worked harder than you ever did, and I mastered my ability while you barely touched the power of yours."

Nathaniel scrunched his face and growled. "That is not what I asked," he said. "I want to know how you knew where we would be!"

Marcus repeated, "I told you. I used my ability. I can become the air around me and move through it. Zeke experienced it first hand at his apartment in Connecticut. I became invisible in the air and followed the kids to you."

Gabe had been right all along. Marcus had followed us the whole time. Why hadn't he revealed himself to help Gabe when he had been shot? I would have to ask him that later when we get out of here. That is, if we got out of there. We could still all very well die a brutal death.

"It doesn't matter anymore!" Nathaniel shouted in frustration. "I won! The Clade and all of its pathetic recruits will die at my hands! I have already killed all of yours, including that boy there." He pointed to Gabe lying on the ground unconscious. After Sarah heard Gabe's name, she began to cry again, and Trish began to too. I had let Gabe down; I had broken my promise to get him out of there safely. I still had to get Gabe's body out of there, somehow. I owed him that.

Nathaniel kept screaming at us. "Only two Clade divisions remain, Marcus! Too bad you won't be alive to celebrate it with me when I kill them all." He looked over to his soldiers and said, "Agents, finish them off."

They all held up their guns pointing directly at us. I looked at Marcus to my left and asked, "Have any plans now?"

He smiled and said, "Actually, I do, for once."

All of a sudden, a gust of wind, that wasn't Marcus, blew past me and impaled an Agent next to Nathaniel. His chest had a hole the size of a baseball blown though him. In fact, the blast from the air was so powerful that it actually dented a part of the helicopter.

"What the-" Nathaniel said as another gust of wind blew past me and killed the man on the other side of Nathaniel.

"Marcus," I said stunned at her power. "Is that…"

"Yes, it is. Now, get out of here! I'll take care of the Agents and Nathaniel."

We didn't need any more prompting and we didn't ask to help. Sarah, Trish, and I sprinted for the trees away from the Nathaniel and back the way we had come from. Two Agents were waiting for us, but another gust of wind blew through the Agent to our left. The other Agent had us in his sights, but I charged up and took care of him by firing a bolt directly into his neck.

"Zeke, that is-" Trish said.

"I know," I cut her off. "It's cruel, but we are trying to stay alive here. All sympathy for the people trying to kill us is long gone."

After all that had happened, the thought of killing an Agent didn't affect me. I felt as if I had become some sort of murderer or serial killer, but I had no other choice. The girl from last night had taken a bullet in the neck to keep me safe, and if I let any Agent live, anyone who died, like Gabe, would have died for nothing. I had changed, but, sadly, it was for the better.

We dove into the tall grass and crawled behind the trees to find Juliette waiting for us when we got up. "Hi, how're you three doing?"

"What! You've got to be kidding" Sarah yelled. "What do you mean by that! Gabe is dead and soon Marcus will be!"

"No, he won't," she confirmed what Marcus had said. "He will be fine. There is a reason why the leaders of the Clade promoted Marcus to lead instructor."

We turned ourselves to face the clearing. Marcus was still standing in the center of the ring of Agents. Suddenly, one of the Agents shot his gun. The bullet impaled Marcus causing him to fall backwards. "Marc-!" Trish yelled until Juliette covered her mouth.

"Shhh," Trish whispered. "Watch."

I looked back to Marcus to find him... no longer there. He was gone. The Agents looked around in confusion wondering where the instructor had disappeared to. I thought he was dead. The Agents thought he was dead. Nathaniel was just as surprised as all of us, so that meant he hadn't even known about Marcus' ability.

We looked around for where Marcus had gone to, but we had no luck. One of the Agents said, "He probably disappeared into the forest to run away with his friends. What should we do Nathaniel?"

Nathaniel was incredibly angry now. He said, "You should find him and the others and kill them-" He paused. We all stopped and looked to see what Nathaniel was staring at off to the side. It was Marcus standing up against a tree trunk. How had he gotten over there?

"Hey, Nathaniel. I bet you thought your Agents could handle me," Marcus said smoothly.

"It doesn't matter now," Nathaniel said. "You shouldn't have revealed yourself. Yet, then again, how would you know any war tactics? You are after all just a kid still."

Marcus laughed, "I may only be 28, but I am still more adult than you." Nathaniel glared at Marcus as he continued. "Aww, still upset that the Head Instructors promoted me to a Head Instructor instead of you, Nathaniel? After all, you are one of the original 100."

Nathaniel responded forcefully, "Doesn't matter anymore, child. I have enough power within the Agency to take down the entire Clade. All that will be left of your foolish society are memories, and I will begin with the execution of you all." He turned to his Agents. "Agents, kill them!"

The Agents began to fire at Marcus again, but the same result occurred. Marcus' body quickly vanished right after he was shot, and then he appeared on the other side of the clearing. He was moving through the air so quickly that it appeared as if that he hadn't moved at all until something disrupted the area he was previously in. It was incredible how well Marcus had mastered his ability. I saw why he had been promoted to lead instructor.

Marcus appeared on one side of the clearing and vanished quickly to the next. Each time he vanished and reappeared behind some poor Agent, he would shoot them in the back with a silenced pistol. Where was the Clade getting these weapons? It was such a cruel way to kill someone, but very effective.

The Agents were quickly becoming afraid of him. There were only eight left when Nathaniel stepped up and said, "I've had enough of this nonsense." Just then, Nathaniel pulled his arms to his chest and began to focus power. Marcus had no idea what he was up to. He just kept zipping from one soon to be dead Agent to the next. Once Nathaniel charged up, he let out a furious cry. "Aaahh!" He swung his arms outward and then he clapped them together. In the area where he was aiming, a small mountain looking piece of ground with sharp spikes sticking out of the sides of it shot out of the ground.

Marcus had no chance of avoiding it. Although his dummy was still on the left side of the clearing, his real body crashed into the small mountain and fell limp onto the ground near Gabe. "No!" Juliette cried out. Marcus lay limp on the ground with deep scratches and cuts running all over his body. His cloak was torn to complete shreds revealing his surprisingly muscular body, also with deep cuts in it. He did not stir as Nathaniel approached him.

Juliette put her hand up to her mouth as she watched Nathaniel approach Marcus. This wasn't a part of their plan. I guessed that they had had no idea about what Nathaniel could really do either. I had thought that he could only slide the earth, not create mini mountains. "How is that possible?" I asked Juliette.

"Nathaniel has the power to slide the earth, so he also has the power to create hills and mountains. I can't believe I have never thought of that," Juliette replied.

"What? How could Nathaniel do that by sliding the earth?" I asked confused.

Sarah answered for her. "Mountains are created by the sliding of tectonic plates which are also responsible for earthquakes. If Nathaniel can slide the earth together from a higher point, then a smaller mountain arises I guess."

That wasn't good news. Could it be that Nathaniel could also create earthquakes? I was afraid for all of our lives and Marcus'. Nathaniel looked down to him, still not stirring. He said to Marcus' shambled body, "See, Marcus. I told you. You, just like all of the other recruits, will fall to me and the Agency. I think I'll stop and see how everyone is doing in the Rocky's. What do you think?" He paused for a bit after mocking Marcus. "What is that? You want your friends to die first? Okay, I can't argue with my old friend."

He stared directly at us even though we were hiding behind some trees. He held out one of his hands and pulled his fist towards himself. Suddenly, the ground slid pulling us towards him. We wouldn't all make it off in time since it was so hard to even move on the sliding piece of earth. I didn't think about my decision; it was just instinct. I pushed Trish, Sarah, and then Juliette off of the sliding earth belt.

"Zeke!" Trish cried out. "What are you doing!?"

I tried to control my voice, but it came out as a scream, "I'm saving your lives!"

They watched me through teary eyes as I got swept through the tall grass and trees and into the clearing. Nathaniel glared at me with an evil grin; a man of contradictions. Five Agents still stood behind him protecting the helicopter from my friends in case they decided to make a break for it. I stopped at Nathaniel's feet still lying on my back.

He looked down at me and said, "You have caused me a lot of problems, Zeke."

"Yeah, well, you did your fair share of giving us problems as well," I said sounding like a smart aleck. I continued, "I bet you're the one that hid Trish and Sarah in that cavern room."

"Of course I did," he said. "I needed you and Gabe here," he pointed at him, "to need my help in finding them and escaping. That is how I got you to trust me, and now, I bet you wish you hadn't."

I wasn't going to admit that he was right. I was terrified and I wished that I had listened to Gabe. It just hadn't seemed like Nathaniel could be an evil mastermind or even that clever. The towel wasn't going to be thrown in yet though. I still had time to distract him enough so that Juliette, Trish, and Sarah could kill the Agents and get on the helicopter.

"Goodbye, Zeke. Oh, and by the way," he said while focusing his power on the ground beneath me. "Your father is alive."

I had known it before he had said it, but it still sent a shock through my body to hear it personally from someone and not just by overhearing it. I quickly snapped out of my daze when I realized that Nathaniel was charging up to kill me. I dove from my hands and feet away from Nathaniel just as another mini mountain erupted from the earth.

I quickly jumped to my feet and waved to the other three to get to the helicopter while I dealt with Nathaniel. They began to move around the outsides while I turned around in time to find Nathaniel taking the mountain and sliding it at me. I dove out of the way of that attack too while I threw a bolt of lightning at his chest. He created another mountain to deflect the lightning.

"Why even try, Zeke?" Nathaniel said cockily. "I am an Instructor, who apparently can surprise you with what I am truly capable of. My ability isn't just sliding clumps of dirt. I can bring down an entire mountain, and you are just a two week recruit. There is no chance."

I kept my distance from him by staying near the tree line. I wasn't going to give up until either the others made it past the Agents and to the helicopter, or I killed Nathaniel in some magical way. If I stalled long enough, I could hop onto the helicopter right when it was about to take off.

Nathaniel moved closer toward me, so I quickly threw another weak bolt at him. He slid the earth under his feet causing him to slide out of the way unharmed. The bolt struck the helicopter creating a small cut in the tail portion. Nathaniel laughed at my attempt and then began to focus his energy on another mountain. I dove into the forest just as another mountain erupted where I was standing.

I began to breathe heavily. My lungs ached with every breath of air I took. I had never been a physically fit kid, just enough to get by. At this point my adrenaline was helping me out a lot; if it hadn't kicked in, I would've been dead. I turned while lying on the ground and fired another bolt straight at Nathaniel's head, but again he slid out of the way.

Nathaniel made a pulling motion with his hand, and suddenly, the ground slid underneath me and soon I was back into the clearing. The earth this time was moving slow enough that I could get up and run. I stumbled awkwardly onto my feet and was about to sprint around the clearing when Nathaniel pulled the earth another way and flung me into a tree.

"Aaah!" I cried out after creating a sickening thumping sound after I hit the tree. I pressed my hand to my forehead and felt warm, wet blood. Juliette, Trish, and Sarah were almost to the helicopter, so at this point I just had to keep Nathaniel directed at me.

"Give up, Zeke!" He yelled out in anger. "Don't make me go full out on you. At least die in a way that you would still have a body left!"

"I'm not afraid of you, Nathaniel. In a war, I learned that true power comes from what you are fighting for. Not how big your muscles are."

"Those are very smart words coming from someone so little and pathetic. You have only known about your power for a month and you already think you know everything there is too know. I'm sorry, Zeke, but true power does come from how big your muscles are as you put it," he replied.

I faced him with a threatening appearance. "Prove it you old coward." I didn't know where all of that bravery was coming from, but it distracted Nathaniel long enough for the girls to get around to the back side of the helicopter away from the Agents.

The battle for the 300 recruit, alive and dead, and especially Gabe, fell on my shoulder.

I hope I don't mess this up.

Chapter 25

Nathaniel sneered at me as he began to charge whatever energy he had left. I soon realized that this was my opening to possibly kill him. I jumped up onto my feet and threw both of my hands at him letting a bolt of lightning emit from all ten of my fingers directly at his chest. Nathaniel was taken by surprise and tried to create another mini mountain to defend from my lightning, but it was no use. By the time the tip of the mountain reached his chin, the bolts had broken through the earth and hit him square in the chest.

"Aaah!" Nathaniel cried out as he flew to the other side of the clearing away from me. He landed with a thud and a scorched hole in his cloak where the bolts had all connected. He staggered slowly back to his feet, but I was already ready for him this time. I threw a fully charged bolt at him capable of leaving nothing but a Nathaniel stain on the ground. Unfortunately, he had just enough strength left to slide out of the way.

The bolt struck a large tree causing it to topple and burn. Soon after, the forest began to take flame, and we were surrounded by a wild fire.

Blood poured out of the hole in Nathaniel's cloak. He wasn't too hurt to fight though which was unfortunate for me because now he would really want to kill me. Noticing my new fear, Nathaniel laughed an almost downright evil laugh. It was one of the scariest moments of my life. The fire created an ominous setting for him and his evil grin.

"What do you think is so funny?" I asked him.

"I'm just astounded at how remarkable you really are. Only two weeks here, and you can already fight a top-level instructor," he said as he walked towards me. The fire continued to spread around us. It was about halfway around the clearing, and the smoke was making it hard for me to breath. Nathaniel continued, "Only two weeks here, and you can stand up against a top-level instructor. To be honest with you, Zeke, I think it is your ability that makes you tough and not your skills or talents."

If he was trying to make me angry and bait me into striking him, it wasn't working and it wasn't going to work. "I don't care," I told him. "As far as I'm concerned, I only have this power to kill you."

"Yes, but what will you do when that power of yours wears out? It will eventually, Zeke, just like it did to Sarah. It probably could have happened to Trish too, but

I "accidently" gave her a low dose of the drug to numb her ability."

Suddenly, I realized what he was talking about. "You gave Trish a low dose of the injection on purpose. It was you that caused that fire in the basement, not her."

"Well, not directly," he said. "But yes. I had to in order for the other recruits, as well as Marcus and Juliette, to stay out of the basement for awhile while I showed you the tunnel."

Again, Nathaniel was proving how he had played me and the rest all along. I felt responsible for our current state because I had pretty much forced Gabe into trusting Nathaniel, and now, he was dead. I wanted to break down and never get back up.

Nathaniel swung his arm towards a mini mountain off to my left and slid it at me quickly. I tried to jump out of the way, but part of its jagged surface caught me in the side. I flew about ten feet in pain until I crashed into the ground. That was when I felt it. The ground began to shake and quake violently. The shaking made it impossible for me to stand up.

Nathaniel said, "See, Zeke? I can create earthquakes. The earth is my domain as it exists everywhere. There is no stopping me." He approached me from the middle of the clearing. I was almost out of time. Why couldn't the girls start the helicopter? He continued walking over the uneven ground and said, "It's over, Zeke! All of your friends are dead. Your mother didn't want you, and now you are about to suffer the same fate as all of them. You will just be a memory."

That's when he charged at me. I couldn't stand at all; in fact, I didn't even know how he could stand up let alone run on this cragged surface. Along with the smoke from the fire, which had now completely surrounded the clearing, the place looked like hell. The heat burned my skin, and the smoke hurt my lungs.

Nathaniel was almost right on top of me when it happened. Trish, Sarah, and Juliette started the helicopter. It whined to life blowing the ever growing fire in circles making a fire like tornado.

Nathaniel stopped to look at the helicopter and then turned to his Agents. "What are you doing! Kill them before they escape!" The Agents heard his orders and began to hop onto the helicopter just as it was going into a hover.

"No!" I cried out. I didn't care about the earthquake anymore. I jumped up to my feet and unleashed a powerful bolt from my palm at Nathaniel. He couldn't react in time. The bolt broke through another one of his mini mountain defenses and the rocks smacked him across the face leaving large bloody scratches as he flew across the clearing.

I began to sprint for the helicopter. Gabe and Marcus were going to have to stay. It ate me up inside thinking that, but I had no choice. The girls needed me now. Two Agents were still sitting outside the helicopter waiting for the other three. I threw a fully charged bolt at one of them. It connected with one Agent and, surprising even to me, it arched and killed the other one. Their bodies smoldered and flamed a little bit leaving a gross rotting smell as I reached the helicopter.

One of the Agents inside the helicopter flew out of the side door with a large hole in his chest. I jumped in to find Juliette firing her air arrows at the three Agents, and

Trish grabbed one of them and lit herself on fire. Sarah just stood in the corner of the cockpit and hoped not to get shot. There was no water around for her to fight, so I jumped out and through her a gun from one of the two dead Agents.

"Sarah! Catch!" I yelled as the machine gun flew through the air.

She caught it with one hand and yelled, "Thank you!" She immediately began to fire at the other two Agents killing them both.

Juliette looked at us all and said, "Okay, Zeke, get in and let's go already!"

I had one foot in the helicopter when I heard the most terrifying sound that I had ever heard. Nathaniel cried out from the middle of the clearing, "No! You must die, Zeke!"

He pulled the ground out from under my foot causing me to slip out of the helicopter and onto the sliding piece of ground. I was dead. There was no more getting lucky. I was surely about to die, but I just couldn't give up so easily. I hopped to my feet, struggling to stay up, and tried to run, but the sliding piece of earth was so large I couldn't get off of it in time.

Nathaniel cried as I neared him, "No more with this ability shit! I will kill you the old fashioned way if I have to."

He got right up in my face and punched me square in the jaw. That blow knocked me off of the sliding piece of earth and onto stable ground. My mouth was filled with blood, and I felt a large bump forming on my cheek. I heard Sarah and the others call out from the helicopter. "Zeke!"

Juliette released an air arrow, but Nathaniel noticed this and blocked that with a mini mountain. He continued at me while Juliette kept trying to kill him, but it was no use. Nathaniel had an impenetrable defense.

My body was beginning to weaken from using my ability and fighting to move. I had double vision and shortened breath by the time Nathaniel jumped on top of me. His knees crushed my shoulders, and I cried out in pain. Another one of Juliette's arrows struck the mini mountain protecting us causing small rocks to shower down on us.

I struggled to break away from Nathaniel, but he was too heavy to throw off. He gave me one more punch to the face causing more blood to spew from my mouth. He said, "Now, goodbye Zeke." He pushed down harder with his knees and then used his hands to summon up another mini mountain right where I was laying.

It was hopeless. I was going to die with a mountain going through my body. I could hear the rumble of the mountain under the surface as it approached. At least I had put up a good fight and had given the girls enough time to escape. The rumbling of the ground and Nathaniel's laughter began to crescendo with my imminent death. I closed my eyes, just waiting for everything to fade away. The next thing I knew, Nathaniel had burst into flames and I was free of his grips.

"Aaahh!" He cried. I rolled out of the way just as the mountain broke through the surface. Who could have saved me? The only person that could turn things into fireballs was…Gabe.

I ran past Nathaniel who was stop, drop, and rolling to keep the flames off him to get to Gabe. He looked so pale that he had to be dead, but he wasn't. His eyes were barely open, and he had a small pulse. It was a miracle.

I grabbed him and said, "I'm getting you out of here. Thank you for the help, but now I'm saving you."

I was about to pick him up when he pushed himself weakly back to the ground. "I can't...go, Z-Zeke. I'm going to die. It was just luck that I was alive long enough to save you. Maybe that's why I'm here to begin with, to save you."

I didn't understand what I was hearing. "Gabe, you sound stupid," I said as tears began to form in my eyes. "You have to come with us. We will save you. I promised you that I would."

"Zeke," Gabe said faintly. "You tried. That's all you can ever ask for." Marcus laid next to him and began to groan and stir. He was alive too. "You..." Gabe began. "You w-will get Marcus and leave me. He can h-help you more than I-I would. Besides, I'm dead already."

I wouldn't accept that. The tears were now rolling down my face, and I couldn't even try to stop them. This was terrible. Gabe was sacrificing himself to save Marcus. I turned to see Nathaniel still struggling with the fire. His face lost some of its skin as it peeled and fell off to the ground.

Gabe grabbed me to stay focused and said, "Hurry, he will put out the f-fire soon. Wake up Marcus and go." He coughed a few more times.

"Gabe are you-" he cut me off.

"Yes!" he coughed more blood up. "Now, g-go. Also, Zeke, just know that I f-forgive you for not keeping your promise."

I looked down at him through my teary eyes and nodded. I let him go and his eyes became lifeless. Gabe was dead. I felt responsible, and I never wanted to leave his body, not in the middle of that wild fire, but I had to respect Gabe's final wishes.

I shook Marcus a few times hoping that he would wake up, and after a few shakes, he did. "Zeke?" he asked weakly. "What's going on? Where is Nathaniel?" He realized and quickly sat up.

"I'll tell you on the helicopter, but we are still in danger. We have to go now!" I grabbed his arm and pulled him up. I stumbled a little bit since I was out of energy, but I had to stay awake. If I passed out, all of our hard work would be for nothing.

I put Marcus' arm around my neck and helped him run to the helicopter. Nathaniel was still struggling with the little bit of fire that remained on him, so we were safe if we could just get on the helicopter in time. Juliette ran out of the helicopter and gave me a hand with Marcus, and, together, we successfully got on the helicopter.

Marcus, Trish, and I sat in the cargo area where the open doors were while Juliette and Sarah were in the cockpit. "Hurry up and get us out of here!" I shouted.

"I'm working on it!" Juliette shouted back. The blades spun faster and faster until finally the blades spun fast enough to get us into the air. Nathaniel had just put out the fire and run over to us as the helicopter was taking off.

His face was terrifying and filled with blood. The skin under his left eye and on the right side of his face below his ear was burned away revealing muscle. His left cheek's skin was gone revealing muscle and a part of his jaw bone. Thankfully, we were well above him by the time he reached us. He cried out at us, "This isn't over, Laufor! I'll kill you, and everyone you love!"

I wasn't worried about him anymore. All I had left on my mind was Gabe. How was I supposed to live after feeling this guilty about Gabe's death? He said that it wasn't my fault, but I knew that he was just saying that to make me feel better. I looked into the cockpit and saw Sarah crying out loud. I wish I could've comforted her, but Juliette was already taking care of that as we flew.

The small part of the forest around the clearing was on fire, but the rest of the forest was fine. How would someone make an excuse for that? I looked to Marcus, and he just said, "I know what you are thinking, but don't worry. The Clade is great at making excuses. We have ties in the government which make any excuse believable."

The Clade had control almost everywhere. It was surprising that nobody had ever caught onto the Clade after all these years of it existing.

We flew over the remains of the Clade hospital. There was nothing left of it except a few bricks and slabs of concrete. Trevor said he would see us again on the side of freedom, but I didn't think we would be seeing freedom any time soon. Looking down at that mess, I didn't think Trevor would be seeing freedom either.

The state of New York whizzed by underneath my feet as I dangled them over the side. All of my experiences while at the hospital passed through my head:

my first day with Gabe, meeting Sarah, my training sessions, recruiting Trish, and all the way from finding Sarah and Trish to escaping the forest. I wondered if Nathaniel was still alive out in the forest, but I didn't want to think about that. I would worry about that later.

Trish sat down next to me and let her legs dangle over the side. After a few moments of awkward silence, she said, "What do you think happened to the other thirty or so recruits from the tunnel?"

"Nathaniel probably told them to go in a different direction and then ambushed them," I said without thinking.

Marcus hit me lightly in the side from where he was laying and said, "I told you, Zeke. You are perfect for commanding in a war. You think like a general and fight like a soldier."

"Thanks," I said. "But I really don't want to hear that right now."

"I'm sorry, but yes, you are right. Nathaniel had his Agents ambush them when they went off into the forest. I grew suspicious of Nathaniel when he just so happened to find the door leading out of the tunnel, and then pointed us to go one way when he went the other. That's how we knew to follow you."

"That was smart thinking," I said to him.

Marcus nodded and went back to sleep. We flew for a little while longer, probably long enough to get out of New York, when I asked Juliette, "Where are we going?"

She answered, "You heard Nathaniel. He plans on destroying the other two divisions of the Clade. We have to go and warn them. We will go to the Colorado base first and then on to the head division which contains our leaders."

"Alright, so we are going to be flying for awhile?" Sarah asked, speaking for the first time since we had lifted off.

"Yeah, I would get some sleep," she replied.

I took Juliette's advice and stretched myself out in the middle of the cargo hold area. Trish lay next to me, and Sarah joined us. After the last two nights and that fight with Nathaniel, sleep felt like a gift from the gods. I was out before anyone could say another word.

I woke up a few hours later still a little tired from the lack of sleep. Outside the helicopter was gray and dark from the storm clouds hanging over us. Rain began to fall and patter against the windshield of the helicopter. Thunder rumbled, and the wind blew.

The weather, to be honest, scared me, so I went into the cockpit where Juliette was still flying the helicopter and asked, "Are you sure we should be flying in this weather?"

She replied, "It's fine. This is a military grade transport helicopter. It can handle any weather condition." I just nodded and slouched in the chair and drifted off again.

I woke up again just a little bit later to the sound of an alarm. A red flashy light quickly got my attention, and I asked Juliette, "Is that supposed to be happening?"

"No, it's not… And I can't figure out why it is either," she kept toggling switches and other buttons trying to get it to go off. Suddenly, the tail portion of the helicopter where my lightning bolt had created the cut in the metal completely broke off leaving just the cargo area.

The alarm grew louder as we spun out of control and fell five thousand feet. The altimeter on the dash spun backwards quickly trying to keep up with our descent.

The three in the back of the helicopter jumped into the small cockpit. Marcus said, "Are we going down? Did we just lose the tail of the helicopter?"

Juliette answered, "We did. I have no control. It's only a matter of time until we crash into the ground."

I clung on to the seat praying that we would live through the impending crash. We had just survived against all odds, and now, our deaths could be caused by a helicopter crash. To make it even worse, I was the one who had shot the helicopter creating the cut in the metal.

Guilt flowed through my veins as we spiraled toward the ground at speeds fast enough to kill us all. No amount of electricity will be able to save everyone on board. We were going to crash. Everything we just got done fighting for was coming to a tragic end.

The centrifugal force was so great that I think I saw Trish and Marcus get pulled from the helicopter and out into the open air to free fall. "No!" I screamed, but my throat was squeezed shut.

Marcus, Sarah, and I were left to a smoking hull of a helicopter doomed to crash into the ground. I opened my eyes a pinch to see the ground just below us. This was it.

To Be Continued…

Coming Soon:
The Human Element Trilogy Book 2: Overload

The helicopter spiraled towards the ground at an increasing speed. Trish and Marcus couldn't have survived the long fall to the ground. My heart filled with agony and grief knowing that I was never going to see Trish again, and, for once, there was nothing I could do.

"Hold on!" Juliette yelled to Sarah and I as the ground finally reached the helicopter causing us to smash hard into the solid dirt. The force jutted the copter causing it to immediately smash into tiny pieces. The grinding sound was so loud I wanted to hold my ears because they stung so badly, but I couldn't. All I remember was the sound of crunching metal and blades scratching against the Earth. I blacked out almost instantly...

Water fell on top of my face. The cool drips were godsend after what had just happened. I opened my eyes to see the helicopter smashed to pieces on the other side of the clearing.

I tried to get up and find the others, but I was too sore and tired. My muscles ached with every movement. I wanted to just lay there for the rest of my life and forget all about the Clade, but that would never happen.

I realize that now. They will always be after you to try to keep you safe, or at least, that's what they think they are doing. If they don't come, the Agents will, and they only know how to do one thing. To kill. Just like how the Agents killed Gabe. How long ago was that?

Thunder ripped across the gray and gloomy sky. When we were all in the helicopter, it was a bright, sunny, day. We could have been laying here for hours or even days. I remember riding through the air in the chopper when the tail of it broke off and we spiraled towards our doom. I guess our dooms day was still a few days away.

How did we survive a fall like that? My hand resting its palm on the dirt made it feel as solid as any ground anywhere else in this world. There was no way that we could've have fallen and all survived. That thought gave me chest pains from the sadness. I wanted to cry at the thought of my friends being killed in a helicopter crash. One that was primarily my fault.

Suddenly, a rustle came from the bushes across the clearing. I had no idea who it was, or even where we were. Maybe this was this person's land, and they weren't so happy that a helicopter just crushed some of their trees. It could even be the Agency coming back for round two when everyone was either weak or dead.

I used all of my strength to lift up my palm and charge a bolt of electricity in my hand in case it was the Agency. The bolt would be weak, but it could give me just enough time to run. I was too tired to make this shock lethal. I feel like a nap may be in store for me if I survive this encounter.

The person cleared the bushes. He was an older man, maybe in his mid 50's with curly gray hair and a large round face. His whole self was round actually. He stumbled out of the woods, but caught himself before he fell to the ground.

He said to me through the pouring rain, "I am not as limber as I once was. I swear these trees are gonna be the death of me." He laughed.

I didn't know who he was, so I didn't let my lightning bolt diminish from my hand. This person was a stranger to me. He could be a good person, or an Agent for all I know.

I pushed out through aching lungs, "Who… are you?"

He smiled and said, "I am the person that saved you from becoming a red stain on the ground." He walked up to me. "Now, put down your hand and let me take you back to my house, so you can rest up and heal."

The person sounded genuine, and I couldn't stay out here in the rain. My body may be able to heal itself from cuts and other gouges, but it can't fight a cold for all I know.

Before I tried to stand, I asked, "Did you... find others?"

"Yeah, I got Marcus, Juliette, and the other two girls. Good thing you crashed in the right spot." He laughed. "I guess there really is a bright side to everything. Now, may I ask what your name is?" He tried to bend down to hear me better. Maybe because his ears can't pick up sound like they used to.

"My name is Zeke, Zeke Laufor," I pushed out.

His eyes opened wide and then he said, "So, you are Greg's kid, huh? Well, isn't that just wonderful." He didn't sound too happy about that. The bolt in my hand grew in strength.

He noticed and said, "Woah! Hey now, you don't have to fry me. Your father and I just never got along much when we broke away from the Agency."

"What?" This caught my attention almost instantly. Anything about my father I wanted to know about, but first things first, "Who are you?" I asked.

"My name is Liam Randalph. Would you please now come with me? Marcus told me all about what happened back in New York. The Agents may be on their way if they noticed the chopper go down, so if you like to live, let's go!"

I didn't get to say another word. He grabbed my non-electrified hand and pulled me up on my feet. The pain in my side made me want to scream, but I held it in. My legs were wobbly underneath my weight, and I felt like I could have collapsed at any second.

Liam began to walk back the way he came when he said, "Are you gonna follow me? Your girlfriends are waiting for you back at my place."

Girlfriends? He was talking about Sarah and Trish. This grabbed my attention and I immediately began to briskly walk behind Liam. He must have noticed a happy expression on my face because he said, "Ah, teenagers. All they care about are girls."

About the Author

Kevin Van Camp is currently a 19 year old boy living in La Crosse, Wisconsin where he is attending the University of Wisconsin-La Crosse. He is majoring in Biology and hopefully will become a doctor someday along with being a writer. Kevin's hometown is Freedom, Wisconsin. No one really knows where that place is unless you live there or in the area of Freedom.

This is the first novel published by Kevin Van Camp. He is very excited about it and he hopes to continue his hobby of writing stories for other people's enjoyment. He began to write this during his senior year of high school. At first, it was just for enjoyment since soccer season was over, and he was bored, but it has become something much more thanks to the support of his family and friends. He never would have guessed in the beginning that The Clade was publish worthy.

He is currently working on other books such as The Human Element Trilogy Book 2: Overload and The Grim Events. Due to his current status as a student in college, the books may take time to be completed and be published, but they will still continue the exciting story of the main characters.

Kevin's hobbies, when he is not writing, include playing video games and hanging out with his friends, playing soccer or any other sports in the summer, swimming, and enjoying a good laugh every once in a while.